SECRETS & LIES

BY JOSH GROSS

ILLUSTRATIONS BY
JENNIE JORGENSEN

TABLE OF CONTENTS

THE DOG HOUSE

Truth is, I'd never wanted a dog. But after we graduated college it was all Emma would talk about. Said it would bring us closer. She refused to validate that I preferred to maintain the freedom to go where I wanted, when I wanted, unencumbered by external responsibilities or the threat of errant poo when and if I decided to return. I didn't even want plants hanging over my head. I explained how a dog wasn't right for us, how our apartment was too small, that she worked too much and I too little to afford one. But based on how quickly she'd trained me to sit and roll over, I was fooling myself to think I had any say in the matter. Of course, I'd never wanted a girlfriend either. And for many of the same reasons. But it's amazing how much regular sex will change your perspective. Especially for chubby, wiry-haired chatterboxes like myself.

After months of debate, she dragged me out to the pound one weekend, obsessed. They were having an end-of-the-year sale. I pointed out the flyer on the door that said their prices were going to the dogs as yet another example of this being a terrible idea. She ignored me, and walked through the doors into the kennel area.

That's where I found Elvis.

I connected with him immediately, because he seemed to be the only one besides me that understood this place. Rows upon rows of sanitary plastic prison cells. Living creatures sold at discount prices to avoid euthanasia. And everyone, dogs and people alike, pleased as punch about the whole affair. Children ran and screamed as their parents smiled on. Dogs wagged their tails at all passersby, desperate for love. It was a dystopian orphanage—a brokedown plastic palace smeared with chunks of fur and shit. Emma had even "dressed up," pulling her favorite black-and-white-striped sweater over her stout frame and straightening her dark hair so it clung flatly to her cheeks flapper-style, as if it was important to prove to the pound employees that the dog would fit with your fashion sense. The only one that didn't seem elated by every bit of it was Elvis.

His face drooped long and low like his skin was two sizes too big, and the mournful look in his eye was one of clear understanding that he had just been abandoned. People say basset hounds just look naturally sad, but that wasn't it at all. Elvis knew the score. He even understood that someone had been a big enough goon to think naming a hound dog Elvis was clever.

Emma was down the aisle, looking at a poofy white mongrel with a rat face, so I had a free moment to examine

Elvis without threat of her seeing my interest and reminding me of all the things I'd said against the notion of a dog in general.

I opened the gate and stepped into his kennel, squatting down to be on his level. He looked at me skeptically from where he was seated in the back. But after several moments, he rose on his short little legs, plodded over to me and flopped himself across my lap sadly.

"Yeah, I feel that," I said, scratching him behind his long, floppy ears.

"What are you doing?" a voice said sharply from behind me. I turned and saw an annoyed looking woman with a bright green volunteer apron.

"I'm uh…I don't know," I stammered.

"Just get out of there," she said. "You can't go into the kennels."

"Right, sorry," I said. I tried to delicately move Elvis off of me, but it was clear he didn't want to be abandoned again and he whined pitifully as I stood him up on his paws. "Just a moment," I said. "I'm having a little bit of—"

"Some of the dogs have diseases," the volunteer said. "Not rabies, but still…that's why you can't go in there alone."

"Right," I said, standing up quickly, brushing brown and white hairs off my pants. Emma was watching over the volunteer's shoulder as I stepped out of the kennel. She didn't look pleased. This was the kind of thing she would probably later refer to as making a scene. "How much?" I said, awkwardly pointing a thumb over my shoulder at Elvis, eliciting a look of horror from both Emma and the volunteer.

"Owen, what are you doing?" Emma gasped.

"What?" I said. "This is the dog. You said I could help pick. This is the dog." They were the ones excited about the end of the year sale. I was just trying to play along.

"You don't even know why he's here," Emma said.

"Doesn't matter. This is the one."

"It matters," she said firmly.

"You haven't even seen him yet."

"Maybe you should get to know him a little bit first," the volunteer interjected. "You know, take him into the outside area and get acquainted?" Emma and I glared at her in sync. We may have fought a lot, but we certainly hated all the same things, which produced a far tighter bond as it allowed us to be ourselves unfiltered. And one of the things we hated in tandem was small people butting in.

Emma stepped around the volunteer. "So you want a dog now?"

"I knew you were going to bring that up," I said. "But it is within the powers of the universe for me to change my mind when the situation fits." Emma stared me down coolly. I think she had her eye on the puffy rat. And without her even saying it, I knew that it would in fact match the drapes, but I didn't care. It was Elvis or nothing. "Just look at him," I said. So she did and immediately her face softened the way so many aging, unmarried, women's faces soften at passing babies.

"Would you like to take him outside?" the volunteer asked.

Emma ignored her, stepped into Elvis's kennel and squatted down to pet him. "What is he here for?" she asked. But I knew it didn't matter. Elvis was our dog.

"Ma'am," the volunteer intonated. "You're really not allowed in the kennels. Please, let's just take the dog into the free-range area, and all of your questions can be answered there. If you really want to take him home, it's required anyhow."

"Fine," Emma smiled sweetly. She stood and stepped out of the kennel, allowing the woman by to put Elvis on a leash.

"Bitch," she mouthed to me, when the volunteer turned her back. I grinned in response. That's my girl.

The volunteer led a stubborn Elvis—he kept looking back over his shoulder at us—down the hall to a door, and outside into a private fenced-in play area. Chain-link fence separated our cage from others, where giddy children and Labradors galloped around in circles, bouncing off of the chain-link and howling like it was a full moon. Elvis looked at them with complete and total disdain. The instant the volunteer let him off the leash, he sauntered back to us and rolled over onto his back so we could rub his belly. Our dog was such a glorious snob.

"I'll just leave you here while I go get his paperwork," the volunteer said. She went back inside, closing the door with a barely perceptible slam.

"You want to come home with us, don't you boy?" I said, rubbing Elvis's belly to great effect. He kicked his legs gleefully, and made noises of contentment. "Come on Em, try it."

Emma looked skeptical as she delicately reached out a hand and gave Elvis a tickle. He responded well and she upgraded to full rub. "God, he really has an enormous penis, doesn't he?" she chuckled, careful to avoid it.

"I suppose."

"It looks like it would drag on the ground," she said. "Loooowrider."

"Whadda ya want? He's got short legs. It's just comparative."

"I know, I know," she said. "But still, it seems enormous, like half his size."

"I'll take that as a sign of acceptance."

"I don't know yet. He's sweet, but—"

"But what? But nothing. He's perfect."

"Look, Owen, let's see what the paperwork says."

"Why? Who cares? Look at him." It wasn't just Elvis's demeanor I could jive with. He was downright adorable. His body was long and low like a drag racer, white with brown and black spots. There were brown spots over his eyes like goggles, and his ears swayed with his movements. He could touch the heart of even the most hardened cat-person.

"I know. He seems great so far," Emma said. "I just want to see why he's here is all. Make sure that it's not because of serious medical costs, or explosive diarrhea or something. I don't want to deal with that. And don't pretend that you do either."

"Yeah, you're right I suppose," I said. "I'll spot you the explosive diarrhea. But if that's not the case—"

"Oh yeah, then definitely," Emma cut in. "He's the one."

"I knew it, baby," I laughed. "I knew it from the first moment you called that woman a bitch."

"I just call 'em as I see 'em," she smiled and gave me a kiss.

Elvis stood back up, and stuck his nose in between us, a friendly, sloppy three-way kiss. I scratched him behind his long, drooping ears, and he craned his neck out happily, his loose thick waddles hanging low.

"How do you do, folks?" a voice said from the doorway. Emma smirked at me, seeing that the woman had sent someone else in her place, an old man in a trucker cap with a flannel shirt beneath his volunteer's apron. "I've got Elvis's file right here, if you'd like to look over it," he gummed.

Emma stood and took the file from the blue-aproned lackey as I ran once around the pen with Elvis trotting along behind me.

"I used to have a basset myself," the lackey said. "Good hunting dogs. Great with children."

I smiled awkwardly in response as Emma silently shook her head no at both options. "We'll take him," she said to change the subject, and handed back the file.

"But no need to gift-wrap," I quipped. The man kept a stone face. "Never mind," I offered. "Just a joke."

"Mm-hmm," he mm-hmmed. "Come with me then," he said, and opened the door to let us back inside. He put Elvis on the leash, and led us to an office to fill out the necessary paperwork and extolling, in triplicate, the Basset's virtues in a hunting capacity as we did so.

There were so many forms that I didn't get around to asking Emma why Elvis was at the pound until we were in the car driving home.

"Divorce," she said.

"Really?"

"Yup. You can read the file when we get home, but the short of it was that neither side wanted him."

"That's the worst thing I've ever heard. What awful people."

"I've heard of worse, like people getting rid of an animal because it doesn't match their new carpet. Now that's terrible." I made sure not to mention the puffy white drape-matching rat she'd been eyeing before I found Elvis.

"Still, divorce?" I said. "That's pretty awful. I wonder if they sent their children to boarding school while they were at it."

"Probably. He's purebred, so I'm sure they could afford it."

"Fucking bankers," I grumbled. "You've got to be some kind of asshole to take a dog to the pound for any reason, let alone one so petty."

"I thought you didn't want a dog."

"Doesn't mean I think they should be mistreated. It's probably why I didn't want one. Was afraid I wasn't up to the task. I wouldn't want to be the one responsible for anything else's life or death."

"Because of—"

"No. Maybe…"

"But you are now?"

"Special case," I said, reaching back and patting Elvis's head. He had spread himself out on the back seat.

"Oh God," Emma said disgustedly.

"What? What?" I said, panicked.

"Nothing," she laughed. "I just think I saw you grow up right before my eyes is all."

"Damn it. Did I really?"

"Only a little," Emma smiled. "You still got a ways to go."

"Good," I said. "You had me worried there for a second."

"I'm sure I did," she snorted, then turned her attention to Elvis for the rest of the drive home.

Elvis and I went on walks every morning. Through the neighborhood, to the park, to the grocery store; we went nearly everywhere together. Work being scarce, and my desire to seek it even scarcer, I had a lot of free time to devote to him. Especially since it gave a semi-legitimate excuse as to why I hadn't found a job that particular day. Emma had been the driving force behind adopting him, but I was the caretaker while she was at work. Essentially, I was her dog nanny. And she could hardly get mad at me for that. Not so long as I had insurance money left and plasma to sell anyhow.

But spending all that time with him was fine for me anyway because he was exactly the opposite of every other dog I'd ever known. He ignored cats and squirrels, walking by them with his nose and tail in the air. He didn't chew on things or shit inside. He didn't bark or cause trouble. He didn't even run away or wander off. I stopped using a leash when I walked him because all it did was get tangled up in his short little legs. He walked along next to me without it just fine, meaning we could go for leisurely strolls together anywhere I liked and have nothing to worry about. He would stop to smell something here and there, but always trotted back to my side the instant he was done.

His only real flaw was that he seemed to like homeless people a lot. Presumably because they smell and hounds are attracted to strong scents. Every day when we walked, he would stop and mingle with the winos that clustered at the stoop on the corner, letting them dote all over him and being incredibly stubborn about moving on. This always prompted the winos to drum up a conversation, once again asking me what his breed was, how old he was, and how long we'd had him and the such. And no matter how many times I told them, the same questions would come again like clockwork the next day as the afternoon's boozing wiped out their memory of asking in the first place.

But Elvis's hobophile tendencies were a small price to pay for everyone's clear jealousy. He was the dog others wished they had. The tired-looking owners of Labradors and Retrievers and Pugs and all manner of others abandoned their loyalties the instant Elvis arrived on the scene, singing his praises and petting him endlessly. People stopped on the street and pointed out of car windows. Some even came out of restaurants, unable to resist sharing a little piece of their lunch with such an adorable pooch.

When Emma would come home from work, I would gush to her about the amazing things we'd done that day and do all I could to convince her to come along on our walks so she could see it first-hand. But she seemed content to cuddle with him intermittently on the couch, intellectually acknowledging Elvis's status as the king of dogs, but never really giving herself over to it. I could never tell if she was overwhelmed by work, or underwhelmed by our pet choice.

And through it all, I just grew more confused. How could anyone not want a dog this amazing?

"I still can't believe those people," I said to Emma over dinner one night. Elvis had been with us for three months at that point, and was currently spread out on the couch.

"What people?" Emma said puzzled.

"Those a-holes who gave Elvis up to the pound." How could she have forgotten?

"You're still on about that?"

"What, you're not?"

"It passed as a point of interest once we adopted him."

"But that's because you haven't come out with us and seen how great he is. I just don't know what they could of possibly had a problem with."

"It wasn't the dog, Owen. It was their marriage."

"But neither of them wanted him afterwards. That's what I don't get. How could you not love him? He's perfect. I mean, except for the winos, but that's negligible. How could they both be entirely passive about him?"

"Can you please give this up?"

"Why?"

"Because, I think you're projecting."

"About what?"

"Oh come on, Owen, you know what about."

"What? About me finding out I was adopted? It had nothing to do with that."

"Fine. It has nothing to do with it."

"It doesn't."

"Okay, whatever you say."

"And I thought I asked you not to bring that up anyway."

"I'd be glad not to. I'm tired of it frankly. You're the one whose been going on about it since we got Elvis." His head perked up at the sound of his name. "Every time the mailman comes or we order a pizza, you've got to tell them all about it. Every time he does something supposedly great, you drop back into rant mode. Even he's over it at this point. If they hadn't given him up, we wouldn't have him. And clearly we love him more, so let's move on." Elvis trotted over to the table and rubbed up on my legs.

"Are you saying you'd fight over him if we broke up?" I said. "Go to kennel court for custody?"

"There's no fight to be had," Emma said dryly. "He's mine." She put a forkful of macaroni and cheese in her mouth in a very final way, not even bothering to look at me.

"Oh, is he now?" I chided. Emma just kept chewing.

Then she leveled her eyes at me. "I paid for him. I pay for his food. You're just the nanny, remember?"

"No need to be snitty," I said. "I'm just saying, whatever happened to a dog being a man's best friend?" Emma snorted laughter. "What?" I said back.

"Like all of a man's things, the woman gets them in the divorce," she chuckled, sadistically grinning at me.

"Well, at least you care I suppose," I said.

"Yeah, it's something," she said. "I'd say you should just take what you can get."

"It's better than those people who gave him up anyhow," I said.

"Oh, good god!" Emma said, slamming her hands on the table. "I thought we were done with them!"

"Well, no, just—"

"Never fucking mind," she snarled. "Just forget it." She stood up and took her plate into the other room in irritation, leaving me scratching Elvis's ears at the table.

I looked down at Elvis and circled one finger around my ear while crossing my eyes at him. "Crazy," I whispered to Elvis. "Your mommy is fucking loco." Elvis hummed contentedly in response, one of his hind legs kicking as I rubbed his throat. "I'm just curious is all. What kind of assholes would give you up anyway boy?"

I looked to him for answers, but Elvis didn't seem to have anything to say on the subject. Maybe he could be content with his creature comforts, but I needed more. The curiosity was eating a hole in me, and one way or another, I was determined to find the dastardly secrets of his former owners. I just wasn't going to bring them up over dinner anymore. Apparently this was the one thing that Emma didn't hate right along with me.

The streetlights outside were just humming to life, providing an artificial twilight to the shadows cast over lush green lawns by the tall trees lining the street. I rubbed my eyes and readjusted myself in my seat, stretching my arms and neck. Elvis and I had been sitting in my car across from 5275 Oak Street, watching, for an hour. Today.

The person working the desk at the pound had looked at me like I was crazy when I offered a bribe for info on Elvis's former owners. Then, like I was crazier, when I upped my offer from four to seven dollars. But after some inspired fast-talking about tracing his genealogy, I was politely, but firmly, asked to leave.

Luckily, I ran into the volunteer who went through the paperwork with Emma and me while returning to my car, and started spinning yarns about all the hunting trips Elvis and I had been going on. I'd personally seen Elvis tear the throat out of a wolverine after tracking him for three days straight. It was quite thrilling. The head was mounted in Elvis's doghouse.

The old man knew the local breeder who'd sold Elvis to his original owners. After a quick trip to a farm just outside city limits (where Elvis and I were introduced to Col. Tom Parker, Scotty Moore, Priscilla, Jesse-Garon, Lisa Marie, Sam Phillips, Lieber-Stoller, and a newborn litter of puppies called the Jordainaires) we were rewarded with an official Graceland Kennels trooper cap—so Elvis and I would have matching floppy ears—and the name of our prey.

From there, all it took was a few minutes on the internet to find out that Lyle and Mindy Malone (the bankers) had separated in none too kind a manner, with the house and children located at 5275 Oak Street remaining in the possession of Mindy. Lyle's whereabouts were unknown. I cursed Emma for her savvy on the politics of divorce as I crouched down low in the driver's seat for my stakeout. I would find the truth about these heartless savages even if I had to forgo all possibilities of employment to do so. There was a mystery afoot.

In order to adhere to the popular literature, Elvis and I shared Chinese takeout the first day. But we switched over to donuts and dog biscuits after he got a case of gas that made his wino pals smell pleasant in comparison.

So far we'd spent a week observing every detail of the life of The Harpy Malone. Comings. Goings. Stayings. We'd researched the layout of her mini-mansion, its shadows and crannies as well as the best bushes to urinate behind. We'd catalogued the school schedule of the children, who we referred to in our notes as Karl and Molly to protect their underage identities. We'd even scavenged some bits of their homework from the garbage. Molly was in serious need of tutoring in math, but Karl showed great promise in his studies of American history and government. An essay he'd written about General Custer seemed to say it all quite succinctly: Custer was a big doo-doo face. I hadn't resorted to peeping in the windows yet, primarily because Elvis had never struck me as the tree-climbing type. All of this information was helping to form a clear picture of who the Malones were, a picture that would be necessary to understand why they would inflict the deep trauma of abandonment on a sensitive creature like Elvis, an understanding that was required before moving on to the next phase of Operation Blue Hawaii.

So far, the picture was an ugly one. It basically boiled down to the Malones being colossal jerks who got rid of him out of pure spite. There couldn't have been any sort of practical reason. There was plenty of room for Elvis in a place like that. Certainly much more than in our one-bedroom apartment. He would have been happy just roaming around the yard or laying on the porch. He wouldn't even have been in the way. And he couldn't possibly have done anything wrong to get banished. It just wasn't in his nature. Not to mention that my examination of their garbage had revealed nothing about allergies. They'd just clearly never appreciated him in the first place. Didn't get him at all. Didn't understand the little things, like how he loved snow, but hated water. The way he'd walk around puddles rather than through them, even if they were only an inch deep. That he'd sing and chirp along to a strummed ukulele or how much he liked waffles. They probably didn't even know that Chinese hot mustard made him gassy or any of the other little idiosyncrasies that made him unique and wonderful, a reversed spelling amongst dogs. These were things that I and I alone seemed to recognize. The nerve of the breeders even letting the Malones take Elvis home in the first place. He'd have been better off with his wino pals than these savages.

And what kind of name was Mindy Malone anyhow? Alliteration is only acceptable for superheroes, and anyone who would give up a dog like Elvis wouldn't have lasted ten seconds in the Justice League. It made me bonkers just to think about it.

The living room light switched off and The Harpy Malone was observed going upstairs. Her shoulder-length, blonde hair bounced irritatingly as she passed by the window. Those who couldn't see the depth of her evil would probably describe her as pretty. Sure, she was less dumpy than Emma, probably because she worked out Tuesdays and Thursdays. And sure, she'd probably been prom queen or what-have-you, the kind of girl who boys like me dreamed of but knew better than to ever talk to directly. And sure, she was probably on the rebound, looking for a quick fuck to get her through these stressful times (but not a replacement father for her children) making it an ideal time to lust after her. But as I could see the malevolence in her heart underneath those perky breasts, I knew better.

I made a note in my log and then glanced at the dashboard clock. Eight o'clock. Shit.

My absences had been explained away by telling Emma that Elvis and I were training for a dog show, and that it may take long hours as I was training him on a specialized course outside of town. When she protested, I told her about the $5,000 prize for best in show and my plans to spend all of that money lavishing gifts of rent and utilities upon her, my temporary office worker princess. She harrumphed off to the other room, but appeared pacified as the subject didn't come up again. Still, I had to return to home base from time to time when the supply of donuts was depleted, or early enough in the evening to ensure that the true scope of my operation was kept concealed and my alibi maintained. Whichever came first. Right now, I was late for both.

I turned the key in the ignition and eased out down the street, waiting until I reached the corner to switch on my headlights.

Emma was wrapped in a blanket, drinking tea at the kitchen table when I got home. Elvis trotted in behind me, and plodded over to her chair, fishing for a petting. Emma stroked his head several times, but gazed off into space dully rather than looking at him.

"Hey lover," I said, kissing her on the cheek as I passed by on the way to the fridge. She pulled away the tiniest bit, but I ignored it. "Big progress today. Real flaming hoop kind of action," I said, rummaging around for something to drink. "You should have been there."

"Yeah," she sighed. "I really should have."

I took some juice from the fridge, and saw that she was still blanking out. "Em, darlin'?" I asked, sitting down at the table. "Are you all right?"

"Why?"

"You just seem, I don't know, off. Distracted."

"I'm fine," she said. "Just, you know, work."

"Stressful day?"

"You don't want to get into it," she scoffed. "It's not worth it. Just forget the whole thing."

"Have it your way," I said cheerily. "Juice?" I offered her my carton. "It's cheerier than tea. Less British."

"No thanks," she said and took another sip. "God save the queen."

"See, there you are," I smiled. "Glad to have the ol' snarky you back."

Emma put her tea down on the table and looked at me seriously. "Tell me something, Owen," she said.

"Yeah, what's that?"

"Are you really training Elvis for a dog show?"

"Of course," I lied. "Big day today too."

"Right, real flaming hoop kind of action."

"Yup."

"So when is this dog show?" She wasn't employing a pointed tone, indicating this wasn't an interrogation to root out my scam—though it certainly could work out that way if I didn't proceed carefully.

"Why?" I asked casually.

"I don't know," Emma shrugged. "I thought maybe I could go."

"Oh right, sure," I said. "Of course you should be there. I'm sure Elvis would love the moral support."

"Or maybe I could even help out with the training. We're supposed to be doing this together and all."

"Oh, totally." Not, fingers crossed and jinx.

"It's just that apparently you have the magic touch with dogs or something—"

"I mean, don't make too big a deal over it. It's not that magic."

"Why shouldn't I? He likes you better than me."

"He does not."

"Come on, Owen, he obviously does."

"Just cause I spend more time with him. And I shower less. He likes smelly people."

"I didn't want to admit that it bothered me before…"

"What, the smell?"

"No, Owen—"

"Why? What's going on?" I needed to change the subject so she'd forget about helping out.

"It's not important," she said. "Just tell me when the dog show is and what I can do to help. I'd kind of like to take some time off from work anyhow."

Sitting there, looking into Emma's unexpectedly, genuinely sad eyes, I knew that the Mindy Malone observation phase was out of time and needed to be wrapped up ASAP. It was time for the confrontation and beratement phase, the part where I rubbed in what a dumbass she was.

"Let me check the calendar and get back to you," I said.

"Okay," Emma said. "Let me know." She stood and took her tea into the bedroom.

Fuck. Sure Elvis walked well, but only because he felt like it, and only when he was good and ready. I was going to have to start extra early the next morning so I'd have time to teach Elvis something. Anything.

Luckily, there was a surge in demand for Emma's temp services that paid too well for her be concerned about the fake dog show, so Elvis and I were able to continue our important work without interruption. She was apparently just as much of a hit at her current office as Elvis was at the dog park.

Though it was hard to say if fate was working for or against me, it was certainly working for someone, as it had been four days since the Harpy Malone showed her face. By now, most would have called the whole thing off. But every passing moment just raised the stakes and made me more invested. I needed to see this through or it all would have been for nothing. So Elvis and I worked on tricks in the passenger seat for hours at a time while watching 5275 Oak Street. He was now nearly able to maintain attention without his name being called. We decided to keep this part of his act secret from Emma, as we decided she might not appreciate its limited scope under the current circumstances. She wanted flash and bang, Elvis sawing a cat in half and pulling bones out of a top hat. But cats were far too skittish for that sort of thing. No discipline whatsoever. Emma didn't ask about helping again. She just came home, drank tea, and went to sleep.

It was odd, but this was the first time I'd felt guilty about the little games we played. There had been something different in Emma's tone, like genuine disappointment. She probably just wanted me to refocus on getting a job. But I still had money saved and didn't see the point of making myself miserable from nine to five every day like she did.

But all of my pondering ceased to matter because I'd just seen The Harpy Malone's car rounding the corner and returning to dock. Ah, a loaded roof rack. They'd been out of town, the sneaky fucks. Well, if that was the case then they ought to be worn out from the trip, less able to mount a suitable defense. They were vulnerable and it was time to strike.

As they pulled into their driveway, Elvis and I stealthily got out of my car so we were hidden from the Malones. It needed to look like we were just randomly happening down the street.

We hid behind the car, waiting until The Harpy Malone looked away. Then we dashed into place and started sauntering in their direction, the only travelers on the long suburban street.

My heart was beating fast as we closed in on our prey. The Harpy Malone was unloading the back of the family car, bent over the trunk, that annoyingly pert hair hanging in her face and hiding Elvis and me from her view. I slowed down just enough so that we wouldn't pass by unnoticed. I even stomped my feet a little, just to ensure she'd be aware someone was approaching and look to see who. Once that happened, she'd see her former dog, perfect and happy with a new owner that appreciated him. She'd see the mutual respect we lavished on one another, she'd see what a sham she was and then she'd learn some sort of valuable lesson about seeing the value of what's going on right in front of her. And then she'd cry for giving up such a prize, making such a mistake. I'd say too bad, you had your chance to appreciate Elvis, and you failed. It was about to happen. It was going to happen—right now.

She straightened up right as I passed by. Perfect execution.

"Oh my God," she smiled, that stupid hair parting to reveal her horrid face and perfect skin. "What an adorable little dog."

"I know," I said. "He is, isn't he."

Just then, Karl and Molly barreled out onto the sidewalk, all giggles and snotty hands. They molested Elvis about the ears and ribs to his great delight and my intense confusion. He wagged his tail and lapped it up. The filthy turncoat. Didn't he understand these were the war criminals who abandoned him behind enemy lines? And ugly war criminals likely to be rife with infectious bacteria at that?

"He is just adorable," the Harpy Malone said, giving Elvis a scratch.

"Yes, he is," I tried once again.

"What's his name," she asked.

"Elvis," I stressed.

"Well hello, Elvis," she gushed and squatted down to pet him. Elvis acquiesced and even rolled over onto his back to allow her the privilege of a belly scratch. She smiled and gave him a quick rub, then stood back up and shooed her kids off of him. "That's enough," she said. "I'm sure this nice man has to be on his way."

"Right," I said.

"Well, have a nice day," she smiled, then picked up her bags and herded the children inside with a straight face and a clear conscience.

What had just happened?

I was still pondering the Harpy Malone's technique when Emma asked about the dog show again over the hastily microwaved leftovers we both jokingly referred to as dinner that night. "I was waiting for you to check the calendar, but apparently you didn't ever do it," she explained, sans eye contact.

"I'm sorry, Em," I said. "I totally forgot." Her interest was threatening to derail the entire Malone Initiative.

"So you don't know when it is?"

"Uh, well, it was supposed to be today actually."

Her eyes narrowed. "So it's done and you didn't tell me?"

"No," I scrambled. "It was, uh, cancelled."

"What?"

"Yeah, rain. You know. But they're going to reschedule it or something." Why was she making this so hard? "So, super-intense training all day tomorrow."

"Wasn't it supposed to be inside? Who would hold a dog show outside?"

"There was a, uh, malfunction in the sprinkler system. So it was like rain. That's what I heard anyhow. I wasn't actually there."

Emma just stared at me, hard and slow. She had to know there wasn't a dog show. But that was just how we did things. What should I tell her I was doing with my days? Committing felony stalking in the suburbs? She'd never understand. We both hated the suburbs.

"You don't want me to be a part of this do you?" she said.

Fuck. There was no correct answer for that question.

"Fuck. Forget it," she went on. "Never mind. I don't even care," she said disgustedly. "I'm over it. Just tell me how he does." Emma took what was left of her dinner to the bedroom in a huff.

How Elvis would do…Who could say? I'd give him the blue ribbon, but I wasn't sure if that would serve to further enrage Emma or not. Sure we'd gone through periods of playful faux-rage or hostility meant to gerrymander that thin line between love and hate. But she seemed genuinely mad, and that had never happened before. I could ask her about it, but I knew that would only elicit an explanation of her "dog show." She'd once called them "relationship lies"; they're things that are better left unsaid because there just isn't any way to say them without incident. They're lies that hurt, but don't count. Mine was a dog show. I didn't have time to figure out what Emma's was. I had to figure out why in the hell The Harpy and Munchkins Malone were playing ignorant and what I was going to do about it before mine unraveled and changed from relationship lie, to lie-lie.

Of course, there really was only one answer. I had to go back.

In the morning, I groggily told Emma I understood her opposition to pet cloning, and that she could count on my support as I kissed her good morning. She told me to go back to sleep, then got up to get ready for work. I pretended to be asleep as she got dressed so I could watch. It was one of the few opportunities I got to see her with her defenses entirely down, and I liked it. It provided dimension and perspective to a girl that had yet to stop surprising me.

Once she was gone, I got out of bed, did a few quick stretches, and got dressed to take Elvis out for his morning walk to the coffee shop.

After that, I loaded him into the car so we could return to our stakeout. Today was Thursday and that meant The Harpy Malone would be outside 5275 Oak Street around 10:30 a.m., fresh from her standard weekly check-in with The Elder Malone for pastries. Elvis and I made sure to be in place twenty minutes early just in case there wasn't much to talk about over said pastry this week. But seeing as how there had been a recent run-in with a certain pooch she'd sentenced to the gulag, I could only imagine she had a lot to get out to a sympathetic ear with the genetic antecedent of her pet care philosophy. I could just imagine those conversations. Tips for flushing goldfish without clogging the drain. Recipes for box turtle soup. Elated viewings of the end of *Ol' Yeller*. Just thinking about it made me angry. I was more determined than ever to squeeze the truth out of The Harpy Malone.

I was right. She was ten minutes late today, probably from discussing Elvis's comeback tour. I made a note in my log, and again stealthily exited the car. The plan was to run the same game as yesterday and try to catch her in the crossfire. Her duplicity couldn't stand up to the rigorous cross-examination I was planning. If she tried to zig, she'd find I'd already zagged. And if she tried to zag, well then, she would pay dearly for her arrogance.

Again, we sauntered up. And again, she turned and smiled.

"Oh, hello again there, cutie-pie," she said gleefully.

"Yeah, he is cute isn't he," I said, snidely raising a single eyebrow.

"Beyond adorable," she said and squatted down to scratch Elvis behind the ears. She hit the nerve that made his hips wiggle. "It's Elvis, right?"

"Right, Elvis," I stressed.

"What a great name for a hound dog," she smiled. God I hated her and her perfect smile. "How old is he?" she asked.

"He's ten," I said, "but I haven't had him that long. Just got him from the pound."

The Harpy Malone gave me an odd look. I was getting to her, I could tell.

"Well, he looks fantastic for being that old," she said. "What is that, seventy in dog years?"

"I dunno," I said. "It's supposed to change over time. All I know is he's too old for someone to turn him out on the streets like they did. Whoever did it must have been pretty cold-blooded."

"Well it looks like he ended up in a good home at least," she countered.

"Yes. Yes he did," I said with a firm, flat tone. She had just been toying with me. I could see that now. And I wasn't going to sit and take it any longer. I followed my statement with a pointed look and perfectly timed breathing.

"Um, well, I'm sure you were on your way somewhere," she said, with a half-smile. "I've bothered you and Elvis long enough."

"It's all right," I said. "I'm not really in a hurry." I'd be damned if I was going to let this charade go on with her at the helm.

"Oh, well, I actually have some—"

"I'm new in the neighborhood," I cut in. "Me and Elvis. We just moved in, on the next block." Take that.

"Oh. The empty house on Oak Street?"

"Yeah, that's the one. We live there, me and Elvis. So, you know, we're out exploring our new turf, and meeting the neighbors. Elvis likes to meet people for the first time."

"Ah, I see," The Harpy Malone said, visibly uncomfortable. She was about to crack. Any second now.

"Well, now you've met me, I suppose," she said, with a giggling head-shake.

"And Elvis," I offered.

"Right, sorry," she said. "And Elvis."

"Owen," I said, icily extending a hand.

"Angela."

My insides were quivering. What an opponent! What a maneuver! Oh, she was cunning, I'd give her that. But she couldn't keep it up forever. I had right on my side and it would always outlast deceit. Plus she had kids to take care of, and probably a job she had to go to sooner or later. I wasn't going anywhere.

I smiled wide. "Pleasure to meet you, Angela," I said slowly and deliberately.

"And it's a pleasure to meet you, Owen," she responded.

"And Elvis."

"Right, and Elvis."

I kept my eyes locked on The Harpy Malone and did my

best imitation of mad Emma, that unblinking, burning probe of a stare that could see through lead. She could be a military interrogator with that stare. I wished she were here. She could have been able to do it right. I was trying, but I think I was succeeding more in putting the squeeze on my face than on my prey.

"All right, well, I'm going to go inside now, Owen," she said. "It was, uh, nice meeting you."

"And Elvis."

"And Elvis." She backed away from me slowly.

I could feel Elvis tugging at the leash trying to follow her, and a panic set in. She was getting away with it. And worse, Elvis was leaning towards forgiveness. I couldn't let it happen. "Just admit it," I blurted out. "Tell me the truth."

"I'm going inside now, Owen," she said. "I think you should leave, just keep moving. We'll forget about this."

"No! I'm not going to forget. Admit it. Admit what you did!" She said something in response, but I wasn't listening. I just needed to punch through her defenses. "Why would you abandon him?" I moaned. "He was so good to you, even now. And you just left him to rot. How could you do it?" My knees suddenly gave out and I realized I was screaming, "You don't know what it's like, to be abandoned, not to know, until a check comes in the mail because they're dead. You have no idea what you did!"

She had almost been to the door, but she suddenly stopped. "I'm going to have to call the police, Owen. I don't know what this is about, but you need to leave."

But I didn't have it in me to move. I wanted to lay right there on her walkway and cry until there was nothing left so I would never have to do it again. But Mindy had a different plan. Her eyes grew fierce and she advanced aggressively.

"Didn't you hear me? Get the fuck out of here!" she snarled with pointing fingers and sharp heels.

Her charge snapped me from my self-pity and I backpedaled, realizing that I needed to regain the offensive, and quickly, or the match would again be Malone's. So I planted my feet, puffed up my chest, and spoke with my leash-free hand waving wildly. "I wanted to confront you, see what kind of monster would abandon a defenseless creature like—"

Then she shoved me, much harder than someone who works out only twice a week should have been able to, knocking me to the ground. "Now scram, before I get my gun," she snarled. She stood firm, pointing down the street away from her house. Two sets of terrified but curious eyes were visible peering through the window behind her.

I stood slowly and dusted myself off. "You win again, Mindy," I said. "But one day, all this will make sense to you."

"My name is Angela, you freak," she said without moving.

"Oh right, got it," I said with a wink. "Who is Mindy? Don't know any Mindys. I gotcha."

"Forget it. Just go fuck yourself," she snarled.

"Yeah, I'll—"

But she was already inside and slamming the door.

I looked down and saw Elvis lazily scratching himself behind the ear. "Come on boy," I said and lead him back to the car.

"What do you think boy?" I said once we were inside. "If you weren't before, I'll bet you're sure glad to be out of there now that you've seen what she's really like."

He grumbled and sniffed in response, so I reached into my pocket and got him a dog biscuit. I should have been mad at him, the Judas, but that was what set me apart from The Harpy Malone.

"Here you go," I said, feeding the treat to him. "Savor it

my friend, 'cause there's only one more left."

Elvis didn't listen though. He inhaled the snack as I started the car and pulled out into the street.

There wasn't a stop sign on the corner, but I paused for a moment there anyway so I could readjust my seat belt and fiddle with the radio. Stopped there for the first time, I caught my first motionless glance at the street sign and suddenly felt like I'd been kicked in the stomach. The white letters said Oak all right, but not Oak Street. This was Oak Court. How the fuck could I have missed that?

I jammed on the gas, tore around the corner in the opposite direction of home, and found Oak Street one block further down. I turned and drove down it, scanning the house numbers intently. Could I have been entirely wrong? What exactly had I been doing the last several weeks?

And there it was: 5275. A grand place fit for bankers and bassets with a Southside Realty Sold sign planted firmly in the yard. While I'd been inadvertently stalking Angela Whoever—Mindy Malone, the horror of hounds, the terror of terriers—had gone on the lam.

I opened the door to my apartment, still barely able to contain my laughter. Elvis and I had howled and guffawed all the way home, but it just kept coming. We were so far past absurd we'd punched through to the other side. And now that we were inside without the distraction of driving, I was free to cackle until the cows came home. Or Emma. Oh god, Emma! I couldn't wait until Emma got home. Dog shows and relationship lies be damned, I was going to confess the whole thing. It was just too good to keep to myself. Fuck, why wait? I decided to call her. This was hot news and I didn't want it to cool even a single degree.

I picked up the phone, but then I heard something in the bedroom and decided to investigate. I found Emma home early and curled up for a nap.

"EMMA!" I thundered gleefully, leaping onto the bed. "You're never going to believe what just happened."

"What are you doing here, Owen?" she said, terrified. That should teach her to nap when there were stories to be told.

"I live here, duh," I scoffed. "But seriously, this is amazing. So remember how mad I was about the—"

"But I thought the dog show was—"

"Oh no, there was never any dog show," I laughed. "You didn't really believe that did you? I thought for sure you knew that was bullshit. But whatever, it's just a minor detail. What really matters is that…" But then I stopped. There was something wrong. Emma didn't look mad; she looked scared. And… bare-shouldered? I picked up one edge of the covers and snuck a peek. "Why are you naked Emma? Were you waiting for me or something?"

"Oh god," she sighed. "Owen, I really…"

Then I saw the blue suit jacket draped over the chair. "Whose is that?" I pointed.

She turned her head to the jacket and then suddenly Emma wasn't the girl I knew. Gone was her capacity to scare me blind and in its place was a sallow shroud of defenselessness. "I thought you were going to be gone all day," Emma said.

"Whose is it?"

"My boss's…"

"And it's not here because you were cold at work today is it."

"No."

"So he's…" But I didn't need to finish. I realized that in all the excitement of my escapade, I hadn't noticed the shower running. But there it was. Swishing and gurgling away, with just the faintest bit of someone humming Heartbreak Hotel underneath. "You, you, just…" I kept moving my lips and tongue to the right positions, but the words just weren't there. It was too much of a jumble.

"Oh, come on, Owen, you had to know this was coming," Emma said, returning to character. She stood up, keeping the blanket snugly wrapped around her as she moved to the closet to furiously dress herself.

"Why on Earth would I—"

"Are you serious?" she cut in, anxious to regain her momentum. "The lies, the unemployment, the blank check refusal to take any part in growing up? Take your pick." Every phrase had been punctuated with a fierce stab into the closet, like she was spearfishing for an outfit.

"So it's a neat haircut and nine to five you want? Like your office pal? God, Emma, your boss? How cliché," I scoffed. "I thought you were better than that."

Emma stepped out of the closet and angrily into a pair of pants she held with one hand, still clutching the blanket with the other. "Owen, if you want to act like a child, then I'm not going to waste my time trying to have a mature adult relationship with you. It's that simple."

She lost her grip on the blanket and it fell to the floor, revealing her bare torso to me one last time.

"What chance would I have against your clear desire to climb the corporate ladder?" I said. "You made your mind up on this long ago. I can tell."

"You've had nothing but chances," Emma said, slamming a shirt over her head. "Not that it made a difference. I telegraphed them to you one after another, and you were just so wrapped up in your own world, you couldn't bother to see what was happening right in front of your face."

"Oh, look who's talking, you believed me about the dog show?"

"I did not."

"Did so."

"Owen, stop it right now," Emma stomped. Her orbit around the room was increasing in speed. "I'll take Phil and we'll leave and—"

"Oh, fuck you," I laughed. "You don't get to leave. You can stay here in stew in your own mess."

"Fine, whatever," she said. "Just whatever."

I whirled, took a step towards the door, and nearly tripped over Elvis. He must have wandered in unnoticed sometime during the previous exchange. He wagged his tail and rubbed up against my leg, then dropped to the floor for a belly scratch.

"You never wanted a dog, did you?" I said.

"Hating all the same stuff wasn't enough, Owen. We needed something to love also." Emma squatted down and gave Elvis a scratch also. "You better take him with you," she said.

"I thought he was your dog."

"He likes you better. We both know that."

"Yeah, but I never wanted one, you know that."

"What happened to him being the best dog in the world, and all that?"

"Too bad I never wanted one, then isn't it?"

"Owen—"

"No!" I shouted, standing up. "There is no way I'm going to take your dog and look at him every day, thinking of you and what you did. Cleaning up his shit, knowing that it's you with the filthy hands. A constant reminder while you're busy living free? No fucking way. You don't get off the hook that easy Emma."

Emma probably said something in response, lots of things at varying levels of volume and anger most likely. It was quite possible she followed me waving the leash and ranting, but I was walking, and I was putting on my jacket, and I was leaving, and I didn't care where to. And that was all. It didn't matter what happened anymore. That was the past. And I'd always preferred to maintain the freedom to go where I wanted, when I wanted, free of external responsibilities anyhow. No baggage to weigh me down. Now I could get back to that. Back to me and my life. I'd never wanted a dog anyhow. Or a girlfriend. And for many of the same reasons. Never. Not even for one second.

It was cold and I put my hands into my jacket pockets as I walked down the street. One of them came back out clutching Elvis's final dog biscuit. I had to stop. There was no air to go forward. My chest felt tight, like it was imploding, being sucked into the little black pit in my stomach. My skin was crawling in the same general direction. "NO!" I shouted, and threw the biscuit to the ground where it shattered into a dozen pieces on the sidewalk. And then I kept walking. I'd never wanted a dog, I kept telling myself. Never, never, never!

ALL SHE WROTE

The car hit the little girl right below the knees.

It was an old, European-style convertible, low to the ground, zipping down the street like a rocket ship. The girl floated above the car free from gravity like an orbiting piece of space debris. The driver slammed on the brakes, but it was too late. Her face had smashed the windshield into a crimson fractal, careening her skyward into a triple flip over the car—a human bowling pin trailing a single thread of gore like a grisly tether. Those watching would later say they were sure she'd be dead by the time she hit the ground. But she wasn't. She hit with a thud and leapt right to her feet, running in nonsensical circles like a headless chicken, weaving patterns akin to crop circles and screaming like her bone was about to crumple and poke through her skin. It was.

A man from the sidewalk café tried to predict her erratic path enough to intervene. He pleaded for the girl to sit still, chasing her with a paper doggie bag he'd emptied onto the street. He told her he could help, that she needed to sit down, that an ambulance was coming—that it would all be all right. But it was futile. Earlier cultures would have labeled her possessed. Then she suddenly crumpled onto the sidewalk she'd been trying to reach in the first place and pounded her fists into the concrete, gurgling gibberish and tears and gasping for air as the skin on her knuckles thinned.

The driver was on his knees in the street, whimpering prayers to a God that his black, heavy metal T-shirt inferred he probably hadn't believed in two minutes ago. He said he was sorry, that he was afraid, that he'd do anything to save her—though he was doing nothing. He just whimpered, "Oh my God," over and over again, rocking back and forth, staring at nothing at all.

Traffic ground to a halt around the stopped car as other drivers got out to catch a glimpse of the ragged flap of flesh sitting on the sidewalk, bleeding from the head and flashing her tibia at passersby. Probably drunk, they muttered to each other.

"How can 9-1-1 be busy?" someone shouted from the café.

Best show in town, someone thought to themself.

A waiter ran into the street, frantically waving his arms at a cop who was passing by. The cop leisurely pulled his car back to a legal parking spot behind the café and sauntered around the scene making comments into his walkie-talkie, eventually squatting down to ask the little girl what her name was. She put down the paper bag that the forcefully helpful man had provided for her to breathe into, and nearly choked on the word "Alice," then quickly put the bag back to her mouth. The cop stood back up and went to talk to the driver (who had converted and was now slightly more composed for the effort).

Across the street, a group of tiny, guilty-looking, slightly grubby faces were watching from the shadows. They huddled close to each other, acting as skittish as minnows when the adults got close to them. They whispered nervously, holding council. A chubby boy in a baseball cap tried to break ranks and step forward into the street, but was grabbed by the shirt collar and hauled back into line. After that, they began to melt progressively further back into the darkness.

By the time the ambulance arrived, her friends had abandoned Alice altogether. And by the time she was loaded into the ambulance, even the man insistent on helping was reseated at the café having his coffee refilled by the waiter, and commenting on the sleek lines of the convertible as an overweight man in coveralls hitched it to a tow truck.

"Not something you see every day," he said to the waiter, who responded that he preferred the bus, no insurance required. The man laughed and didn't leave a tip.

The next day the paper read: *Accident reported at 2300 Siskiyou Blvd. Ten-year-old girl taken to hospital for minor injuries.*

THE MISSION

There was something I'd really wanted to ask John. I knew there was. It had lurked inside of me at school every day for the last week, but I was terrified of the myriad of possible responses it could evoke should I dare voice it; it was a desire best kept camouflaged until the time was right. It was big. I knew that. But here—alone with him in my room, the timing right, all the pieces in place—the point of my elaborate setup had vanished.

He tapped the bowl of the pipe onto his palm, making sure it was empty, then put it down on my desk and looked at me with that glimmer of pot-induced genius, the kind that sober people might refer to as "so crazy it just might work."

"We should totally fight crime," he said.

It seemed logical to me. Go with the flow here.

"Okay, sounds good," I said cheerily.

"We'll need masks," he continued methodically. "That should go without saying."

"Masks. Check. I can handle that," I piped up.

"But I'm saying it anyway, cause, well, you know…it needs to be said." He nodded to himself with the smug satisfaction of outsmarting no one in particular.

"Yeah…that was key." John was like an oracle and I felt lucky to be in the presence of such a mastermind.

We stood up off my bedroom floor, but stalled momentarily when we reached apogee. What were we doing exactly? It went without saying…but how would we know what was going on without saying it…then I noticed John rummaging through my closet and suddenly snapped back to now.

"Oh yeah, fighting crime," I said out loud.

"And we're going to need capes," John added.

"Capes. Totally. I can dig it." I was digging it.

"Do you have any capes?"

"Ummm…I think I'm fresh out," I said slowly, trying to extend the sentence long enough to remember if I did, and where my mother would keep the supply of crime-fighting capes in that scenario.

"Can we use sheets?" John asked.

This was a tough question. "Umm…I think so, but I'm not quite sure."

John gave up his search through the closet and turned back to me. "Where are the masks?" he asked, relentless in his inquisition. Obviously he was a born leader, a big man on campus, a skinny man, a buffalo on the range, a shrimp on the barbie, a ninja master, a tiger burning bright. Wait, what's a barbie? I thought those were dolls. Why would you put shrimp on a doll?

John whistled and snapped his fingers in my direction like the soundtrack to a Three Stooges film. "Dylan," he whistled. "Hey, Dylan. Masks?"

"Oh yeah. Uh…well, you know, that's just really hard to say for certain. I mean, who's to say in this day and age, really? I mean, you tell me?" The look on John's face said it was now my turn to be the smug one.

"Hmmm…" John said scratching his chin. He slowly drifted out of the room "hmm-ing" to himself all the way.

I collapsed back down into my chair. This was exhausting! My mind just couldn't keep up with everything that was happening. I turned off the overhead light, and switched on a desk lamp. Better. Magic in fact. Now I could think clearly with only the flip of a switch. Glorious! Like Edison, but backwards. What if I could do Einstein backwards too. Could I stop the bomb? Or…or…but, oh yeah, what was it I was going to do tonight? It wasn't fighting crime; it was something about John and me…Something I wanted to tell him…or was it something I wanted us to do together? There was a reason I invited him over tonight. Something backwards maybe? What was it? I rubbed my fingers in circles on my eyebrows, scrunching my face up in concentration for several minutes trying vainly to solve the puzzle, but losing myself in visions of an elaborately planned sandwich big enough to feed all of Ethiopia. I barely noticed when John came back into the room.

"This should do the trick," he said, showing me an armful of makeup. "I went to meditate on the toilet and found all this in the bathroom."

"That was in the bathroom?" I said incredulously. Would the wonders of my house never cease?

John gently pulled my hands away from my face and told me not to move as he leaned over me. Dread coursed through the veins in my neck as he tried to paint a mask on my face with a variety of different substances, eventually settling on an eyebrow pencil. It tickled. Suddenly, I panicked. I was going to lose an eye. Or die of asphyxiation from the makeup fumes. Or from being so close to John and forgetting to breathe. I closed my eyes trying to ignore the feeling of John's fingers slowly creeping across my face, discoloring it like spilt coffee spreading across a rug. His breath was hot on my forehead and my concern shifted to worrying that I might sweat off my mask before it ever got the chance to conceal my identity from the forces of evil. Would that make me a failure in his eyes? A crime-fighter's civilian identity is their most guarded secret. How pathetic to be outfoxed by your own exocrine system. Betrayed by your own bodily functions. Is that how old people feel when they try to fight crime? At least colostomy bags could double as a weapon. Right? Right?

"Okay, now you do me," he said, straightening up and handing me the pencil. We switched places and I tried to keep my hands steady as I drew a raccoon mask on his face, carefully tracing an outline and filling it in. He'd been so meticulous with mine that I felt it was important to measure up.

I finished and stepped back to survey my work, but John was out of the chair and out the door again before I had the chance. This time he came back with towels.

"See, when you take a shower and dry off with this, it will be like washing it so no one will even know that it was used as a cape," he said as he tied a pink bath sheet adorned with umbrellas and ducks around my neck. "It's brilliant." He did have a point there. John then tied a large dark blue towel around his neck and beckoned for me to follow him out the door.

We walked through my house and John picked up assorted objects along the way, hanging some on his belt, and handing me others so I could do the same. A roll of masking tape, a bungee cord, a large BBQ spatula, a Swiss Army knife, rubber dishwashing gloves and some Post-it notes, "for sticking messages on the chests of criminals that we tie up and drop off in front of the police station," he explained.

I was beginning to think he'd done this before. He seemed so knowledgeable and confident. Was I not his first sidekick?

John looked at me and gave me the pointing-to-his-eyes, mine, and-then-forward, move-out sign they use in movies. We silently slipped out the front door to terrorize the criminal element. We made it all the way to the curb before John turned to me and admitted that he wasn't really sure where one would go to fight crime. So he hadn't done this before. A change quickly came over me, a bouncy self-assuredness that comes with donning the fabled cape and spatula. I felt confident, clearheaded, and ready to do battle with the forces of evil. And what's more, I knew the answer to our problem.

"The first thing we should do," I boomed, all chin and no hand signals, "is to take to the rooftops so that we can put one leg up on the edge of a building and observe the city, searching out evildoers." This image was consistent throughout all the relevant literature. No respectable crime-fighter worked on the ground.

John agreed, and we set off skulking through the back alleys and railyards of our small town. We had yet to procure the funding for the amphibious, nuclear-powered crime-scooters, equipped with rocket launchers and stealth technology, the necessity of which we discussed on the walk.

Ten minutes later, we reached the center of town and began furtively working our way through the storefront shadows, sideways-stutter-stepping from nook to cranny and back again, eventually working our way around into the alley behind the ice cream parlor.

It was a dirt alley, almost more of a lot—an oddly shaped space formed between buildings that was too uneven to serve any purpose other than housing dumpsters. The dumpsters were on high ground right next to the building, and could easily be used as a stepladder to grab hold of the rain gutter. From there, we could simply hoist ourselves into the history books as the first vigilante justice group to hail from a town with a population under fifteen thousand. Look out Holmes County, there's a new Sheriff in town. Well, two Sheriffs. Sheriffi, perhaps? No, that doesn't sound right. How does that work? What is the plural of Sheriff?

There was a cacophonous, smashing sound, like a plastic bag full of windows hitting someone in the face, as the dumpster lid crashed down into the garbage. I shook my head clear and saw John trying to scramble up on top of the slick plastic lid. He struggled for secure footing and nearly fell off the dumpster, eventually using the metal edge as a launching point to reach the gutter and hoist himself onto the roof. I followed his example and cautiously scaled the green behemoth, wincing at the pungent smell of rotting vegetables wafting from within as I pulled myself up onto the roof.

John had already raced to the other side and assumed the

position of one leg up on the edge, leaning forward attentively, scouring the city streets two stories below for the black scourge of criminal malfeasance. Backlit from the street below, John glowed with a thick, white aura that would put fear into the hordes of evildoers intent on plundering the ice cream parlor. He was a majestic sight to behold and I didn't want to be left out. I ran forward anxiously to get in on the action. I quickly threw one leg up onto the edge and whipped my head into position, equipping my face with my best sneer to taunt our prey lurking below.

The street was empty.

"There's no one there," John said disappointedly.

I quit my sneer and looked down again, and upon confirming his hypothesis, grunted in agreement. We were unprepared for this contingency. Spatulas and masking tape could not combat the lack of evil. We both continued to glare dully at the street below, John's aura still ironically shining bright.

"I guess we should just remain vigilant," I said.

"Yeah. I guess," he replied blankly.

We kept watching the empty street for several minutes, hoping something would happen. And then something did.

Headlights pulled into the alley behind the ice cream parlor and parked. Someone got out of the car and a voice crackled indistinctly through a walkie-talkie as the beam of a flashlight began probing the area.

John's eyes widened at me in terror. "Fuck! It's the fucking cops," he whispered in a panic. He dropped to his knees and crawled clumsily in one direction, then back again, then back in the original direction once more. I stood paralyzed, an urban possum. I felt the flashlight beam stab across my eyes, then saw John frantically beckoning for me to get down. He was huddled behind a small chimney. I quickly crawled across the roof and squeezed up against John to fit behind the only available hiding spot. He threw his dark blue cape over the both us and we froze, clenching every muscle and orifice, trying even to stop our breathing from giving us away. My face was pressed up against his chest and I could hear his heart thumping like a drumline. There was no way the cops wouldn't be able to hear us. Our bodily functions were like a stampeding herd of elephants. I'd known back at the house it would come to this end. A crime-fighter should always trust their instincts.

John shuddered as we heard the cop clamber onto the dumpster, tracing his flashlight lazily back and forth across the rooftop, sweeping the area. Apparently satisfied, the beam clicked off.

The walkie-talkie belched a short burst of static. "Looks like it's all clear here. False alarm," the cop said.

"Roger that," the radio crackled back. "Continue with scheduled patrol route."

"Roger," the cop said.

The dumpster creaked with the shift of weight signifying a dismount. I breathed a deep sigh of relief. It was over. We'd survived. Then, I suddenly sucked it back in as I realized the reason the dumpster was creaking was because the cop was climbing up onto the gutter, not down.

Footsteps thudded across the roof, moving closer. Each one seemed to shake the foundation of the building and the marrow of my bones. I prayed to Stan Lee to get us to safety. I wanted to throw off the cape and run, to scream, to confess to being on the grassy knoll in Dallas that day, anything to make this terror end. Was he a sadist? The super-criminal we'd been searching for? Cop Man? The devil in blue? Oh God, this is not how I wanted this night to turn out. This is not where I'd envisioned things ending up when I first saw John on stage in the 9th grade talent show last week: crushed against him on a rooftop, about to be jailed and sent to rehab, with so much undone, unsaid, unaccomplished. I squeezed John tighter with the approaching doom. He squeezed back and I closed my eyes, knowing this was the end as the footsteps became deafening.

Then, unexpectedly, they became quieter. The cop passed by us, moving to the edge of the roof and stopping. I opened one eye and strained my ears for any possible clue to comprehend what was happening. Was this another dirty cop trick? Was he about to holler, "olly-olly-oxen-free"? What? What, damn it! I was ready to burst. Why wouldn't he just bust us and get it over with? How long could he keep up this sick game?

"Do you see anything down there, Robin?" he said breaking the silence.

"All clear, Batman," he answered himself, altering his voice slightly.

"Good work," he said in the first voice, then paused for moment and took a deep, sad-sounding breath. "Back to the Batmobile, I guess. The poor man's up, up and away…"

He walked back across the roof and climbed down to the alley, calling in a return to patrol on his walkie-talkie as he did so. We heard him start the car and pull back into the street, all the while staying huddled beneath John's cape. We let another thirty seconds go by to be sure he was gone, then stood up and bolted for the edge, practically jumping off the roof and sprinting for the unpatrollable shadows of the railroad tracks with nearly superhuman speed.

We reached the tracks several minutes later and collapsed panting onto the rough gravel, not caring how much it hurt because we'd somehow eluded capture; we were now safe.

And suddenly, I remembered what it was I'd wanted to ask John, the whole point of our hanging out tonight. It seemed stupid now, and childish after what we'd just been through, but at this point I figured there really just wasn't anything to lose. So I turned to him, sweaty, mussed, lying in gravel, clothed in a dusty towel, and asked what I'd been aching to ask for the last week—ever since we'd first met at the school talent show.

"John…do you think you could teach me how to play guitar?"

QUESTIONS

When I was seven, I asked my mother how she and my father decided whose last name to use when they got married. She told me it was traditional for the woman to take the man's name. I told her that didn't seem fair and that when I got married, my wife and I would choose whose name we liked better. She ruffled my hair in that motherly way and brushed past my plan with similar abandon. Though I would like to claim pure intentions of promoting social equality by the age of seven, I can't deny that I was partially motivated by my desire to shed the last name Gross, which had caused me nothing but trouble since I had entered public school two years earlier.

When I was nine, I asked my mother why people were so upset about abortions—if they didn't like them, they could just not have them. The car in front of ours glared angry slogans from the bumper, demonizing any sinners who might dare to tailgate. She told me some people didn't think that was good enough; they believed abortion to be child murder. I told her it seemed fishy and that people should be able to decide for themselves what happens to their body. She did not respond, but again ruffled my hair. Though there were no ulterior motives behind this line of questioning, the answers she gave stopped an equal distance short of satisfying.

When I was twelve, I asked my mother why she didn't draw anymore. I'd found some of her sketches from art school hidden in a box upstairs. She had wanted to be a medical illustrator and seemed to have the talent to do so. She told me nothing, but she answered in the form of changing the subject, saying it was time for dinner and mentioning what the weather had been like that day. I told her that I didn't understand how someone could give up on their passions so silently and completely, and that real estate lacked soul. She passed the peas.

When I was fifteen, I asked my mother why she didn't own any music, how it was possible to get through life without so much as a single album. I couldn't think of anything sadder than a life devoid of melody. She told me that things are different when you are grown up, and that she used to have a fantastic record collection. I asked what happened to it and once again she passed the peas.

When I was nineteen, I asked my mother why she didn't go out to the movies or have any friends. I said that since she was divorced and my sister and I would be leaving, she would soon have no one to talk to. She told me she was tired after work and that she preferred to stay home. Like so many of her other answers, I was skeptical, but when she turned on the television the subject seemed to be as officially closed as if she had actually ruffled my hair.

When I was twenty-two, I stopped asking my mother questions with the word *why* and instead refocused on questions with simple yes or no answers like *can I have some money for rent?* and *can I have some money for electricity?* While these questions might not have yielded the intellectual weight of my existential inquiries, I found their answers to be far less nebulous and much easier to implement in the complexities of the modern world.

When I was twenty-six, I asked my sister what the hell was wrong with our mother—why had she given up a career in art, a fabulous record collection and all vestiges of interest in social interaction, current events and cinema? I couldn't understand why she did any of these things, or how anyone could go on each day living such an obviously horrendous life. My sister told me that my father had made my mother sell her record collection because many of the albums had been gifts from ex-boyfriends, he had refused to let her use their car to attend art school, and that the same general patterns of overbearing emotional self-interest he'd inflicted on us had been visited on her tenfold. My sister didn't specifically use the word tenfold, but made assorted statements to that effect and then changed the subject.

My life has always been full of amazing, strong, passionate women—women who have taught me how to play the guitar, who drink and fight like livers and knuckle-skin are going out of style, who are brazen enough to make art despite a total lack of talent, who throw the first rock, who change their names to Hank, who run newspapers and play the drums, who start literary magazines and organize zine symposiums, who write novels and traipse about South America on a whim while riding motorcycles and helping people in the third world. These are women who stay out as late as they like every night of the week and whose record collections could never be sold because they are a physical part of their soul.

My mother is not one of these women. She's more keen to pass peas than start a revolution. But I often wonder how things would have been different if she'd just refused the last name Gross.

BRAD

Brad was an imposing presence—the kind of guy I imagined I would meet at a bar over a game of pool, if I could go
to bars to play pool. He oozed confidence. This was because
he had proclaimed himself king of all that he could see. Even
here in juvenile lockup, he still saw himself as royalty. And as
royalty, it was easy to exude confidence. It didn't even matter
whether or not anyone else treated him as such—although
most did—because as king, his opinion was the only one that
mattered.

His imposing presence extended beyond just his attitude.
Brad was six-foot-two and wide at the shoulders, with bright
red hair and a full beard at the age of seventeen. He kept a

towel draped over his neck as if he'd perpetually just finished lifting weights. There was always a toothpick in his mouth. Where he came across the contraband toothpicks was a mystery, but they were an effective tool to establish an air of superiority. However, the most definitive thing about Brad was that he was a full-blooded Irishman and wasn't shy about it.

"The Irish can drink, fuck and fight better than anyone else in the world! And I'm as Irish as they come. What else is there in life?" Brad would boast to anyone who dared to be incarcerated in his presence. He would lean back in his plastic lawn chair with his thumbs grasping his shirt, tugging on imaginary suspenders as if he were Mark Twain relaxing on the deck of a riverboat. "That makes us the best in the world." He really just recycled those three nuggets of bravado. It might have been more convincing had he diversified his portfolio of cultural superiority. Personally, I thought he was making a good argument the Irish were also the best braggarts.

No matter the topic, Brad made ethnicity part of nearly every conversation. He liked to compare—mostly so he could show why the Irish were the best.

"The Irish can do whatever they please. Who's gonna stop us? You can't outdrink us, you sure as hell can't outfight us, and we fuck enough to raise one hell of an army. We could conquer the whole damn world. Who's gonna stop us?"

Obviously the legal system had been overlooked in this line of logic.

Brad either really liked to pick on me, or to argue with me. I was never sure which. Sometimes it was kind of like a "pigtails in the inkwell" situation, as if he liked to try to dominate me out of affection or camaraderie. But whatever the reason,

I never cared for being picked on and pushed back at every opportunity. However, since he was twice my size, all I had against him was my Jewish wit, which (to make a tired analogy) takes to an argument like a fish to water. Or, to make a racist analogy, like an Irishman to a bottle of whiskey. So we usually turned to arguing, which was fine, since we had to pass the time somehow.

"The Jews can write, produce, and direct better than anyone else in the world!" I would joke, mocking his cultural pride. I really couldn't care less. It was just fun to argue with such an exuberant opponent.

"Who cares?" Brad would snort defiantly. "The only movies worth watching are about drinking, fucking and fighting, and that is Irish territory."

No one else in this place could have gotten away with swearing and boasting quite so loudly as Brad did. He had been in Mac for a long stretch on some sort of sex offense. I never found out which one. But it was long enough for the staff to recognize him as nothing but a loudmouthed braggart—exactly the kind of guy they met after work over games of pool at bars. They almost seemed to find his bravado as entertaining as he did.

"The Vikings," I said to him one day. Football was on the television at the time, which made the connection in my brain. "The Vikings were better at drinking, fucking and fighting than the Irish."

"There aren't any more Vikings," he said.

"Casualties of drinking, fucking and fighting my friend."

"That doesn't mean—"

"The Vikings used to get drunk and have sex on the dinner

table at feasts in between fights. The Irish may drink and fight, or drink and fuck, but they don't do all three at once like the Vikings."

Brad hooked his thumbs into his imaginary suspenders and snorted off to the dorm room where he could get away from me and my Jewish insolence.

Brad never spoke to me again. I've always thought that meant I won.

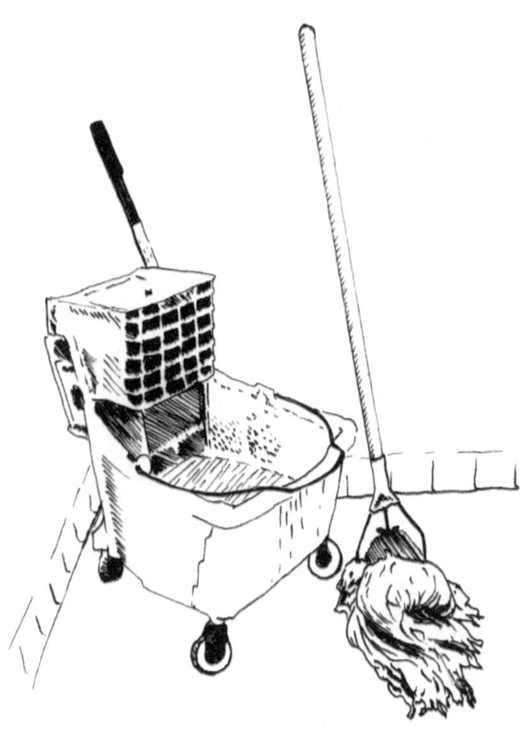

DEAD AIR

No matter how many electricians were called in to address the problem, the lights had flickered in the news writers' pit at CWBC for more than twenty years. People joked that it was the ghost of the former nightly news anchor, Reed Bancroft, who was every bit as dedicated to the network in death as he was in life.

"Copy for Bancroft!" they would shout ceremoniously when the lights flickered near deadline. A white sheet with eyeholes had been hung on the makeup room wall for so long that it was eventually framed.

And though none of the trained skeptics that worked in the newsroom actually believed the building was haunted, they kept the folklore alive as a form of reverence for a man who had practically built the Countrywide Broadcasting Corporation, winning more Peabodies than the rest of the network combined. His reporting on the Korean War was a standard part of broadcast journalism curricula at universities across the country, and many claimed that his steady reassurance had helped steer the nation through the turbulence of the sixties. They never spoke of his decline into alcoholism and senility, or his claims that the network (and the news in general) were under attack from evil spirits and that he, and he alone, could do anything to stop it. They only said that he had eventually died of a heart attack at his desk one night while preparing copy for the evening's broadcast, a dedicated newsman to the bitter end.

The only person who actually believed Bancroft haunted the building was Leroy Jackson, the night janitor. And the reason Leroy believed it was because he had to put up with it every damned night while he was cleaning the building.

A wispy grayish Bancroft appeared at his desk every night at 1 a.m. sharp with a wispy grayish snifter of brandy and wispy grayish cigar that emitted wispy grayish smoke. He read his copy out loud to himself several times over in his soothing trademark baritone, then clutched his wispy grayish chest and pitched forward, dissolving into wisps of gray on the desk. At 2:30 a.m. sharp, he would stomp out through the closed studio door telling a nonexistent producer that the whole world was going to hell before fading into the carpet. After that, Leroy would have to spend the rest of the evening contending with a variety of random ghostly rebroadcasts of the Korean War and all manner of petty vandalism. Once, Bancroft had even covered the bathroom stalls with lewd ectoplasmic graffiti about

Korean barmaids and a weather girl fired long ago. Leroy had spent hours spraying and scrubbing only to have it inexplicably fade from existence at 6 a.m.

At first, he hadn't minded. The reports on the war were a free education the working-class Leroy had missed out on in his youth, and there was a certain allure to being the only one privy to the situation at hand. Sometimes he would talk to Bancroft about his day, or what he'd seen at the movies recently. Occasionally the ghost would respond, offering a thumbs up or down, though it was more common for him not to. Once they'd even passed a wispy grayish flask back and forth, sharing stories about girls they'd known once upon a time. Leroy never understood how the spectral liquor had worked, and felt there were some things it was best not to question.

But over the years, the novelty faded as the mental decline Bancroft had displayed in life continued in death. He became a serious annoyance as he slowed Leroy's work down considerably with violent rants about 24-hour cable networks and beatniks in go-go boots, as well as frequent and ironic commentary about the threat posed by evil spirits. It was all compounded by Leroy's decision to give up drinking after a bad fall, an act that made Bancroft's activities seem less mirthful, and often packaged them with a splitting headache.

Leroy finally had enough on the day when all the toilets violently expunged themselves towards the ceiling, geyser-like. There were rumors of pay cuts and Leroy wasn't in the mood for any more shit.

He knocked on the office door belonging to the floor manager, Jill Masterson, the next morning. "'Scuse me, Miss Masterson. You got a moment?"

She waved him in and pointed to a chair without removing her eyes from a thick binder that lay open on the desk in front of her. "One moment," she said.

Mountains of paperwork covered every flat surface including the chair she'd directed Leroy to sit in. Not wishing to disturb any potential order that might exist, he sat delicately on top of the stack of paper like it was a child's booster seat.

After several moments, she clapped the binder closed. "All right, what is it?" she asked impatiently.

"Well you see, Miss Masterson, it's that ghost," Leroy said. "He always botherin' me, making extra messes to clean and talking foul 'bout that ol' weather girl. I cain't take no more. That ghost needs to go."

Jill gave Leroy a steely once over. "You mean the ghost that flicks the lights on and off?"

"I can't rightly say if that's the same one, 'cause when I around he more prone to drinkin' and making a mess, but it's prolly the same fella. Bancroft's his name, I think."

"Oh my god, oh my god, oh my god…" Jill said, burying her face in her hands and sucking in a long angry breath.

"Whatsa matter, Miss Masterson?" Leroy said. "You need some water or something?"

"Leroy," she wheezed. "You do a good job. And I sympathize with your medical situation—"

"Well, thank you."

"Right… but if you come to work drunk again, I'm going to have to let you go. Do you understand?"

Leroy's jaw dropped, shocked. "I ain't had a drink for near on two years now, Miss Masterson, ever since I hurt my hip." Leroy protested. "I'm telling you, it's that ghost that folks on the day shift always going on about."

"I'm serious Leroy," she said. "No more."

Leroy looked at Jill's set jaw and stacks of work and realized she wasn't going to come around. "All right," he said with a smile. "I understand."

"Thank you," she said. "Now if you don't mind…" She re-opened the thick binder and turned her eyes back to the desk.

"No problem," Leroy hummed pleasantly. He stood up slowly, taking care not to dislodge any of the paperwork he'd been seated on, and left the office. "Sheet," he grumbled once he got into the hall. "Guess I'll have to figure out how to take care of ol' Bancroft myself."

Problem was, Leroy didn't have the first clue what to do. Once, he'd seen a movie about some scientists with laser backpacks they used on ghosts, but that seemed like it would only make a bigger mess to clean up, which was exactly what Leroy was trying to avoid. He asked a gypsy fortune-teller he passed on the street, but the gypsy wanted $100.

"I tell you I'm a janitor and you ask for that kind of money?" Leroy laughed. "You don't know nuthin'."

He chuckled all the way home, despite being no closer to finding a solution to his problem.

So when he got home, he started looking through the yellow pages, under *G* for ghost. Leroy's eyes were immediately drawn to a large ad for the Society of Professional Organizations of Occult Kinesis or S.P.O.O.K. It sounded official and offered a free consultation, so Leroy picked up the phone and made an appointment for that afternoon.

The address listed in the phone book was in an alley behind

a downtown pizza parlor. A small neon sign glowed the letters S.P.O.O.K., advertising a narrow staircase down to the basement. Feeling he really had nothing to lose, Leroy limped down the stairs and let himself in the door. When Leroy stepped inside, instead of a waiting room like he'd expected, he found himself in a tiny room with bare concrete walls and bright red carpet. There was a skinny, young man in his mid-twenties, with stringy blonde hair and glasses that looked thick enough to be cut from the floor of a glass bottom boat. He was seated behind a lavish oak desk that stood in stark contrast to the room itself. He was wearing a thick, velvet smoking jacket and there was a hammock in a darkened corner.

He nearly jumped from his seat. "You must be Leroy," he said excitedly. "Come in, come in, come in. Let me get you a chair." He pulled a matching oak chair from a darkened corner and offered it to Leroy.

"Thank you," Leroy said, sitting down.

"No, thank you," the young man beamed. "From what you told me on the phone it sounds like you have a genuine repeating kinetic spectral orb with corollary pareidolia on your hands. It's not everyday that we come across a case like that."

"I dunno nothing 'bout no orbs," Leroy said. "Really's more like a drunk ol' white guy than an orb, but you're the expert."

"Oh, right, sorry," the young man said. "That's just what we scientists call them, is orbs. I probably should have explained, but I got so excited I got ahead of myself. Oh jeez. I haven't even introduced myself yet," he babbled. "Sorry. I'm just so darned excited here."

"It's really no problem," Leroy said.

"I'm Charlie, Charlie Hort, of the Society of Professional

Organizations of Occult Kinesis, or S.P.O.O.K. for short." He extended a hand.

"Pleased to meet you, Charlie," Leroy said, accepting it. "So you think you can help me out? 'Cause I tell you, work is getting awful hard lately, what with my bad hip and that darned ghost, or orb, always fussin' about. He made all the toilets explode one night. That ain't no way to behave. I don't care if he is dead."

"Well, hopefully we'll be able to take care of that for you," Charlie smiled.

"So, you know, I don't mean nothing by this, just curiosity is all, but you look kind of young, you know," Leroy said. "How long you been at this line of work?"

"Uh, well, long enough," Charlie said.

"So, your organization has helped a lot of people with problems like mine then?" Leroy asked.

"Every case is different," Charlie said. "But I'm pretty confident we can help."

"I see. How many cases you had though?"

Charlie paused, mentally mulling something over. "All right," he eventually said. "You've got me. You'll be the first, which is why I'm so excited. I've been waiting for a case for months now."

"So, there ain't really no organization in the strictest sense of the word?"

"Oh, yes. Yes, there is. However, at the moment, it's just me. But I really do know what I'm doing," he pleaded. "Look, I've got spectroscopes and EMF meters and there's a thermographic camera around here somewhere," he said gesturing around his office. "It just came in the mail the other day and I forgot where I put it, but I know it's here. I even went to M.I.T."

"Mmm-hmm," Leroy said. He looked around the office,

taking it all in slowly. "To be truthful," he said, "I just got me one question."

"What's that?"

"What you chargin'?"

Charlie smiled. "Special free introductory offer. Good for today only," he said.

"Then, Mister Hort of the S.P.O.O.K., you got yourself a deal."

Leroy left the S.P.O.O.K. office with a stack of pamphlets Charlie gave him to read through on haunting and cleansing rituals before they met up again that night for Leroy's shift. It all seemed like a bunch of new age hooey, chanting and making offerings and the such, but Leroy had to be honest with himself that the situation was strange enough in its own right. Adding some hand holding and incense on top of things wasn't that far a leap into the farcical.

Leroy met Charlie at the loading bay door at midnight. He was carrying a large duffel bag full of supplies and wearing a pair of mechanics coveralls with plastic safety goggles over his thick-lensed glasses. "Just in case," Charlie said, tapping the goggles.

"In case of what, is what worries me," Leroy grumbled. "Hurry up in here 'fore someone thinks you're robbing the place."

They took the service elevator up to the news floor and Charlie busied himself setting up a variety of instruments to collect data.

"What's all this stuff for anyhow?" Leroy asked.

"Electromagnetism. Ultraviolet radiation. That sort of thing."

"Mr. Bancroft's more grayish than violet. Kinda transparent really.

"No, it's—"

"You'll see when he shows up though."

"At one?"

"Every damn night. I even tried changing the office clocks once, but he kept showing up at 1 a.m. on the network clock. Don't know if it means anything, but it's set to Central Standard Time."

"No, not really. Sorry."

"Ain't no worries," Leroy said with a smile.

"Wait, did you say Bancroft? As in Reed Bancroft?"

"Yessir. That's the fella."

"You never said it was Reed Bancroft. He's a legend."

"Does it matter?"

"No, I suppose not. It's just exciting, really. My first case is a celebrity."

"Mmm-hmm," Leroy droned. "You need me, I'll just be down this way emptying out the trash cans." Leroy went back to work as Charlie calibrated his instruments. At 12:59 a.m. he put down his mop and shuffled over to Charlie, pointing to Bancroft's old desk. "That's the one," he said. "Dunno whose desk it is now, but used to be Mr. Bancroft's, I suppose."

"So that's where he'll appear?"

"Every damned night," Leroy said sourly. "So what we gonna do when he shows?"

Before Charlie could answer, Bancroft materialized at his desk, sipping his whiskey and sucking at his cigar. "New York City officials awoke to a firestorm of criticism over their handling of the garbage workers' strike," he rumbled. "No, no, no…that isn't right at all. It lacks poetry, panache." Bancroft scribbled something on his vaporous news copy and prepared to begin again.

Before he could, Charlie stepped forward directly in front

of him, spread his arms wide and shouted, "Spirit! I command you to cease what you're doing and leave immediately!"

"Sorry," Bancroft said. "I'm on deadline."

"You're…huh? What?"

"I said, I'm on deadline. It's part of work. Something I'm sure you beatniks don't understand, and frankly, I don't have time to explain to you."

"Uh, please leave?" Charlie offered, his voice cracking slightly.

Bancroft suddenly clutched his chest and pitched forward, shattering into thousands of smoky particles that spread out and dissolved into the desk.

"All that big talk about M.I.T. and all you do is ask him to leave?" Leroy said. "You gotta be kiddin' me. I coulda done that."

"Well it worked didn't it? He's gone, isn't he?"

"Aw sheet, that didn't do nothing," Leroy said. "'Cept for tellin' you off, this the same stunt he pulls every night. He'll be back again in a few hours, 'cept now he'll prolly be all hot and bothered and make an even bigger mess."

"Well, there's more to try. That was just the first step," Charlie said desperately.

"Let's hope so," Leroy scoffed. "'Cause right now I'm starting to want my money back."

"But I didn't charge you," Charlie protested. "Oh…I just got that."

"Good. That means you ain't completely slow," Leroy snorted. "He'll be back over there in an hour or so, and I gotta try and get these floors in order 'fore then." Leroy took his mop and walked to the other end of the office, calling back over his shoulder. "Holler if you need something. But my suggestion is your time be best spent coming up with a better plan."

Charlie didn't say anything though, just went about checking his instruments against charts in an old leather bound book and making notes on a pad until it was nearly 2:30 a.m., time for Bancroft's second appearance of the evening.

"It's nearly time now," Leroy said, parking his cleaning cart between some desks. "What you got in store for us next? A readin' of the Declaration of Independence?" he chuckled.

"Okay, I get it," Charlie said. "This is all very funny to you. But this is all stuff from really authoritative texts. Some of it dates back hundreds of years."

"I ain't no expert, but seems to me since we got a modern ghost on our hands, you might need something new."

"Well, ghosts are supposed to be afraid of vacuum cleaners," Charlie offered. "We could try that."

"I'm the damned janitor and you think I ain't never run a vacuum cleaner in here before? What kind of fool are you?"

"Look now," Charlie stammered, "this is tricky business and it doesn't always work the first time."

"How you know? This your first time out, remember? Sheet. I been dealin' with this ghost for near fifteen years now. This point, I s'pect I know more than you."

"Except how to get rid of him."

"Yeah, well you got me there," Leroy said. "Though I ain't sold you know a thing about that neither."

"Well that's 'cause we haven't tried this yet," Charlie said and hung a large string of garlic around Leroy's neck. "And, this…" Charlie produced a large stick of sage incense, which he shoved into Leroy's hands and then lit. "You wave this around the office while I get out the holy water."

"Holy water! Now we're talkin'," Leroy said. "For a moment

there, I thought we was making a pizza 'cause ghosts don't like Italian food." Satisfied, he shuffled around the office with a renewed vigor, waving the sage bundle wildly, as if the goal was to bludgeon Bancroft with it should he happen to materialize in its trajectory. Maybe there was hope after all. When Bancroft appeared a moment later, Leroy even hollered, "You had it now!" waving the incense around like a sword. "Get 'im, Charlie!"

But rather than douse the specter in holy water like planned, Charlie began ringing a bell and clapping his hands.

Bancroft didn't even slow down, only snarled, "This is a newsroom, not a damned Turkish coffeehouse!" before fading into the carpet, leaving a large stain of ectoplasm in his wake.

"What was that?" Leroy demanded. "You were supposed to make with the holy water and instead you started going on like some damned Hare Krishna."

"Will you please stop being so critical? This stuff is supposed to work," Charlie said. "I don't know why it isn't. We could try scattering rice on the floor so the ghost has to stop and count it. They're supposed to hate that. Or maybe painting the door red."

"Painting the what? You trying to get me fired?"

"No, just—"

"I think we's about done for the night Charlie. I gotta get some real work done so I don't get in no more trouble with Miss Masterson come morning." Leroy started gathering up Charlie's instruments and ushering him towards the elevator.

"Wait, wait, wait, wait..." Charlie said dragging his heels "Maybe he has unfinished business."

"Oh yeah? Like what?" Leroy scoffed.

"Um, doing the news maybe?" Charlie offered.

"Aw sheet. I didn't miss a thing not going to school did I?

That's even stupider than the rest of your ideas. It's time for you to go, boss," Leroy said, shaking his head. He hurriedly shepherded Charlie toward the elevator. Bancroft would be back soon and Leroy fully expected to have his hands full when it happened. He was already mentally calculating how many extra mop buckets he would have to prep, just to be safe.

"But what are you going to do about the ghost?" Charlie whined. "Let me try again please? Please?"

"You had your chance kid," Leroy said. "Now I gotta get back to work cleaning up and finding a new ghost hunter that can actually help."

"Oh, come on, you have to give me another chance. No one else has ever taken me seriously. Not the other ghost hunters, or my professors or even my parents. I was practically laughed out of M.I.T. Just, I'm begging you, Leroy, please don't give up on me now. I just need some time to figure out what we're dealing with here. Please…" Charlie seemed so pitiful that Leroy felt truly awful, but he didn't really have any choice in the matter. He had a mess and an angry ghost to deal with. There just wasn't time to play nursemaid on top of things.

"Sorry kid. You gave it a good shot," he said. "Go back home and order yourself a pizza." Then Leroy softly pushed Charlie backwards onto the elevator, watching the tears fog up his goggles as he sank silently down out of view.

"Good grief," Leroy said. "I guess you really do get what you pay for." He turned back around to fetch his cleaning cart and saw Bancroft floating, watching him with a mischievous smirk on his face. "I know, I know," Leroy said. "I's in for it now, ain't I?"

"Yeah," Bancroft smirked, "you are."

"Well, let's get to it then," Leroy said. "I ain't gettin' any younger."

When Miss Masterson saw the state of office the next morning, she sent Leroy to take a breathalyzer. And though he blew clean, the only thing that kept her from firing Leroy anyhow was a memo from HR explaining that she should consider herself lucky he didn't want to sue.

That next evening Leroy brought a bottle with him to work for the first time in years. If he was going to be accused of drinking on the job, he might as well do it. And he certainly wasn't going to share a bottle with that contemptible ghost again. Not after what he'd pulled last night. Drinking buddies don't stain chalk outlines into the carpet with ectoplasm or dump garbage in the air conditioning.

When Bancroft finally showed, practicing his lines as usual, Leroy's only response was to lift his bottle slightly in his direction, adding a respectful nod before taking a pull. After the previous night, he'd come to the conclusion that it was impossible to predict what the ghost might do. It was better to just wait it out and then figure out what needed to be cleaned up afterward. After all, some nights Bancroft had been nearly innocuous, barely lifting a pencil, much less overturning a file cabinet or multiple file cabinets depending on how the war was going that evening. The way Leroy figured, the less he did, the less likely he was to be labeled a beatnik agitator—which had historically been a factor in incurring the full consequence of Bancroft's annoyance.

Things got off to a good start as Bancroft rolled through his dialogue and sipped his ethereal whiskey obliviously before doing his nightly misty meld with the desk and retreating behind the perceptual curtain. Leroy remained stoic, sipping away at his bottle and waiting for the second act, which happily also passed without event. Leroy was beginning to think his plan might actually work. All he had to do was be patient. He settled down into an office chair to rest his hip and finish his bottle.

The spectral news that night focused on one particular offensive in 1952. It had apparently been crucial to the war effort, though ultimately unsuccessful. After several updates, the ghost looked annoyed and sat down on a chair next to Leroy, inasmuch as ghosts can sit.

"Aren't you going to say anything?" Bancroft said. "Why don't we talk about the movies like old times?"

"No sir," Leroy grunted. "I's sick of you and your lousy attitude, always calling me a beatnik and the such."

"Why don't you quit then?"

"Pooh," Leroy snorted. "'Cain't get no other job with my hip all janky like this. Lucky to even still have this one with the way you always carrying on."

"Sorry, but I have to protect the newsroom from evil spirits."

"Well, ain't that about the pot and the kettle," Leroy cackled. "You worried about evil spirits, when you spend every night pouring 'em down your gullet."

"My job is stressful," Bancroft said. "You beatniks don't understand the pressure I'm under."

"Your job? Who is you kidding man? You dead! Been dead long enough that you ought to be used to it by now too. But you's still going on about the Korean War every night. It's shameful livin' in the past like that."

"World affairs are of a paramount importance."

"Okay, whatever you say Mr. Dead Man," Leroy grunted. "Why don't you just do whatever you's going to do and let me be, so I can get about my own business?"

"No," Bancroft said firmly, though he was clearly somewhat shocked at Leroy's audacity.

"No?" Leroy scoffed. "Whatsa matter, out of ideas after them stunts you pulled last night?" he laughed.

"No," Bancroft sneered. "I've got some real doozies stored up, censored government reports and stains you'd never get out, even with bleach. You'd have to replace the carpet altogether."

"Well, get to it then," Leroy challenged. "I ain't got all night."

"The news desk doesn't kowtow to business interests," Bancroft replied pompously. "We're an independent agent."

"Oh, forget you," Leroy snorted, tossing away his empty bottle. "I'm so fed up with your nonsense. Why don't you just wreck the place and let me do my job already? Like this," he exclaimed, knocking a large stack of papers to the floor. "Or this," he said, overturning an office chair. "See, it's easy!"

"You've totally lost it pal," Bancroft muttered. "I can see the copy now: 'A local janitor got so confused he made a mess instead of cleaning one. Film at eleven.'" Bancroft paused momentarily. "No, we can punch that up a bit. How about…'The CWBC offices were vandalized today in a manner befitting a rogue beatnik horde, though it was later discovered that a disgruntled janitor in the midst of a nervous breakdown did the damage. He claimed the office was under attack by evil spirits.'"

"I just cain't take it no more," Leroy howled drunkenly. "Get out! Get out! Get out!" he screamed, hurling anything within reach at Bancroft. Coffee cups, books and keyboards all whizzed through the air at the misty news anchor who was still rattling off potential copy for his satirical broadcast in his thundering baritone.

Finally, Leroy launched a large stapler that sailed right through

Bancroft's smirking face, punching a hole in the wall behind him.

"Damn! Now see what you've done," Leroy shouted, stamping his feet. But instead of responding with more potential headlines or accusations of beatnik sympathies, Bancroft dissolved silently into the air, leaving Leroy to wallow in his own mess.

Leroy looked around to be sure Bancroft was gone, then hobbled over to inspect the wall to see if it was possible for him to repair the plaster before morning. But when he looked in the hole, he recoiled in horror as the withered face of the corporeal and very dead Reed Bancroft stared back at him. Panicking, he covered the hole with the closest thing he could grab, then ran from the office as fast as his hip would carry him, leaving a commemorative framed copy of Bancroft's head shot covering up the hole in the plaster that his body was hidden behind.

Leroy called Charlie over and over again, and getting no answer, eventually went down to the S.P.O.O.K. office and pounded on the door until it was answered by a bleary-eyed Charlie dressed in his smoking jacket.

"Let me in, dammit," Leroy said. "We got us a whole new set of problems."

"But I thought you didn't want my help anymore."

"You may be a world class fool, but you's the only one who believes me, and we on a schedule, so you gonna have to do."

"I don't know," Charlie said. "You really hurt my feelings."

"And I'll hurt 'em again if you keep acting the fool. You gonna help me out here or not?"

"Okay," Charlie said excitedly. "Just let me get my shoes."

They got into Charlie's battered Volkswagen Karmann Ghia and sped back to the office where Leroy showed Charlie the body hidden behind the plaster.

"Oh jeez," Charlie laughed, "This makes total sense."

"What are you talking about? Don't nothing about this make no kind of sense at all," Leroy thundered. "Ghosts doing the news and bodies in the wall. All I want to do is mop the damn floors in peace."

"No, no," Charlie laughed. "I mean it makes sense why the other things we tried didn't work. Clearly Bancroft is still here because his body is still here. If you want him to go away, then his body needs to be buried properly. You should probably tell your boss to have him exhumed from the wall."

"Uh-uh," Leroy said flatly. "She'll just ask what I was doing drunk, tearing up the walls looking for dead guys. How I'm gonna explain that one? I'd be fired before noon."

"Well…" Charlie said, staring off into space. "I guess we could do it ourselves then. Are there any tools around to get him out of the wall?"

Leroy was about to protest when he realized he had passed the point of no return long ago. He was practically in the capitol city of No Return by now. "Yeah," he said. "I think there's a sledgehammer and some plaster down in the boiler room."

"Why don't you go get the tools and I'll start clearing some space," Charlie said, hanging his smoking jacket over a nearby office chair.

"All right," Leroy said. "What's he doing in there anyway?"

"I couldn't really say," Charlie said quizzically. "I've heard of bodies being interred in walls to ward off evil spirits before, but that went out of style in the 1700s."

"Yeah, he's always going on about protection from evil spirits, saying that's his job."

"Really?" Charlie said, incredulous. "Do you think he did this to himself? Maybe in his will?"

"I dunno," Leroy said. "People round here sure are fond of Mr. Bancroft, prolly 'cause they ain't spent much time with him lately. But I'll reckon if that's what he really wanted, some fool at the network woulda let him. I'm starting to think college messes with y'alls heads something fierce."

"He was certainly famous enough to pull something like that," Charlie mused. "Oh well. We probably oughta get to dealing with the body now and figure the rest of it out later. Otherwise, we won't be done by morning."

"True, true," Leroy said and started towards the elevator. But just before he got on, he stopped and turned back. "I'm sorry I yelled at you, Charlie," he said sheepishly. "You ain't dumb. You been real nice to me and I appreciate it."

"It's fine," Charlie smiled. "Really."

After Leroy brought up the tools from the boiler room, things moved quickly. Charlie busted through the wall with the sledgehammer while Leroy cleaned up the messes he'd made earlier that evening. They hurriedly plastered the wall back up and scooped the crumbling body into a black plastic trash bag to load into the trunk of Charlie's car for the trip to the cemetery. Leroy knew he wouldn't be back before the stuffed shirts showed up in the morning, but things were clean enough when he left that no one was likely to notice—especially compared to the state the office had been in after Bancroft's offensive the previous night.

Leroy and Charlie found a nice secluded spot in the back corner of the cemetery and set themselves to digging silently. By the end of the first two feet, Leroy's hip started bothering him enough that he sat the next two feet out, but he joined back in to finish the rest.

After they put Bancroft in the hole and filled it back in, Leroy took a small bouquet of cyclamen flowers from a nearby headstone and laid them at the foot of the soft dirt mound. The sky was just beginning to pinken as the sun peeked over the horizon.

"Should we say something?" he asked Charlie.

Charlie stared ahead blankly for a few moments, then clearly, steadily, he spoke. "Peshawar, Pakistan—Pakistani attack helicopters have shelled militant hideouts in the northwestern Swat district, killing thirty rebels, the military said on Sunday."

Staring straight ahead, Leroy grabbed Charlie's shoulder to stop him. "What's that you going on about?"

"It's the headlines," Charlie said. "It seemed the appropriate memoriam."

"I meant like magic words to make sure this ornery fool stay dead this time."

"Oh…" Charlie said. "No. This should do it."

"Good," Leroy said, and limped his way back out of the cemetery and towards the nearest bus stop. He was in serious need of a shower and more than ready for bed.

When Leroy returned to work the next evening, he finished the floors in record time, whistling cheerfully as he gave them a much-needed coat of wax he'd been putting off for weeks. The next night he scrubbed clean all the grout in the bathrooms, even polishing the chrome pipes on the urinals. Leroy felt like he'd been running with weights on all these years and he was finally free to sprint for the finish line. Over the next two weeks, the office started to sparkle in a way that no one had thought possible—though the white-collar jokesters credited the ghost of Reed Bancroft for the act, as the lights continued to inexplicably flicker. Miss Masterson even commented that she was glad Leroy had been able to quit drinking and told him he'd receive a quarter raise if he kept it up. But Leroy didn't mind. His job was easy now. His life was easy now. His hip even felt better than it had in years.

The only problem was that free of Bancroft's interference, Leroy was running out of stuff to clean. He regularly finished with his work by 2 a.m., which left more than four hours until his shift ended at 6 a.m. to do nothing but sit and stare out the twelfth floor window at the city lights below, reflecting on his life so far and what bits of it he had left. Leroy had no wife or children. His parents were long dead. He had a brother somewhere out west, but didn't have the first clue how to contact him. Leroy now went blocks out of his way to avoid walking past the liquor store on his way to work. Things may never have been easier for him at work, but he was starting to realize that Bancroft had been the closest thing he'd had to a friend. Work had become unbearably lonely without him and his nightly old broadcasts. He even found himself jumping and cringing at strange noises he heard from corners of the office, scared they might be the evil spirits Bancroft was so concerned about.

After two months, Leroy decided he couldn't take it any more. So, after he finished the floors, he took a shovel from the boiler room and made his way to the secluded spot in the back corner of the graveyard where they'd left Bancroft. Grass was starting to grow in over the mound and the flowers Leroy had laid at the grave had deposited seeds that had just begun to sprout tiny pink and white buds.

"All right," he grunted. "You been in timeout long enough now. Let's just hope you learned yourself a lesson or two." And then he plunged the shovel into the soft dirt and began to dig.

PRIVATE PARTS

It was a perfect summer night with the moon high in a cloudless sky and a perfect view up Janelle's skirt as she climbed the fence, wobbling slightly at the peak. She was unapologetically free of underwear. Not that it mattered in the slightest. Though it may have been awhile, I'd been over that mountain and seen all there was to see many times before. And even if I hadn't, she started stripping the instant her feet hit the ground on the other side, revealing her asymmetrical nipples, her moles, the diamond pattern of her sandy pubic hair, the contours of her hips, her topography in full, to any and all lurking in the park that night. Though I did notice that a tattoo had appeared on her shoulder since I'd seen it last.

"Mmm-hmm," Sam grinned, playfully backhanding my chest. "That's my girl." He shoved his half-empty bottle of wine into my hands and launched himself up the chain link, nearly vaulting over the top.

"Toss it over," he said after touching down on the other side.

"There's no cork," I replied. "What if it spills?"

"That's why we have more," Sam laughed. "Just toss it."

"Okay." I carefully lobbed the bottle over the fence, doing my booze-sopped best to keep it from spinning or flipping, trying to keep it perfectly upright. Somehow, despite the watery slurring of my muscles, it worked. The bottle slid into Sam's waiting hands, a perfect Willy Mays basket catch that didn't spill a drop.

"See?" He grinned. "You just gotta have faith. That's what I do, and things always seem to work out. Hang with me and you'll always have fun."

"Okay," I grumbled, slightly jealous of his easygoing swagger. "I'm coming over." I grabbed the chain link and hoisted myself up, tightly gripping the plastic bag with the second jug of wine in my hands while clinging to the fence. There really wasn't anything to worry about. It was simple chain link, five feet high, and not even any barbed wire on top. It was almost like the city wanted people to break into the pool at night. Why else would they have put it in a park, submerged in a gulley and surrounded by tall trees that totally obscured it from street view? Everything Sam and Janelle had pitched to me a half-hour earlier at the bar during their invitation was accurate. It really was too easy.

Once my feet touched down on the other side, I also began disrobing, though unlike Sam and Janelle I left my clothes neatly folded in a pile, rather than as trailmarkers leading to the water's edge.

Janelle was already in the water, and Sam was going up the water slide. I could see a tattoo identical to Janelle's on his shoulder.

"Watch, it's just like I told you back at bar," he beckoned from atop the ladder. "Nothing funnier than naked dudes on a water slide." He threw himself down the ramp, feet akimbo, and his thumb plugged into the wine bottle to keep it both pure and readily accessible. When Sam reached the end, he went airborne, flopping backwards with his balls swinging free in the night air.

It was pretty funny.

Naked, I popped open the second jug of wine, and took a long sip. The air was pleasantly warm but I didn't expect the water to be.

"Jesus, Nick, quit dragging your feet and get in already," Sam hollered. "It's life and you're busy missing it."

I padded to the rim and started to dip in a toe, but was interrupted by Sam's insistence that I do it all at once. "The water slide," he said, slapping the water, then chugging from the bottle again. "The fucking water slide. It's the heart of the whole bit."

"Fine, fine," I said and climbed the ladder. I sat down carefully and pushed myself forward, clutching the recapped jug of wine to my chest like a baby. When I reached the end, I realized it wasn't through any intention of his own that Sam had flopped over the way he did. The slide kicked you up at an odd angle, splaying your limbs and particulars in all directions for natural comic effect, and creating maximum splash upon contact with the water. It was a little kids' pool after all.

When I surfaced, both Sam and Janelle were laughing at me.

"It just never ceases to be funny," Sam cackled. "Your balls are just floating free like they're in zero gravity or something. It's space camp for testicles."

"God, it's warmer in here than I expected," I said, treading water furiously to keep the jug from sinking me.

"The pool sits in the sun all day, warming up the water," Sam said. "Why this place isn't packed every night of the summer is a mystery to me."

"Probably because it's trespassing," I offered.

"It's a public park. I'm a member of the public," Sam grinned. "I just keep different hours than most, is all."

"Hey, you opened the red yet?" Janelle asked, clutching the pools edge.

"Yeah," I said.

"Well, bring it here then."

I paddled over to Janelle, her naked body shimmering beneath the water, and hoisted the jug up onto the deck for her to drink at her convenience. I was going to drown if I held onto it much longer anyhow.

"I'm going on the water slide again," Sam announced proudly while sloppily paddling one-handed towards the edge. His penis flopped around like a rudder steering his torso as he lopsidely propelled himself toward the slide. The sillier and more difficult it became, the happier he seemed. The whole affair was so preposterous, I couldn't help smiling.

But Janelle wasn't smiling. "Hey," she whispered to me. "Sam doesn't know about you and me, so don't say anything, okay?" She unscrewed the cap and took a long pull from the jug.

"Why?" I said, then took my turn with the wine.

"I just don't think he'll take it well," she said, her voice still hushed. She flinched slightly as she caught some spray from

Sam's floundering. "Things are still fresh is all."

"What difference does it make?" I asked, but Janelle pressed a hushing finger to her mouth. "Right, sorry."

"It's fine."

"Just, I haven't even seen you for a year, and you just met him, right?" I said softly. "I don't know, when were you married? It came as such a shock when I ran into you, I didn't even think to ask."

"Two weeks ago."

"And you met when?"

"Three weeks ago, at Floyd's."

"Wow..."

"I know," she said dreamily. "We both grabbed the same beer at the bar, thinking it was ours. Next thing you know, we're talking, then getting tattoos, and suddenly we're married. Everything's been sort of chaotic ever since."

I saw that the wine was still in my hand, so I took a long drink, then set the jug back on the rim. "It's...well, it's impulsive." I handed her the wine.

"That's what makes it fun." Janelle took the jug and drank long and full, gazing dreamily at Sam as he clambered out of the water. "It's intoxicating to have all that energy and chaos focused on you for a change, to just let yourself get carried away in it."

"At least now I know where the tattoo came from."

"Checking me out were you?" She smirked. "Do you like it?"

"Does it mean anything if I do?"

"No."

"I like it then," I said. "Wouldn't have expected a pterodactyl, but you must have been pretty carried away in things to get married so quickly, so a wacky tattoo doesn't surprise me at all."

"I married him because he asked," Janelle said firmly. "It's just nice to be carried away in the process. And I happen to like pterodactyls, one of the many things you don't know about me."

"I thought you said it was chaotic."

Janelle laughed and took another sip of wine. "See for yourself," she said and thrust it into my hands. I took the jug in both hands, hoisted it high, and drank as I sunk, then kicked my feet to get back up when I ran out of air. Janelle was grinning at me. "Captain goes down with the ship?"

"Something like that," I said and set the wine back on the deck. "But you're happy, right?"

Another drink, and a look-away she probably thought was subtle. "Of course. Why wouldn't I be happy?"

"BALLS AWAY!" Sam thundered as he shot off the end of the slide, colliding with the water, making a loud slapping noise and an aquatic eruption. He surfaced like a shot, wine bottle still clutched tightly, grinning wider than ever. "Did you see that, baby?" he shouted. "Like a fuckin' A-bomb!"

"It was great, baby," Janelle offered.

"This is life, man. This, right here. We should be doing shit like this every night," Sam said. He swam to the edge by Janelle and me. "Other people are just watching TV or some bullshit. And, of course, the real irony is that they watch shows of people doing shit like this rather than just going to do it themselves. Everyone knows the pool is right there, and still no one." He put the bottle to his lips, but found it empty. "Aw, fuck it," Sam said and tossed it over the fence to the grass where it bounced off into the darkness.

"Some people like TV," Janelle said.

"But not us," Sam grinned.

"No. Not us," Janelle echoed.

"What about you, Nick?" Sam asked. "What's the deal? We scooped you up with us so quick, I never even asked what your deal is."

"What do you mean, what's the deal?"

"The deal, the skinny, the hot poop, man. Who are you? What do you do? You got a girl waiting for you at home? 'Cause if so, I'm telling you now, she's going to be waiting awhile, 'cause we're going late tonight!" Sam held a hand up to Janelle for a high five, which she ignored.

"No," I said. "No girl. Not anymore."

"Why? What happened?"

"Oh, you know," I said uncomfortably. "Life, I suppose."

"Yeah, I been there," Sam smiled. He grabbed the jug of red and hoisted it high. "To life." He took a quick drink and offered it to Janelle, who passed it on to me.

"To life," I agreed.

Janelle pushed off from the wall and paddled towards the center of the pool. "I'm going to float," she announced sourly.

"Okay babe," Sam said, again drinking deeply. His capacity for wine was truly impressive; my head would have been bobbing even if we weren't in the water.

"So what's life?" Sam asked.

"'Scuse me?"

"What's life? Like, what happened?" He offered me the wine, but I didn't take it.

"I, uh…a job," I said. "There was a job offer."

"You or her?"

"Me."

"And?"

"And it was in Africa," I said. "Temporary, but in Africa."

"She didn't want you to go then? Got all nesty on you or something?"

"Something."

"You gotta start using full sentences, buddy," Sam said. "The whole point of wine is to initiate rambling, run-on monologues, to tell people how things really are, how they really are. And here you are, the one-word wonder."

"Sorry."

"Shit must be defective or something," Sam said. He took another sip and swished it around his mouth. "I dunno. Seems fine to me. Maybe you just need more." He thrust the jug at me.

"Maybe," I said.

"Maybe," he mocked.

I put the jug to my lips and sipped, but when I tried to set it down, I found that Sam was holding it up to my mouth with a wide grin on his face. I sucked air in through my nose, gulping and chugging for dear life as wine poured into my gullet, seeping out of the edges of my mouth and pouring down my cheeks in tiny rivulets. Sam relented, and I tore the jug from my lips to gasp for air just as I thought I could take no more.

He set the jug on the side. "Now, try again, friend," he said. "What happened? Well, catch your breath first, I suppose. But then…"

"Fine," I wheezed. "We just had different priorities is all."

"How so?"

"She said that after Africa, there would just be another Africa. Or an Alaska. Or Chicago, or Kansas even. That there would always be a big opportunity somewhere and I would always want to take them. And if I didn't, I'd resent her for that."

"And?" he prodded.

"And she was right." I drank again, this time on my own.

"She wanted to keep you home?"

"No," I said, "she wanted me to want to stay home. And I couldn't do it. I went. And now I'm back. And she's gone."

"I see."

"Yeah."

"Life," Sam grinned.

"Life. That's all."

"Don't worry," he said. "It happens to the best of us." Sam took the jug from me, sipped quickly and set it on the edge. "Now, after all that, just one question for you, Nick."

"What's that?"

"How did it feel sharing your feelings with another naked man?" His eyes were locked into mine, completely serious.

"Nothing funnier than naked dudes on a water slide," I laughed.

"Not a damned thing," Sam agreed. "Not a damned thing." He pushed off towards the middle paddling on his back. "Look out baby, sharks in the water," he announced.

I pushed off the wall gently, floating on my back and looking up the sky. The air and water were both warm, soft and soothing (even with the thrashing sounds and playful shrieking of Janelle falling victim to Sam's shark attack). The waves rocked me gently up and down, like being adrift on the ocean. I didn't understand why Janelle wanted our past to remain discreet. Sam seemed all right to me. And it was clear everyone had moved on. They sounded happy. I felt happy. Even the moon looked happy as it loomed large and bright overhead, slightly hazy from spray kicked up by Sam's forbidden horseplay that rained down in a fine mist.

Then the words *cut it out* drifted out of the din. But they drifted back in just as quickly, and between the wine and the waves I wasn't sure they'd ever even been there at all. Only that the playful shrieking was gone, and only the thrashing about in the water remained, punctuated with the word *stop*.

I let my feet sink back below me and started treading water to get a better view of what was going on. But all I saw was Sam and Janelle cuddling up against the wall. Shark-lovers.

"Nick doesn't mind, do you?" Sam said.

"Mind what?"

"See, I told you," Sam said to Janelle. "It's cool."

Janelle hoisted herself up and sat on the rim, tucking her knees to her chest. "I want to go," she said.

"What? We just got here," Sam protested.

"I'm cold," she said, "and I want to go."

"Come on, baby," he said, and touched her leg. "What about Nick? He doesn't want to go yet either."

"Then you two can have fun together," she snapped. "I'm cold." Janelle scooted back from the pool and stood up. Her skin glistened in the moonlight and her hair was hanging around her face in wet strings as she planted her feet firmly, arms crossed and crotch exposed. "I'll wait in the car or something." She strolled around, picking up her clothes and clutching them to her chest in a bundle.

"Damn it," Sam said, hopping out of the pool, a small river following behind him. "Why do you have to be like this? Everything was fine."

"I'm just cold."

"How are you cold? It's like ninety degrees!"

"I just am," she snapped, throwing the bundle onto the ground.

Sam answered with a harsh glare, locking his eyes right into hers with a previously unseen ferocity. But he suddenly broke into a wide smile. "Fine, see you there," he said. Then he strolled over to the jug of wine and took a large swig.

Janelle pulled her T-shirt down over her head, then donned her skirt and shoes. She clutched her bra tightly in her hand as she stomped back to the fence.

"Have fun," Sam chided. "Nick and I will be fine, won't we Nick?"

"Great," Janelle said, tossing her bra over the fence and once again flashing us as she flipped over the top. "I'm sure you two will be very happy together."

"Actually," I said, "maybe we should get going."

"Why? 'Cause of her?" Sam protested. "Don't take it seriously. She pulls this shit all the time. I'm trying to break her of this anti-social crap, but whatever. No sense ruining our night over it."

"No, it's not that," I said. "It's just that I have a job interview in the morning, so I should probably get some sleep."

"Oh yeah? Where at this time? Indonesia? Disneyland?"

"Here actually," I said, "down at Hancock's. I kind of wanted to stick around for a bit."

Sam shrugged and snorted in semi-approval. "Whatever," he said, taking another drink and then chucking the rest of the jug over the fence. "Home can sucker you like that."

We got out of the pool, and Sam and I dressed ourselves in silence. We both climbed back over the fence and soggily trudged through the darkness back to Janelle and the car. And for the first time that night, I felt a light chill in the air.

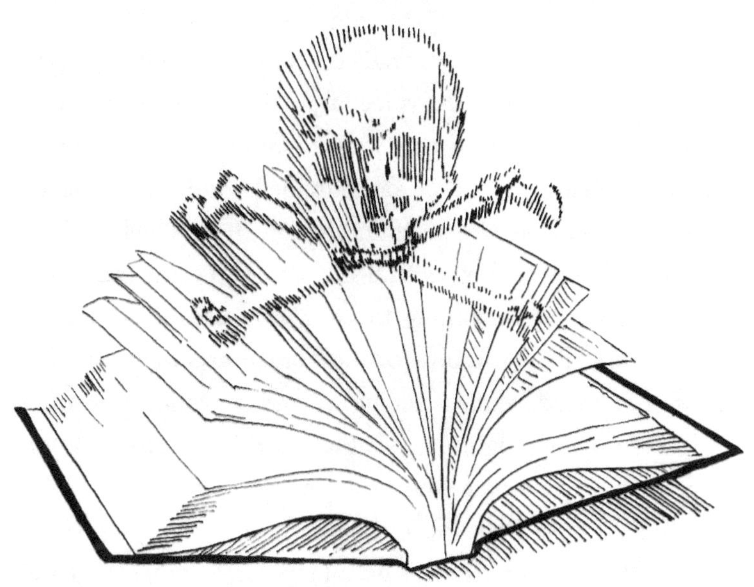

THE CURSE OF
THE FAILED NOVEL

He tells me that he wrote a novel once, that he knows it's no big deal, that everyone's done it. It doesn't even require talent, just the belief you have some—a belief so rampant it's best described as an epidemic.

Andy's is a classical Greek dialog between the state of nature and contemporary pop culture. Judith's is an existential first person narrative told from the perspective of processed food. His mother's is a scathing imagining of an alternate reality of the life left unlived by a middle-aged housewife whose children have left home—which she claims is more archetypal than autobiographical. He says the words people use to describe their novels are generally every bit as meaningless as the work itself, that they're divorced from definitions. People insist the novels mean what they want them to at the time, regardless of what ideas the words contained within the avalanche of the unpublished actually represent. Black is white. Up is down. Orwell is Huxley. It all stems from the arrogant notion that they have something to say, a story somehow uniquely free from the constraints of the human experience of being born, eating, drinking, sleeping, breathing, working, dreaming, loving, fucking, fighting, eventually writing a bad novel and finally dying over the whole sorry experience.

Then he says that his is different.

Of course, he tells me, we all say ours is different but his really is, even though none of them really are. Still, his is. It's cursed.

He tells me that everyone who's read it has never spoken to him again, and he's not talking about publishing industry people avoiding his phone calls. Friends, lovers, family—gone. All whose eyes have skimmed his words have skipped town or his inner circle. Five readers. Five dropouts from his life.

He tells me that his friend Michelle was going to school for publishing, intending to be a book editor, and she offered to look it over in exchange for drum lessons. Shortly after delivering her a smartly bound copy of the manuscript (which he had made just for her, along with a specially purchased red pen), before she could have read more than a few chapters, she stopped arriving in his basement on Tuesdays at three. Her phone number stopped working without report, she disappeared from class, and never returned the manuscript, her thoughts on it, or the pen.

He fell in love with an English major, a "writer" herself. Mad with passion and poetry, they exchanged books. Hers, a blip of novella length, was read in an afternoon and reported on over dinner. His, a full novel of a solid one hundred and five thousand words, needed more time for full analysis, time it would never receive. She gave her novella and her love to a rival by Chapter 7. He wondered if Michelle had also been on Chapter 7, thinking it a shame because the exposition and backstory had barely faded at that point. It didn't really pick up until Chapter 9.

He tells me that his roommate's mother was a professional novelist, that they'd met and gotten along, and he wanted her to be his mentor. However, he didn't want to give her his novel until it was at least readable enough for people to reach Chapter 8 or she might not be interested in helping him. Instead he gave it to her daughter, his roommate. She promptly moved out in the swarm of meritless allegations roommates always make against one another upon exit. He didn't know what chapter she was on, only that she didn't pay the electric bill when she left.

He tells me that her mother moved shortly after, to a deserted tropical island to write.

There was another interested publishing student he knew—Erin. He tells me that he resisted, because by now he'd caught on to the curse (at least in some sort of kitschy way). Soon after the papers left his hands, those to whom they were delivered would leave his life. He would lose a friend and a nice pen. But she insisted, saying that knowledge of the curse neutered its power, and not only would she reach Chapter 8, she would read every single word. She'd scour for grammatical and logical errors so that when the manuscript was returned it would be covered in so much red ink it would look like a mutilated corpse. She said he could call her a butcher. He flirted, saying he wasn't sure. The curse had already claimed three, but Erin was sure.

She was wrong. There was an incident. He was never clear on the details, only that she lost her scholarship, and she had to drop out of school and return home. The ritual murder of his words was a lost desire for her. The manuscript languished in a box in her parents' garage.

He tells me that was about the same time as when his grandfather wanted to see what sort of crap he was paying for at that fancy school of his grandson's. He begged his grandfather to want something else, because he knew what would happen, and it wasn't fair to ask him to shoulder that responsibility. But his grandfather was a solid fellow of the Greatest Generation, adamant, resolved and of the deeply held conviction that superstition was for queers and pinkos. He practically tore the pages from his grasp. He tells me that he never knew how far his grandfather read, only that it was far enough for him to make up his mind that it wasn't only superstition that queers and pinkos wielded, it was also the florid nonsense dribbled onto those cursed pages. Though his grandfather said he would finish paying the bill for school because he'd made a commitment, he also said that if the words contained within those pages were how his grandson really felt about his family then he was no grandson of his, and he never would be again.

He tells me that was when he knew the curse was real. And though the obvious course of action was to shred the manuscript, delete the file, disconnect from the internet to ensure the curse could not escape, remove and burn his hard drive while reciting the proper incantations to cleanse it of evil spirits and finally scatter the ashes to the four corners of the Earth to avoid its supernatural resurrection, he couldn't bring himself to do it. It was his novel, his work. One hundred and five thousand emblems of his soul made concrete. One day, there might be a time or situation that could defeat the curse. He could be quarantined in a room with another, jailed, or married. Then the reader could not leave and he could watch them absorb every last syllable. It was possible. He hoped.

So you see, he tells me, though it may contain the same bullshit, the same arrogance, the same self-aggrandizing departure from reality, and though cursed might just be an equally meaning-divorced word to explain the qualities that drove his readers away from his life, his novel is still different—it is cursed. Even if cursed is just a word.

He tells me that this is why he never mentioned it before, because he wanted me to stick around, and all powers of positive thinking, trust and human intention were powerless against his apparently complete and total lack of talent or soul.

And then it's there, on the table between us, four hundred printed pages with a black plastic copy shop binding and a big red bow. There is no pen.

He tells me that he wishes this were about trust, about art, about love, but it isn't. He tells me that he found the letters, that he knows I'm leaving him, that at least this way he can rationalize it, lay blame, say it's not him that drove me away. It's the novel, the cursed and failed novel, the one that's waged a war against him for years now. The ruthless enemy that will stop at nothing to destroy him. The one he must eventually master or die trying. He tells me that he needs to understand it and this is the only way for it all to make sense in his head.

He tells me he knows his desires probably mean little, but still he hopes I'll read the whole thing, and to remember that it doesn't really pick up until Chapter 9.

He tells me he is sorry—then he is gone.

THE CAT BURGLAR

"There's a party over at Tanya's apartment tonight," Cassie said, keeping her gaze on the stock of new hammers she was slowly pricing with a label maker. "It's Thomas's birthday."

"So?" Jill sneered from where she was performing similarly menial labor down the aisle.

"So, it might be fun."

"Somehow I doubt it." Jill punctuated her doubt by violently pricing a cordless drill with a slashing motion.

Cassie stopped pricing hammers and turned towards Jill who was now crouched down, attacking a herd of routers with her price-gun and mumbling, "20 percent off," with each stab.

"Don't you want to see Thomas turn one?"

"Not in the slightest," she stabbed.

"But Tanya's your friend—"

"Ugh. Please," Jill groaned, ceasing her assault and turning to speak directly to Cassie. "You're my friend. Tanya is just someone I have to put up with for political reasons."

As if on cue, Tanya walked past the aisle on her way to the register with a greedy smile and wave. Jill cringed at Tanya's attire as she waved back sarcastically. All of the employees at Hometown Hardware had to wear the same bright red vests, announcing their willingness to answer customers' questions in bold yellow letters across the back, but it seemed to stand out on everyone other than Tanya. The gaudiness of the vest was perfectly matched with the overly hair-sprayed mess of raggedly bleached curls on her head and the buckets of blue makeup slopped around her eyes like a parabolic dish. Not that Jill thought the vest or tan work boots were doing much for her own appearance—often described by her mother as scraggly or dykey—but Jill thought that, unlike all the other employees, Tanya might have purchased the vest on her own before she'd gotten the job as a cashier.

Once Tanya was safely past the aisle, Jill's cheeks flopped back to scowling and her waving hand dropped heavily back to her side.

"And her sister's kid means even less to me," Jill said, rolling her eyes. "If there's anyone I'd ever hoped wouldn't breed, it would be the two of them. Continuation of that bloodline hardly seems like an occasion worth celebrating; it's more like a day of mourning."

"You don't really mean that," Cassie sighed as she returned to stretching out the hammer-pricing task as long as possible.

"Yes I do."

"Well, whatever," Cassie shrugged. "Will you go with me or not?"

"No. Anything involving Tanya is bound to suck and anything involving going to her house will suck even worse."

Cassie stopped her torturously slow, hammer pricing once again, and walked down the aisle to address Jill more intimately.

"Please?" she said.

Jill stopped her slaughter with the price gun. "Why are you pushing this?"

"No reason," Cassie said sheepishly.

"OMG. It's a boy, isn't it?" Jill laughed. "Ick! What possible attraction could there be to a boy that would hang out at Tanya's house?"

Cassie's face went a little red and she made panicked motions to shut Jill up as quietly as possible. "Look, will you go with me?"

Jill wrinkled up her nose and puffed out her cheeks in disgust at what she was about to agree to.

"Okay," she said. "But this is your birthday present this year," she added with a laugh. "Maybe next year's too."

Cassie smiled and strolled back down the aisle to price her hammers, cheerily finishing the job in no time at all.

Jill sat at the computer later that evening, concentrating on opening the pupils of her eyes as wide as possible to let the radioactive glow of the screen soak into her, hoping to actively meld her consciousness with the online world as her fingers danced furiously across the keyboard.

Another vapid day at work. The things we do for money continue to amaze and disturb me. Taking orders from a troll like Marsha, for example. "Perk up! Take initiative! Smile!" It's a hardware store, lady.

No one wants to be there, so let's quit pretending. Why is it that bosses are so stupid as to think you want to be at your job? No one does. Who would willingly submit themselves to eight hours of mind-numbing drivel, like answering stupid questions from fat people about nails while their stupid, fat children giggle when their parents ask what kind of screws I would recommend unless they absolutely had to make the rent. As soon as we get enough money to move to the city, Cassie and I are out of there. But until then—

The computer bleeped, announcing an instant message from AwesomeAussie389.

"Sup?" it bleeped.

"Just updating the old blog," Jill typed back.

"Boss still a bitch?" came the lightning-fingered reply.

"Duh," Jill said out loud and made the accompanying duh-face at the screen as she typed.

Another guest was announced, and this time it was the doorbell that bleeped.

"Gotta go. My ride's here," Jill typed hurriedly. "Back later." She closed the IM window without even looking at AwesomeAussie389's response.

Jill quickly clicked on the tab to publish her blog entry, drumming her fingers in irritation as the hourglass icon acknowledged that the tiny bits of information, which made up her post, were still trudging onward through a processor that was nearly ready to put out to pasture. Jill had worked her computer day and night for years, thinking that an A.I. would have likely collapsed from exhaustion while processing all her commands. Only a drone could keep up with the strain of managing her online life. However, a new computer would have to wait until after enough moving money had been saved.

Twenty-two whole seconds later, Jill's entry posted. She closed her web browser and bounded towards the front door as the doorbell rang again.

Jill opened the front door and found Cassie giggling as she pressed the doorbell button yet again.

"Hey, my mom's asleep," Jill said sternly.

"Just saying hello," Cassie grinned.

Jill scanned Cassie's outfit: a tight-fitting, light green skirt, embroidered with a floral pattern, and a spaghetti-strap tank top that accentuated her cleavage. Shiny black, two-inch heels were on her feet, and the barrage of barrettes she usually wore at work were on hiatus.

"Let's go," Jill said in a knowing, motherly tone. She closed the front door and walked towards Cassie's car, content in her faded jeans and second-hand, button-up shirt over a tank top. Jill had an inkling that she ought not to wear anything that she wouldn't mind stained—not only with the bevy of liquids that came with small children, but also with the shame of spending time around Tanya off the clock. Cassie hit the doorbell one last time with a giggle, and then quickly followed Jill to the car.

Cassie ignored the road to fiddle with her hair incessantly during the drive, adjusting the rearview mirror to analyze her bangs, and once, actually winking at her reflection. Through a massive personal effort, Jill managed to keep her groans to herself and rolled her eyes only in the direction of the window.

They parked the car outside the Vista View apartments, then got out and made their way up the stairs, where Jill turned to Cassie and made a final plea.

"Last chance. We could still make the late show at the

Cineplex," Jill said with a pleading grin. Cassie smiled back, but opened the door and went inside without a word. Jill shrugged to no one and followed suit.

First birthday parties shouldn't be so decadent. Thomas was mysteriously asleep in a car seat set on an end table as two boys in their late teens attempted a two-man juggling act with open cans of beer (to the delight of Tanya's sister, Danielle, and several others seated on the grimy couch). Empties were liberally distributed around the room, and it was slightly hazy with a misty mixture of sweat and smoke, making it five degrees warmer than the other side of the front door.

The bottom of Danielle's arm jiggled a little as she sloppily waved hello. Her face was a battlefield between her acne and the thick layers of cover-up that were probably causing it, and ringed with the same ragged, seaweed-esque mop that crowned her sister. Secretly, Jill thought that Danielle looked like an over-inflated Tanya, as if she had sat on one of the air compressors at work.

Jill suppressed a smirk as she moved forward into the apartment, each step bringing her feet a new consistency with the settling of her weight. She followed Cassie into the kitchen where an unidentified teen boy clad in a filthy, black sweatshirt was face down on the linoleum. Jill thought he would probably regret it later as she peeled her feet from the floor like Velcro to step over him. Cassie opened the refrigerator and came out with two beers, handing one to Jill who was cautiously leaning against the one spot on the counter she deemed safe.

"Do you want a glass?" Cassie said, opening a cabinet.

"Are you joking?" Jill said, pointing to the overflowing sink. "I feel like I should be wearing a HazMat suit just to be in this place." She thoroughly wiped the mouth of her beer with her shirt, then opened the can and took a sip.

"So, ready to go?" Jill chirped.

"We haven't even seen Tanya yet."

"I know! And if we hurry up, we won't have to."

Cassie rolled her eyes. "Don't be an ass," she said and stepped over the unconscious boy to exit the kitchen. "I'm going to go find Tanya."

Jill scowled at Cassie's back. When her back was gone, she scowled over the counter at the people on the couch. When they remained oblivious, she scowled at the kitchen, and then finally at the unconscious boy on the ground.

"Just you and me, I guess," Jill huffed.

A roar of approval came from the next room as the juggling duo pulled off their most sophisticated move to date. Jill turned to watch, just in time to see a second attempt at the move douse the couch-dwellers in beer. She laughed out loud and spilled her beer on the sleeping boy.

"Oh, I'm sorry," she said quickly and wiped her spill with her hand. He didn't move. Jill stared at him curiously for several moments, then peeled one foot off the floor and nudged him with her toe. The boy grunted softly and moved his arm.

"Fantastic," Jill said and took another drink, then readdressed the unconscious boy. "But I feel like if this thing between us is going to continue, then you should have a name. Unconscious Boy just won't do. So I think I'm going to call you Juan-Pablo. Does that work for you?"

Juan-Pablo said nothing.

"Excellent," Jill said and nodded to herself, then took another sip.

Cassie came back into the kitchen, her arms crossed and her face blank.

"No Tanya?" Jill asked.

"I think she's in her room, but the door's locked," Cassie said and picked off a piece of paper that had been speared by her heel.

"So where have you been?"

"I needed to pee," Cassie said. "And you won't believe this—"

"Oh, I'll believe just about anything," Jill laughed.

"All of Thomas's dirty diapers are stacked behind the toilet," Cassie said with a disgusted look on her face.

"Are they separated into still usable and throw-away piles?"

"That's disgusting," Cassie said.

Jill made a sweeping gesture with her hands as if she were a model displaying the apartment on an infomercial, but Cassie ignored her, visually searching the living room instead.

Jill snorted and tipped back her can, finishing its contents. "You need another, Juan-Pablo?"

Juan-Pablo said nothing.

"Yeah, me too," Jill said sourly.

"Who's Juan-Pablo?" Cassie asked.

"Nobody," Jill said. She opened the cabinet beneath the sink to toss her empty into the trash can.

A skinny ball of fur rocketed out the door and past Jill. She turned her head and saw that it was a tiny undernourished kitten that had run by, straight into Tanya, who'd scooped it up and was now chastising its attempts to escape with revolting baby talk.

"Oh, so cute. He tried to get away," Tanya grinned. Her face looked atypically flushed and slightly shiny. "Isn't he cute," she announced to the equally shiny-faced boy standing behind her.

"You keep your cat under the sink?" Jill asked.

"Only when people are over to keep him from getting away," Tanya said with a smile. She petted the cat roughly and picked off a piece of food that was stuck in its fur. "So kind of a lot, I guess."

"How despotic of you," Jill smirked, "I mean, considering the libertine nature of the surroundings."

"You're so funny, Jill," Tanya giggled. "I like the way you're always making up words." She turned to the boy again. "Isn't she funny?" He nodded in disinterested agreement, very obviously trying to avoid looking at Cassie.

The kitten mewled pathetically as Tanya bent over and shoved it back into the space between the trash can and the ironic containers of household cleaners. Cassie glared at the back of Tanya's neck, the tag of her inside-out T-shirt like a flag.

"I'm really glad you and Cassie came over," Tanya beamed as she stood up. "We don't get much chance to talk at work."

"No, we don't," Jill replied.

"Have you been here long?"

"Long enough," Cassie interjected. "In fact, we kind of have to get going. We promised Zach we'd stop by his house tonight also."

"Oh, is he having a party too?" Tanya asked hopefully.

"No, just, you know…a few people," Cassie said. "And we're a little late. We just, you know, wanted to say hello."

"Oh, well thanks for coming," Tanya said glumly. She pushed an unexpected hug on Jill. Caught unaware, Jill warily patted the moist spot on Tanya's back with the tips of her fingers, then squirmed loose as quickly as possible. Tanya turned to hug Cassie, but she was already working her way through the rough terrain towards the front door. Jill forced a goodbye smile to Tanya, then quickly followed Cassie, bounding over the clutter like a mountain goat, jubilant to be on her merry way.

Cassie stomped down the stairs without a word and silently handed her keys to Jill as they reached the car. There was no hair fiddling or winking on this drive. And the only impulse Jill had to resist was to say, "I told you so." She managed. Barely.

Jill returned to her computer as soon as she walked in the door. Cassie may not have been in the mood to talk about it, but the real world (the way Jill thought of the internet due to people's much less filtered depiction of their opinions and personalities online) would be dying for this: the skank from work, dirty diapers, and Juan-Pablo. It was practically enough for a whole website.

Three IM windows popped up nearly instantly, and Jill filled AwesomeAussie389, Britknee_Spears, and the CrayolaKid in on the events of the evening. She finished things off by blogging a lengthy list of steps that would be necessary to purge the grime and evil spirits from Tanya's domicile, including extensive plastic surgery and napalm somewhere in the middle.

Her fingers aching, Jill finally stumbled off to bed around three in the morning, where she flopped face down and slept without even untying her shoes.

"You know, I've been thinking," Cassie said to Jill several days later. They were both busy pricing lengths of PVC pipe in their signature styles: foot-dragging and fist-swinging. "We should do something about that kitten."

"What, like last rites?" Jill said. "I could look them up on the internet later."

"No," Cassie said softly, scrutinizing a sale tag. "We should steal it."

Jill cackled and nearly missed her pass with the price gun. "The purpose of that being?"

Cassie continued her slow rhythmic pricing for several moments before answering. The gun rang out on the pipes like a distant jungle drum, a nearly hypnotic pulse that she seemed unable to stop. "To save its life," she finally drawled.

Jill stopped savaging products and looked at her friend. Cassie's schemes and attempts to talk Jill into them were typically whimsical in nature, even the mildly criminal ones. They were always delivered from a slyly grinning mouth, or a mischievously twinkling eye. When she proposed the move to the city to Jill, her goofy lead-up would have made most think she was proposing marriage. Today, this wasn't the case. Cassie's eyes were cold, distant gravity wells. On a closer inspection, even her pricing seemed especially lackluster.

"You're serious?"

"You know that Thomas has worms."

"Then why do you want us to steal the cat?" Jill said. "It's the baby you should be worried about."

"We can't take Thomas," Cassie sighed. "Kidnapping."

"Well, the cat's burglary," Jill threw in, "and we could call child services."

Cassie ceased her hollow pricing effort and shot Jill a frustrated glare. "But child services is a really big deal. Tanya won't even notice the cat's gone," she said. "Didn't you see the way she only wanted it to show off? She doesn't care about the kitten at all."

"I'm not disagreeing with you," Jill said sympathetically. "I'm just not sure that stealing Tanya's cat is the wisest idea you've ever had."

"Look, Tanya and Danielle are going to visit their parents

this weekend," Cassie said undeterred, "and the lock on their door doesn't work, so all we have to do is stop by and get the cat and leave a window open or something. She'll think it ran away."

Jill paused for a moment, taking in Cassie's resolute posture. Was this something Cassie was determined enough to proceed with on her own? Or was it like the time when they were seventeen and Cassie made Jill sneak out of her window at 3 a.m. to help her silently load her possessions into the car without an explanation. That was the last time Jill had seen Cassie's eyes so forcibly dry.

"How do you know their landlord hasn't fixed the lock?" Jill asked.

"Tanya said they haven't told the landlord because then they'd have to explain how it was broken, and she thinks they'll get kicked out if they do."

"How was it broken?"

"One of those boys did it," Cassie said. "I didn't get the details."

Jill was getting frustrated. Cassie apparently really had thought this out thoroughly.

"So what are we supposed to do with a cat then?" Jill asked.

"We'll find it a better home," Cassie said.

"Where?"

"Anywhere."

"Anywhere?"

"Anywhere is better than under the damn sink," Cassie said, almost yelling. She managed to catch herself when the volume of her first syllable jumped dramatically, but it was perilously close. Jill thought she could just barely see something twitching in Cassie's neck.

"Are you sure this isn't just about revenge?" she asked.

"Yes," Cassie said through her teeth.

Jill chanced a disapproving leer at her friend's lie.

"Okay," Cassie admitted, softening just a bit. "Maybe a little."

Jill grinned. "Well, then I'm in," she said. "I'm no good Samaritan, but revenge I can swing."

Cassie's neck returned to normal, and a look of deep relief settled into her face as she began to once again thump out the bright orange message that PVC pipe was on sale this week, each pass with the gun returning her eyes one pixel closer to sparkle.

The idea of cat burglary grew on Jill throughout the day as Marsha bellowed orders to move this and price that with all the delicacy and tact of a tack hammer. Comparatively, a life on the lam held romantic allure. She and Cassie could traipse about the countryside, liberating woebegone kitties from skanky slutrags, and give them to children with cancer or small town shoe stores who needed some sort of adorable mascot to draw in business.

Cat burglary definitely qualified as a life less ordinary, and after all, Australia was made up of criminals and AwesomeAussie389, was well, awesome. That night, Jill went home and began her blog with the sentence, *tonight begins my criminal career,* which segued excellently into yet another extensive and expletive list of reasons she was dissatisfied with her current station. That lasted late into the night, until she eventually parted ways with consciousness, fully dressed as usual.

The job—a slang term Jill had found online for burglary— had come and gone with little ballyhoo, not that they'd expected much. In reality, the process of walking into a house, picking up a cat, and walking out was hardly college-level coursework. Any fool could have pulled it off. However, the adrenaline from those forty seconds was just now wearing off as Jill stared at the kitten, curled into a ball on her lap. He was purring contentedly after a meal and a bath—which Jill had insisted upon to cleanse evil spirits, and the possibility of lice, before she agreed to provide temporary lodging. She smiled to herself and began to type.

The operation was a success. Code Name Mittens was liberated from enemy territory at 2300 hours, and is now recuperating at home base after being debriefed. Now that he's over the wall, Mittens is free to let everyone know that he loves balls of yarn without fear of political suppression and hopes to one day pursue a career in hotel management.

Jill stopped to wallow in her own self-amusement. This is why she liked the internet. Other people didn't seem to be nearly as amused with her as she was by herself. Her blog, written under an assumed name (known in her offline life only to Cassie), was a way of guaranteeing an appreciative audience. Of course, CNM seemed to be soaking her up as well.

"You really are adorable," she said, stroking Code Name Mittens, "but we have to give you over to a neutral third party. I want you to know that now, so it doesn't come as a shock. But it doesn't mean anything about you and me, okay?"

CNM swished his tail lazily back and forth in understanding. It was all kosher with him, just as long as he wasn't under the sink without a litter box where Tanya had left him for the weekend.

"But seriously," Jill added to her entry, "does anyone out there want this cat I stole?" Then she hit the button to publish and got up to use the bathroom, carefully picking CNM up and depositing him on her bed. By the time she got back, AwesomeAussie389 had already flung two cents her way.

"You really stole a cat?"

Jill sat down at the computer and chuckled to herself. "You were my inspiration Aussie. XXOO."

"'Cause all us Aussies are criminals?"

"No, just hoping to impress you enough to get a date. Perhaps dinner and cyber mugging?"

"Cheeky bugger!"

Jill laughed out loud. Then another message window popped up, from Crayola_Kid.

"Is that 4 real?"

"Hey CK!" Jill wrote back. "Yup."

"You should take that post down," the kid wrote.

"Why?"

"The cops busted a friend of mine for tagging from his blog posts."

"Easy, paranoia face," Jill smirked to herself as she typed. "We left the window open so Tanya will think the cat ran away, and I post under a fake name. Only my friend Cassie knows about my blog—which is why she's never mentioned, coincidently."

"Just don't say I didn't warn you. 1984 police state, yo. We'll all have chips in our arms and barcodes on our necks before you know it."

"L-O-fucking-L!!! You need to get a life, CK. I'm going to sleep." And Jill did, taking her shoes off beforehand for a change.

Monday morning was awkward for Jill. Not because she felt guilty, but because she was curious if Tanya had been effectively misdirected, and felt compelled to make a number of attempts at casual conversation just to see if she mentioned anything. She asked how Tanya's weekend had been, if anything was new, and if it was nice to be home again. The questions were of a nature so atypical to her personality that Jill felt like a charlatan, like these pathetic attempts at conversation were the wool she was pulling over Tanya's eyes, not the theft of her pet.

Despite Jill's inquiries, Tanya never took the bait. She grinned like a child, and gabbed away gleefully as if she and Jill had been the best of friends for their whole lives. Jill was beginning to think that perhaps Tanya just hadn't looked under the sink yet, until right around closing time. She casually mentioned that her kitten was gone and had probably been hit by a car to a male customer buying superglue who seemed eager to be empathetic to her loss. As soon as he'd gone, Tanya smiled and gave a thumbs up to Jill on the register opposite her.

After that, CNM wasn't mentioned again, nor was Jill the slightest bit concerned. She reported her findings to Cassie, who nodded silently, and to AwesomeAussie389, who demanded a 10 percent royalty for being the inspiration behind their conspiracy. Jill told him there was no way to give him 10 percent of a cat through the postal service, that it was just unsanitary and would therefore be hypocritical considering the nature of the theft. He then demanded that CNM embark on a lecture tour about his time behind enemy lines, or to be groomed into a fancy show-cat, so his winnings could be divvied up between partners. To this, Jill wrote a blog profiling AwesomeAussie389's history as a cat fancier, the baron of the litter industry, and a general poof. AwesomeAussie389 was amused to say the least.

Three weeks had passed since the heist and CNM was still camping out in Jill's bedroom. It was apparently a bear market for slightly used kittens, but he hadn't been doing much to encourage prospective, adoptive cat-parents either. He hissed at a woman who appeared to wash her blond hair in salt-water like Tanya, and wouldn't come out from under Jill's bed for a nice old man who needed some help with mice. The man didn't say where the mice were living, but it seemed implied that they might congregate in the cabinet under the sink.

Cassie had been little help despite her promises that CNM would fly off the shelf like so much orange-tagged PVC pipe. She had been mysteriously distant of late, taking several sick days from work, and keeping mostly to herself while she was there. Crayola_Kid said she was probably part of a secret test group that had drugs mixed into their drinking water, or she might be a double agent for the NSA.

"What possible sense does that make?" Jill had asked.

"To monitor who is buying building supplies," CK replied, as if it should have been obvious. "The cat theft was just a way to be able to blackmail you later if you try to rat her out."

Jill thought it was much more likely Cassie was just depressed. Grant Williams had cheated on her in high school, and she'd behaved with similar detachment. CK said Grant was a well-known pseudonym for Oswald, at which point Jill pointed out that Crayola_Kid was a really stupid online handle. CK became mysteriously drowsy and stated that he was off to sleep, although Jill thought he was most likely going to surf porn sites until the sun came up over wherever his parents' velvet-draped basement was located, and then retreat to his "coffin."

The following Monday, Jill was called into Marsha's office. She passed a sobbing Tanya on the way in.

"What happened to her?" Jill asked as she sat down in front of Marsha's desk.

Marsha had a stern look on her already stern face. The tips of her chestnut brown hair were spiky strands, like barbed wire around her solidly set squarish jaw. Jill half-expected tumbleweed to blow across the prairie grass thickly coating Marsha's upper lip. Marsha swiveled her computer monitor to face Jill, who found herself face-to-face with her blog.

"What's this?" Marsha barked.

Jill's abdomen suddenly felt icy cold and she had a deeper empathy for road kill.

"I don't know," she stammered.

"Really?" Marsha humphed. One of her catcher's mitts spun the monitor back in her direction and she squinted slightly as she read off the screen.

"Says here that Marsha is a brain-dead troll who probably needs medical assistance to take a dump. Further down here, it says that Hometown Hardware is a good place for teen girls to meet ex-convicts willing to knock them up, and down here it says that the décor would be more appropriate with Nazi flags instead of American. Are you sure you don't have anything to say about this?"

"So it's mine," Jill blurted out. "Who cares?"

"Who cares?" Marsha's fist hit the desk like a ten-pound sledgehammer—$12.95 on orange-tag sale. "You're busy telling the world that I'm a Nazi troll and you think I don't care? You stole Tanya's cat and you think she doesn't care?"

Jill sneered at the mention of Tanya caring about anything. Marsha continued to huff and puff with a fresh vigor.

"That poor girl's been crying for three weeks, thinking her

cat was dead—"

"Oh please, she's crying because she found out someone got the better of her," Jill snorted. "She's been fine."

"Shut up, Jill," Marsha ordered. "Your whole damn generation may think you're entitled to something, but not from me, you're not. You're sick and you're fired."

"You can't fire me for this," Jill snapped.

"And why not?" Marsha blazed.

"How about a little thing called the first amendment?" Marsha just laughed at this. "How did you find it anyway?"

"Oh, that's not important," Marsha said.

"That's my private blog, and what I say in it while I'm off work is my business."

"As my employee you are my business, and what you say about this business is my business. And I make it my business to know what's being said to the whole damned world."

"You don't own me," Jill sneered.

"Not anymore, I don't. You're through here, and if you don't have that cat back to Tanya by five today, I'm calling the police as well." Marsha wore cruel teasing hints of a smile, tempered by the cold control of a crooked politician.

Jill fought to control the spasms of her upper lip and the gaskets around her eyes.

"Fuck you," she quivered.

"Right back at you, you spoiled, little snot."

Jill locked her eyes into Marsha's, a firehose for a raging blaze. Marsha was venomous, resolute and rapturous. Jill didn't know what she was even fighting for. She hated this place and everything about it, and Marsha possibly even more than Tanya.

"I quit," she spat. Marsha snorted back at her.

"You can't quit, I already fired you."

"Oh, never mind!" Jill roared in frustration throwing her hands in the air. She stood up, deliberately kicking her chair over in the process, and then stomped out of the room.

She continued to stomp all the way home, by way of the main street downtown, just so other people on the sidewalk could scram out of her way. She refused to cry out in pain when she stubbed her toe kicking her door open, and then stomped down the hall to her room, cursing Marsha as she did so.

Jill went inside and saw that her stomping had caused enough vibration to shake her computer awake. The screen humming to life and the crunchy chatter of the RAM standing at attention only made her more furious. She picked up a book and threw it across the room, then another, and another, each time feeling more satisfied with the sad sound they made as they bounced off the wall and landed in a spread-eagled mess on the floor, pages bent or torn and bindings compromised. Then she tipped over the whole bookcase, feeling a power over the ideas and feelings of others that she'd always been afraid to admit that she desired.

CNM emerged in a panicked dash from underneath Jill's desk where he'd been curled up. As soon as Jill saw him, her savagery died and she crumpled to the floor. Jill's face was a waterfall, and every tear that she'd kept dammed up since she'd stopped skinning her knees and failing spelling tests gushed out her face in a torrent, emotional levees broken and humanity so long denied, now undeniable. How could she have been so stupid? And how was it that Crayola_Kidd had been right? She'd been a rock, an island, an algebra equation even—and it had all come to a crushing end over a stupid cat.

CNM approached and nuzzled Jill's leg cautiously. A smile broke through her sobs as she scooped him up, squeezed him tight, and gave him his final bath sitting on the floor of her bedroom.

Jill was surprised to see Cassie sitting with Tanya at the display patio table outside of Hometown Hardware. She hadn't worked that day. Jill thought perhaps Cassie been called in to cover Jill's shift after she and the store had parted ways.

Tanya put on that infuriating grin of hers when she saw Jill trudging up to the table with the open duffle bag she was using as a makeshift cat carrier.

"Hi," Tanya chirped.

Jill, feeling unconversational to say the least, just glared back, then delicately set the bag on the table and sat down.

"What's in the bag?" Tanya said. Cassie's eyes rolled and she scrunched up her neck, but said nothing.

"Mittens is in the bag," Jill said dully, "along with a litter box and some actual cat food."

"Oh, he doesn't need a litter box," Tanya giggled.

"Then don't use it," Jill groaned.

"That's so cute you named him Mittens. We hadn't gotten around to naming him yet, but maybe we'll stick with Mittens." She reached into the bag and picked up the squirming kitten. "What do you think about that, huh Mittens?" Tanya cooed.

Jill looked at Mitten's squirming pathetically against Tanya's grip and wondered if there was any way to measure which of them disliked Tanya more.

"So, we're done here then?" Jill asked, and looked back and forth between Tanya and Cassie. Cassie looked oddly nervous, avoiding Jill's gaze and keeping one hand clasped against her neck.

Jill stood up to leave and made a minor head twitch to Cassie in the direction of Cassie's car, indicating that they should head in that direction.

"Wait, Jill, there's something I want to say to you before you go," Tanya said.

Jill winced slightly and stopped. Cassie was still seated. "Yes?"

Tanya took a deep breath and put on her most pleasant face. "I just want you to know that I really don't hold this against you, and that I really hope we, you and Cassie and I, can still be friends." She said the words so genially, so unassumingly, so plainly and with such mind-numbing ignorance that Jill felt a jet of lightning shoot from her heart to her fingertips, and then bounce up to her eyeballs—a white-hot electric urge to bash Tanya in the face with a hammer that flashed through her whole body like a strobe.

Jill tried to look at Cassie's reaction, but found only the side of her head, her face purposefully turned away. Her hand was no longer guarding her neck, and Jill could see the purplish-yellow remnants of a small hickey. This time there was no electric shock. Jill's whole body felt like a block of rough hewn wood.

So Jill looked deep into Tanya's big dull eyes, surrounded by her big dull face and big dull hair, and mustered up the only response she could.

"Sure," she choked. "Sure."

Jill turned and walked away, stepping softly the whole way home, where she picked up the things she'd strewn across her floor earlier and packed a suitcase. Then, with the case in hand, she walked to the bus station and boarded a bus for the city, leaving her computer to rot with the rest of the town.

THE RISE & FALL OF THE WALLY JOHNSON ACT

House Resolution 417, popularly known as The Wally Johnson Act, passed late in the evening in a special joint session of Congress.

Sponsoring congressman, Rep. Rick Stanford (R-MN), told the assembly that the best way to honor the young man, whose death had touched so many, was to take steps to see that the tragic events of February 14 would never, ever, ever be repeated.

Due to the general silliness of the proposal—making it illegal to break someone's heart—all of the elected officials present believed themselves to be the only ones who had voted for it, only to discover afterwards that it had in fact passed unanimously. No one wanted to be seen as supportive of heartbreak, especially not the kind that drove twenty-two-year-old Wally Johnson to throw himself from his fifteenth floor apartment window. He landed on a sidewalk café table where a divorce support group was having its weekly meeting, a meeting which was being filmed for a feature story on a popular TV news magazine program and which captured every grisly detail of the tragedy on film.

None of the incumbents wanted a reputation as being coldhearted—not in an election year anyhow.

A national furor erupted immediately after the president signed the bill, when it was discovered that almost no one in Congress had read it. Some congressional members believed it to be a non-binding statement that the United States of America stood against heartbreak. Some believed it to be a new tort code, bringing heartbreak under the umbrella definition of emotional damages for which one could sue. A few believed it to be a form of criminal assault. However, whatever they believed the bill to be, they had all voted for it for the purposes of appearance. As such, no one was willing to be the first to retract their support for it lest they might be accused of waffling, being a flip-flopper, or even of having philandering or playboy sympathies.

Instead, they claimed that on review, it didn't go far enough and pushed for stricter regulations—a war on heartbreak.

Stanford himself said the bill was only the first phase of a bold new direction for the country, one free of misery and cruelty, both of which were harmful to the economy.

Broad new powers were awarded law enforcement officials to monitor all of the usual suspects, and a special new federal prison nicknamed *The Honeymoon Suite* was constructed.

Within weeks, quarterback was the most dreaded position in high school football squads. Church groups began protesting the opening of romantic comedy films as vile propaganda, nothing less than attempts to poison the minds of vulnerable children by the Hollywood elite.

No one was more vocal in their support than the Catholic Church, as the Wally Johnson Act caused divorce rates to drop sharply. No matter how much they hated each other, couples were wary of risking the jail time.

It quickly became a dark age for daytime TV as tabloid talk show hosts were convicted of conspiracy and racketeering by the score. Conversely, it became a golden age for pop music, as record companies were now willing to sign more talented but less attractive acts. A memo to A&R reps, later acquired and published by the BBC, insisted on a minimum weight of 220 pounds for potential new artists to ensure they wouldn't have to seek political asylum in France like so many boy bands had already been forced to do.

However, after a few months, it became clear that the blue and red states of America were in no way united, that they were in fact cleanly split on the issue. Those who supported the heart's irrational freedom in all it's glory and horror were labeled as homewreckers and sociopaths, and those who believed in respecting other's feelings were denigrated as brainwashed Orwellian minions. Public school teachers, already under fire for their incitement of childhood crushes, were now subject to rigorous review panels as to whether or not their lesson plans were biased on the issue of heartbreak. Shakespeare's sonnets were dropped from curriculums nationwide and the percentage of class time devoted to math increased by 30 percent.

The national discussion expanded when several prominent social conservatives wrote op-ed pieces insisting that the bill was tantamount to special rights for perverts, as it exempted homosexuals, who weren't actually capable of loving one another. Gay rights groups responded that they were every bit as capable of bitter, drawn-out, and devastating separations as heterosexual couples, citing statistics from a recent study in the Netherlands. A peaceful mass-breakup was scheduled in San Francisco, but turned violent after the governor sent in the National Guard.

Sandra Jackson, Wally's mother, rejected the legislation perpetrated in her son's name and staged a sit-in, camping out on Rep. Rick Stanford's lawn, vowing not to budge until America was once again "free to love 'em and leave 'em." Her crusade was not widely supported and an attempt was made on her life by an assassin later found to have sixties flower-child ties.

A coalition of out of work therapists and chocolate manufacturers marched on Washington demanding compensation. Or revolution, whichever came first. They brought mini-workout trampolines, branding themselves as rebounders. Rick Stanford laughed off their protest, calling them "buggy whip manufacturers" in a televised interview, and insisting that profiting off the misery of others was fundamentally anti-American.

The talking heads on TV debated misery-profiteering back and forth for days. The liberals insisted that capitalism was nothing more than creating the illusion of misery in conjunction with the belief that a product can abate it, and the conservatives contended that life is inherently miserable and capitalism is in fact the solution. The Greens tried to say that both life and capitalism could be what you made of them, but no one listened. The dialogue had become a din, a rhetorical slush so thick and garbled that none of the viewers had understood a word of it, only the emotional charge it was infused with.

However, the zeitgeist all came to a stunned and silent halt when Rick Stanford was eventually caught having an affair with a male intern. His wife, Mary, told the media that devastated as she may be, she was declining to press charges. All she wanted was to move on.

She was quickly drafted into running for her husband's vacated House seat (he had fled to Syria, as it lacked a formal extradition treaty with the U.S.) and ran on a platform of pain equaling growth. Pop art posters and T-shirts featuring her image and the word despair were everywhere. Now armed with an icon, opposition to the national climate grew swiftly and Mary Stanford was elected in a landslide.

In her first act as an elected official, Mary sponsored a bill revoking the Wally Johnson Act, which passed unanimously, allowing Americans to once again gaily wreck each other's lives on a whim—looking back at the recent years as a dark confusing interlude in which they let their compassion run wild, distorting reality and opening the door to tyranny, a door that was now thankfully closed.

HEADLIGHTS

Nate recognized the girl as she lazily spun circles in the middle of the street like a ballerina atop a music box that was winding down. She had been at the party, where he'd brushed past her in the kitchen on his way to the bathroom, then failed in his attempt to say something witty about the incident during his return trip. The kitchen was a tough room. Consequently, Nate spent the rest of the evening trying to avoid her and everyone else for that matter. That way, it was easier for Nate to question why he had even bothered to come to a party in the first place, and even easier to vamoose when the host, an acquaintance from his trigonometry class, kindly told everyone to "get the fuck out" after discovering a broken personal item.

The girl spotted Nate and powered down her rotation. She pointed a finger towards him with a similarly lazy movement, smiling as she squinted one eye closed like she was sighting a rifle at the crotch of a sitcom villain.

"I remember you," she said, "the awkward boy from the kitchen."

With the slow drizzle glowing softly in the streetlight, the reflection from the shiny wet blacktop lighting her from all angles and her arm extended in pose, Nate thought it kind of looked like a scene from a snow globe.

"Um, yeah. That's me," he replied lamely.

"What's your name again?" Her diction was as relaxed as her demeanor.

"Nate," he said mostly to his toes. "Nate Stevenson."

"Excellent. A pleasure to make your acquaintance, Nate." She lowered her arm as she spoke, but Nate still thought she looked like she was in a snow globe—a very pretty snow globe. She continued, impervious. "Now, Nate, I have a very important question for you. Are you ready for it?"

"I think so." He was sure he wasn't.

"Nate," she said seriously, "this is crucial and I can't have you only partly here for this question, so I'm going to ask one more time. Are you ready for this oh-so-important question?"

"Okay," Nate said, feeling even more sure that his readiness would be insufficient now that real magnitude was involved. "I mean, yes."

"Are you sure?"

"…Yes."

"Okay, have…you…seen…a red hatchback anywhere around here?"

Nate knew it was the wrong answer before he said it, despite its accuracy. "No."

"Damn it!" The girl stomped one of her feet in irritation, then threw her arms up in the air. "Losing your own car is the height of embarrassment." Then she went back to turning in circles and searching the neighborhood for evidence of her car.

She abruptly stopped circling. "Hey, wait! I know! Why don't you help me find it?" she asked.

"Well…I mean, I was going to go home," Nate said, trying to avoid the inevitable further embarrassment he felt lurking in the back of his throat, waiting for the right string of words to pass by so it could hitch a ride out of his mouth and into infamy. Judging by her reaction, Nate had managed to say something funny despite a deluge of historical evidence of the impossibility of the act. He made a mental note not to write home about it.

"Oh, you don't want to go home, Nate. That's like giving up and admitting that there's nothing better out there. It's a big world and home is inevitably the least exciting place in it."

"Aren't you on your way home?" he rationalized.

"Never," she said indignantly. "Unless, of course, by home, you mean someone else's."

"So, you're off to another party then," Nate said, thinking that she seemed like the kind of girl who was never lacking in parties to attend.

"Everywhere is another party, Nate. It's all in how you look at things." She appeared not to be short on snappy comebacks either. "But, it just so happens that tonight, that other party happens to be another party at…someone's house…who was that again? Oh yeah—Andy!" Her tone switched quickly from jubilated to saucy. "Wait, why are you so interested, Nate? I thought you were going home."

The new personal record of four drinks that Nate had consumed decided to answer for him. "There's not really any rush. I guess I could try to help you find your car first." It felt like there was a six car pile-up in the back of his eyeballs from the sound of his own words.

"There's a thin line between gallantry and creepiness, Nate," she said looking him over.

"Never mind, I guess," he said over his shoulder.

Her eyes rolled as her tone turned conciliatory. "Oh, don't take it personal. I just fancy myself as the peanut gallery from time to time. An extra set of eyes would be appreciated."

She took him by the arm and planted her heels firmly.

"Shall we?" she asked.

Nate didn't really know what to say, so he nodded nervously. The girl winked at him, then tugged him down the road, cheerily humming square dancing calls to herself.

They promenaded down the block, sashayed around the corner and back again, and when they failed to make progress, turned round and round—a step Nate felt his stomach could have lived without. The girl suddenly stopped turning and a wide grin spread across her face. She dropped Nate's arm and started zigzagging down the street towards a destination indetermin-able due to the erratic pattern of her flight plan. Holding on to Nate had apparently served purposes that weren't purely musical.

"I found it!" she said, exuberantly pointing at a blue four-door.

Nate followed behind, slightly confused. "You said you were looking for a red hatchback."

"Did I? Well, I guess that would explain why I had so much trouble finding my car wouldn't it? As I no longer own a red hatchback, I was busy looking for somebody else's." She giggled about this softly to herself, and started digging into her purse for her keys. "Well, Nate, it was nice meeting you, but I have to be off, unless, of course, you want a ride to Andy's house."

"No. I don't know Andy and I should probably just go home anyway."

"Suit yourself. But remember what I said about home. It's just plain lazy. Oop, here they are," she said, pulling her keys out of her purse and promptly dropped them directly on the ground. The girl bent over to retrieve her keys, and then began the process of clumsily trying to unlock the car door.

The word lazy had stung Nate just a bit; it was his mother's justification of his failure to achieve her goals. His irritation almost caused him not to notice the travesty of coordination taking place in front of him. When he did, all the proprieties polite society and network television had filled his head with rushed to the foreground.

"Wait, you're not really going to drive are you?"

"Why not?"

Nate was momentarily unsure what to do in the face of such powerful logic. "Well…I mean, you barely found your car."

"It happens to mall shoppers everyday. They still drive." She was like a verbal linebacker.

"Yeah, but I mean, you're really drunk."

"You don't say." The girl wore a slightly puzzled look on her face, unsure of the motives of Nate's resistance. Then she turned the sauce back up to high. "Do you have a car, Nate?"

He looked at the ground when he told her he didn't, as if riding the city bus was a mark of shame. But this conversation ending was what he felt would really mark him.

"Well, then that, as they say, would appear to be that," she said.

Nate took a deep breath and stepped out onto a limb.

"I could drive you," he offered.

The girl smiled suspiciously at him. "Gallant or creepy, Nate?"

"What?"

"I said, gallant or creepy? Which one is it?"

"Um," he paused, not liking the sound of either. "How about safety-minded?"

"Creepy it is."

She tossed Nate the keys but then stopped him as he was about to unlock the door that had given her so much trouble earlier.

"How do I know you're not drunk too?"

Nate wasn't about to let her know that he'd broken his all-time record of three drinks this evening, so once again, he let that fourth do the talking.

"Comparatively, I don't think it matters at this point. You can't even unlock the door."

"Walk a line."

"What?"

"I said, walk a line. I want to see you walk that line right there." She pointed at a spot in the pavement, then quickly repositioned her pointer finger towards a crack when she realized that she wasn't actually pointing at anything. "Okay, you may have a point," she conceded.

"Thanks," he said, and started for the door.

"Nuh-uh," she said, stopping him. "Walk the line first."

"But…" He gave up. The unwavering look on her face told Nate there was no point. She wanted to see the monkey dance. Nate gritted his teeth and started down the line, sure that it would be his undoing. He was so busy fretting, that he didn't even realize he'd reached the end of the crack until he'd gone three steps too far.

He looked back to the girl for approval. Another party-evacuee down the street had caught her eye, and she wasn't even watching Nate's triumph of balance. He scowled in her general direction. When forced to perform, monkeys prefer an audience. She seemed to notice him out of the corner of her eye and turned back.

"Close enough," she said with another wink. Nate began to wonder if she suffered from chronically dry eyes.

Nate unlocked the car door, but stopped himself before entering.

"Wait, before I do this, I feel I should ask what your name is."

"What a shame," she replied heavily. "How fabulous it would be to have gone the entire evening without you actually knowing my name simply to mock social conventions. It's Annie, by the way."

"Annie." He weighed it on his tongue. Everything seemed to check out. "It's certainly better than calling you the girl."

"My parents seemed to think so."

Nate opened the door and started to enter when Annie stopped him, a genuinely concerned look on her face.

"Wait, before you get in, I just feel I should apologize for the state of things inside first."

"Why? What do you mean, it looks fine." There were a few items of clothing and notebooks in the backseat, but other than that it looked like any secondhand car a young person would have: the tears in the upholstery not yet requiring seat covers and the floor was slightly more than dirty bare metal. A single air freshener hung from the rearview mirror.

Annie managed to scoff and slur at the same time. "Oh, you would say that, wouldn't you. Look, a car should be an accurate representation of the owner, and the truth is it's just not an Annie-car yet."

Nate was puzzled, as he'd never owned a car. "Why not?" he asked.

"It's too damned clean."

"Well, they do say cleanliness is next to godliness."

Annie scoffed and slurred yet again. "You can tell *They* that I generally consider my filth, and more specifically, the filth I keep collected in my car, to be a bold statement of my atheism."

Nate's awkwardness was fading as he realized that he'd never been so amused by a person in his life. "I see," he said.

"Do you?" She fired back flirtatiously. Her brass was disarming, but Nate, now trying on his helpful hat, felt he should offer some sort of response or possible solution.

"You could always mess it up, you know."

"You mean, play God?" Annie smiled, clearly amused at the amateur level of his attempt.

"I guess."

Annie slowly mouthed the word *no*, wagging her finger for extra emphasis.

Nate grinned and sat down in the driver's seat, then leaned across and unlocked the passenger door for Annie, who slid into the seat with a well-practiced drunken flop.

"You should feel lucky, Nate. I don't let anyone drive my car, and I just met you," Annie said as she buckled her seat belt.

Nate turned the key in the ignition, feeling the vibration of the floorboard signal the engine's acquiescence.

"I do feel lucky, Annie," he said as he put the car into gear and pulled out onto the tree-lined street slowly, remembering to turn on the headlights.

"I'll bet you do," Annie whispered to herself, and watched as the fog from her breath slowly enveloped the dim reflection of her coy smile in the passenger window.

Nate reached the intersection at the end of the block and realized he didn't know which way to turn—other than to Annie to ask for directions.

"Where exactly is Andy's?"

Annie had been deeply absorbed in her study of the window, but turned back towards Nate with a deeply perplexed look on her face.

"You know, I don't actually know," she said wrinkling up her nose. "Probably should have thought of that earlier."

Nate's mental engine stalled at this roadblock. The needle on the tachometer however, settled casually into idle. "Uh, well… where do you want to go then?"

Annie's head lolled back on her shoulders and she seemed to ponder the ceiling, as if she were looking for directions in the fabric. When she came to an answer, she spoke slowly as if each syllable carried independent weight.

"Washington."

That wasn't what Nate expected, but what did he have to lose? The cold reality of his dorm room was all that awaited him outside the car. Annie had been brutal enough to point that out earlier. Washington was another state, but Oregon technically ended at the Portland city limits, so it wasn't really that far.

"Okay," he said. "Why not? Let's go." He almost believed himself.

Nate flipped on the blinker and pulled out into the intersection in the direction of the freeway. The dense green canopy of moisture-laden trees and the rickety old houses of southeast

Portland whipped past them on the road, feeding the enthusiasm for foreboding adventures to ill-defined destinations. Annie's breath shortened in anticipation as they steered towards the freeway. She exhaled as Nate pushed the shifter into fourth gear to merge onto Interstate 5 heading north. She gazed dreamily out the window, speaking to Nate's reflection as the engine sang alto.

"I love the on-ramp. No matter how scared you are, once you make the turn, there's no way out of it. It's the only thing that ever stays true to its word. Always on, never off. On-ramps are an industrial-aged metaphor for destiny."

Nate thought he detected a tinge of sadness in her voice. But lacking context to address it, he decided to press on with the mission and only mention the issue if it became pertinent. A subject change seemed more appropriate. At least he thought so. Interaction had never been his strong suit. Of course, neither were cues. In fact, anything involving people or communicating with them had always given Nate trouble.

Annie turned the stereo on softly and returned to her post at the window. "So, um, what's your story Annie?" Nate blundered in response.

"I'm not quite sure what you mean."

"Well, just, you know…tell me a little about yourself."

"Do we really have to talk? You already know my name." Her tone was oddly centered, considering the seeming pointedness of the words. A marked change had come over her since entering the car. Her jubilance seemed to have given way to the melancholy of returning sobriety.

"We're going to be in the car a while is all," Nate offered. "It might help to pass the time."

"That's assuming that time needs to be passed," Annie said flatly. "Besides, what is there to tell anybody that hasn't already been told before?"

"Well, no one told me." Nate's comeback involved repressing a self-satisfied chuckle. He reeled it in when he realized Annie wasn't on board; she was still talking to the foggy reflection.

"We're all the same underneath, living out the same stories again and again, thinking they're exclusive to our existence, that we are somehow special and unique when in fact we are nothing but a series of the worst kind of clichés strung together end-to-end until our eventual demise." Annie paused for a moment, then her head lolled back towards Nate. "But enough about me. What's your story, Nate?"

He didn't miss a beat. "Oh, I go to Portland State, majoring in math—"

"Emm…college, how novel." Annie yawned.

Nate scrambled to get his story back on an approved track. "But, I mean, I don't really know if that's what I want to do with my life or if it's just what I wanted before I started or…hey wait, you didn't answer my question."

Annie reached into her purse and pulled out a pack of cigarettes and a lighter. "You're right," she said, putting one in her mouth. She held the pack out towards Nate, offering.

"No thanks. I don't smoke," he said.

Annie gave a half-hearted shrug then sparked the lighter. "Suit yourself," she said and returned to her intensive study of the soggy freeway shoulder, the cherry glowing through the foggy glass like a light house for an asphalt sea. Nate was left to hang on her lack of response. He only lasted a few seconds.

"Well, don't keep me in suspense here, Annie," he said invitingly.

"I'm the worst kind of cliché there is," she sighed.

"What's that?"

Annie took a deep drag from her cigarette and turned back to Nate. Smoke curled out of her nostrils and drifted along her cheeks like a ridiculous mustache. She smiled coyly and exhaled slowly as she spoke.

"All of them," she said matter-of-factly.

"I see," said Nate.

"Do you?"

Nate chuckled awkwardly to himself, feeling Annie's eyes boring into him as she calmly sucked in a load of oxygen to replace the smoke. Right when he was sure he couldn't take it anymore, she attacked.

"I write terrible poetry. I dream of being an actress despite having never actually acted. I reject religion as an act of rebellion against society and talk about it as if it's a revolutionary act instead of a petty jab at my parents. I only shop at second-hand stores that cost more than retail. I have too many pairs of shoes. I do things before they're cool, and I look down on people who do them once they are. I read books written by junkies and call them art rather than desperation. I cried when I saw *Titanic* and I cried even more when Kurt Cobain died. I tell people that my life, and theirs, are nothing more than a series of clichés strung end to end until our eventual demise." She punctuated people's lives with soggy limp hand motions that brought her down from the climax. "I even have been known to fall in love with the wrong guy, then get drunk and run away in the middle of the night when it doesn't work out."

"Is that what we're doing now?" Nate asked nervously.

"I don't know what you're doing here. I can only speak for

myself," she replied dryly. Then her eyelids fluttered at him as if her still-warm monologue never was. "Have you ever been to New York?"

"No."

"Neither have I," she said mournfully. "Would you like to go?"

Nate almost looked behind him to see if she was talking to someone else. "What, now?"

"Yes." For a girl who liked to wink, Annie's flat gaze could rival even those without eyelids. "How much money do you have?"

"I don't know, thirty dollars, maybe."

She snorted in disappointment. "That wouldn't get us to New York, but it should be enough," she said definitively.

"Enough for what?" Nate felt lost at sea.

"Why, for whatever comes our way, of course." She might as well have patted him on the head and offered him a biscuit.

"What's coming our way?"

"I don't know," she shrugged. "Whatever it is though, I'll wager it's not going to cost more than thirty dollars." She added another trademark wink.

"I guess not." Nate conceded with a weak smile, but this time he gave her a wink along with it. Annie's eyes locked casually into Nate's and he felt as if the space between the pitter and patter of each raindrop was stretching further and further apart. It was betting time in a game of emotional poker, but Annie's poker face broke into a wide grin and her attention turned to the bridge they were barreling towards. She quickly cranked down the window and climbed halfway out of it to scream at the green sign announcing the state line.

"NOOOOOOOWWWW LEAVING ORRREEEGGG-GOOONNN!!!"

Annie slithered back into the seat and cranked the volume up, singing along with her eyes closed, rocking her head back and forth, clearly lacking any knowledge of the lyrics and loving every second of it. Guitars were thick in the air; a dense sonic fog swirled around the car in time with the throbbing in Nate's head. It was three choruses in before Annie returned the volume to only slightly above normal, just loud enough to cover up the ringing left in their ears.

They were now past the Columbia River bridge and rolling down the freeway through Vancouver, Washington, a city constructed almost entirely of sterile pressboard and guarded by impeccably edged lawns with browning corners. Crossing the river into Washington was more than just passing over the state line—it was a different state of being from the wildly unkempt fauna and the rickety, tightly clustered and vibrantly painted old houses dripping with tetanus on the south side of the river. Annie must have had a paradigm shift in mind when she pitched the destination.

"Washington achieved," Nate said cheerily.

"Indeed," Annie muttered.

"Well, what now?"

"Let's just keep going," she said and returned to gazing out the window. All the cheer of Annie's sing-along seemed drained from her words. Even if Nate had wanted to go home, he couldn't have. All he could muster to say was an okay. He wanted to believe it didn't matter to him, that he was only out here because he didn't have anywhere to be in the morning, but he knew that wasn't true. He was out here because he knew that when whatever this was ended, the reality that he'd developed a closer relationship with the fake people in the audio sections of his textbooks than with anyone else during his five months at PSU would really hit home. So he drove on in silence, watching the rain creep sideways in long streams along the top of the windshield beyond the reach of the wipers and relishing the moment as the skyward-reaching commercial signs of Vancouver gave way to the dark roadside forests of rural Washington.

The silence was broken by the electronic pings of Annie's mobile. One hand flopped limply into her purse and emerged with the phone. She looked at the name on the screen and silenced the ring with a noise of disgust, then deposited the phone back in her purse and lit another cigarette (again with a pack-waving gesture of offering to Nate, who shook his head no).

Annie inhaled noisily, as if she wanted to consume the cigarette in quarters. She exhaled in the same tone parents use to express "disappointment" in a child brought home by police. Nate felt he had to break the tension somehow.

"So tell me Annie, what's a cliché like yourself doing in Portland anyway?" he said, attempting to sound casual.

"You know, the old same-old-same-old." She shrugged and took down another fourth of her cigarette.

"Um…tell me about your parents," Nate responded.

"They had sex, I came out. Other than that, they didn't contribute much to my life."

Nate was out of ammo. Luckily the void was filled by the sound of Annie's phone ringing again. She grabbed it from her purse and silenced it for the second time.

"Who was that?" Nate asked.

"Nobody," Annie said curtly and glared at the dashboard. "We need more booze." She started rooting around the clothes in the backseat and came back with a near empty, unlabeled bottle of wine halfway corked. She yanked the cork out by hand and finished off the mystery wine; the look on her face suggested she solved the mystery. She took another fourth of her cigarette to try to numb the taste, then held the cigarette out to Nate offering him a drag. He shook his head no, so she snubbed the butt out in the ashtray and leaned back in the passenger seat, her eyes fixed on the windshield.

"I love the rain." She spoke softly like it was more important for the words to come out of her mouth than to go into anyone's ears. "It's what keeps me in Portland. I've known it from the first time I came here. It rained for a whole week straight, like sadness falling from the sky. It was perfect."

"It rained the first time I came here too. It wasn't sad, but it was what made me decide to move here."

"How could the rain here not be sad? It's so wonderfully thick and dreary that it drives people to become serial killers or rock musicians. That's the whole point of it. That's why we're here."

"I know," Nate said. "That's the beauty of it. It liberates you from network television morals. I realized that when I was here with my parents on tour and we got lost somewhere on the east side and just drove around for hours. It was one of those days where it wasn't raining all that hard, but it never let up, not even for a second. We didn't have anything like that in LA, so I was completely enthralled, hanging my head out the window and breathing in the moisture. As we were driving down this little side street, I looked out my window and saw a guy wearing shorts and mowing his lawn in the rain. There were no movie cameras or people he was trying to impress by being a different. He was just mowing his lawn. It was a completely ridiculous thing to be doing and he just didn't care. That's when I decided that I wanted to live in Portland. It's the only place someone would mow their lawn in the rain."

"That's the stupidest reason to love rain ever," Annie quipped. "It's good for mowing lawns in?"

"Hey," Nate said, feeling stung, "I was young."

"Oh yeah, how old were you?" Annie's wit was getting revved back up.

"Nine."

"You were nine?" she exclaimed, shocked.

"Yup." Nate suddenly knew where this was going and kind of regretted bringing things in that direction.

"You decided where you wanted to go to college when you were nine?"

"Well, I didn't pick the college until later."

"Jeez. I even waited longer than that. I was fourteen when I took off. How could you live your whole life already knowing what you're going to be doing with it? That sounds so miserable."

"It's because I knew what I'd be doing with my whole life if I didn't pick something else and the idea of that made me miserable."

"So you ran?"

"Yes."

"And what were you running from?" She had asked the dreaded question.

"You'll laugh."

"No, I won't." Annie shook her head as if this was a cashback guarantee of her commitment to oppose mirth.

"Yes, you will," Nate said, shaking his head right back at her. "And you'll laugh even more when you realize the irony of your laughter." He'd been down this path before and knew it ended up somewhere sour, but Annie was enthralled.

"You make it sound so tantalizing," she purred. "What were

you, Nate Stevenson the math major, so afraid of that you started formulating escape plans at age nine? It's simply unfathomable."

"Fine, you really want to know?" He knew there was no way out of it now.

"Yes." She said it sincerely but had difficulty suppressing a smile.

Nate took a deep breath through his nose and let it fly: "Comedy."

"Comedy?" Annie looked puzzled.

"Yes. Comedy," he said whimsically. "Stand-up comedy."

"I don't get it."

"My parents wanted me to be a stand-up comedian."

She didn't laugh. In fact, Annie still looked confused but in more of a sympathetic manner, like she wanted to laugh to make Nate feel better by lightening the situation, although she clearly understood that it was the wrong choice.

"That doesn't seem so bad," she said. "Better than a lawyer anyhow."

"No, no, no," Nate said, attempting to correct her. "You don't understand. My parents made sure my first word was *hayo*. They made me carry around a keychain that made an electronic rimshot noise. If I wanted something to eat, I had to work it into a knock-knock joke. They even made me go on Star Search when I was eight. The limo driver said that no one had ever cried on their way *to* the studio before."

Now there was no doubt about it. Annie was very obviously suppressing her desire to chortle. "Well, were you funny?" she said through her teeth.

"No, God no!" Nate fired back. "I'm so not funny that it's not even funny. I overheard the judges saying that my act was like being behind the scenes at an accountant's convention." Nate now looked truly despondent as he expounded. "But you know how parents are. Their child is always the most amazingly talented child ever to walk the face of the Earth and nothing, especially not the pleas of the child itself, can convince them otherwise. Can you imagine staying in LA, living like that? I just wanted somewhere safe and sheltered and orderly, without PR agents, and Botox, and paparazzi, and headshots and all of it. A place where people are willing to mow their lawn in the rain because they just don't care about impressing anyone. Somewhere where you can just be yourself…even if you aren't that interesting."

Annie didn't want to laugh anymore. "I guess I'd have run too," she said.

"Didn't you?"

"All the way from Arkansas," Annie conceded. "But not from anything as sinister as stand-up comedy. I ran just for the exercise."

Nate exhaled in approval and then started to shake his head. "It was too much. They wanted me to live their life, not mine. And I'll never measure up because math just isn't something that young men should be interested in. But I like it even if it doesn't win friends or influence people. I don't care if it's boring. Math makes more sense to me than people. It's consistent… soothing. But they don't understand, so I have to lie to them. I told my mother I had a girlfriend just to keep her off my back. But then they wanted to meet her so we had to break up and now I have a new imaginary girlfriend just to placate their need to pry and meddle. Her name is Susan Hendrake. She's a twenty-year-old theatre major from a small farm town in eastern Oregon who wants to work off-Broadway, because it's less about glitz and more about real art. Now they are pressuring me to meet her. I'm going to have to get her a movie role so she can leave me. Do you have any idea what that's like?"

"No." Annie seemed almost embarrassed in her response, like she'd announced her arrival at someone's bedroom window with the intention to peep.

Nate didn't seem to notice. "They even think I host an open mic night on campus."

"Mine don't think of me."

"Maybe you should become a stand-up comedian," Nate suggested. Annie smiled.

"I'd need a mentor," she said. "Someone who knows the business inside and out, possibly who hosts an open mic night and can give me a foothold in the business."

"Perhaps my parents are willing to adopt," Nate scoffed.

"Better late than never, I guess." Annie shrugged.

"Sometimes it's better never."

"Sometimes," she whispered and again resigned herself to the solace of billboards announcing tax-free cigarettes and the unbroken lengths of barbed wire that floated up and down on the terrain like waves.

They drove in comfortable wordlessness, the dotted yellow paint on the road whipping past and being absorbed into the inky abyss, a soothing hypnotic constant. Annie lit another cigarette.

"I love driving at night," Annie said softly after several minutes. "It's like the world ends with the beam of the headlights, like whatever is happening is the most significant event in the world. Every song you hear becomes the best song ever recorded and whatever is being said is unbelievably profound, even if it's really just inane chatter."

"Are you saying this has all been inane chatter?"

"No," she said, eyes forward. "I'm saying that it's all been profound on a level that the rest of the world can never hope to understand. It's just you and me out here and no matter how eloquently we explain things, no one else will ever get it." Annie paused momentarily. "We have to find a mountain."

"What do you mean? We're surrounded by mountains," Nate replied, slightly puzzled.

"I mean we need to get off the freeway and go to the top of one of these mountains," she clarified.

"Why?"

Annie inhaled deeply. "To hear a song," she replied, "and songs always sound best on mountaintops. It's in their nature."

"What song?" Nate couldn't fathom how Annie switched gears so quickly and completely.

"Why, Nate," she said flirtatiously. "After my little speech just a second ago, it should be perfectly clear that it's the best song ever recorded and nothing less."

Nate realized he deserved that.

Annie took the kind of drag from her cigarette usually reserved for Hollywood ingénues, circa 1940, then casually turned the butt around and held its business end between her finger tips in Nate's general direction. Not really knowing why, he leaned his head over and accepted a shallow nearly hack-free drag, then mustered up a half-smile that smacked of acquiescence.

Annie grinned and lit another smoke in glee, shoving the first one between Nate's lips. It hung down from the corner of his mouth, Bogart-like. The smoke irritated his eye in the best possible manner as Nate eased the car onto the first available off-ramp—a practical older sibling of the on-ramp, always nagging one to slow down and pay close attention to the available options rather than charging madly onward, come what may, towards the possibility of greatness.

The off-ramp begot a country lane that meandered past a smattering of lackluster houses—less of a town and more of a way station of sorts. From there, they found a turnoff leading into the trees and the darkness above the artificial lights. There were fewer houses along the road but it was clearly slotted for more. The crest of the hill overlooking the freeway was a paved street cleared of obstructive trees, with lots marked off for developers and driveways already cemented.

Nate parked the car in one of the driveways and switched off the car and lights, leaving only the glow of the few stars brave enough to poke through the clouds to see by. That light had been traveling for thousands of years to shine on Earth. Letting some punk clouds muck things up at the last second would have been awfully defeatist.

Annie bolted out of the car immediately, telling Nate to wait behind as she closed the door. Nate leaned back in the driver's seat and looked at the ceiling, pondering how he'd found himself in this situation. Perhaps the dome light knew. If the car represented a sealed reality as Annie had suggested, then the dome light could be interpreted as God. It couldn't hurt to ask.

"Give me the answers I seek," he whispered, afraid of embarrassing himself to an audience of none. Predictably, the light said nothing in response. So Nate started looking in the back seat to see what wisdom the ancients had buried in Annie's pile of clothes and knickknacks. He found a notebook, and like all people left to wait in a car would do, he leafed through it lackadaisically, brushing disinterestedly past poetic personal accounts of mornings after, underlined phone numbers and items to do both crossed off and left undone. Annie's phone rang yet again. Nate gave a quick panoramic glance but Annie was nowhere in sight, so he picked up the phone to silence the ringing and snuck a peek at the caller ID. Tyler's name looked him square in the eye and was silenced by a stroke of Nate's thumb for its insolence. If only all conflicts could be resolved so simply, he thought, and went back to flipping through Annie's notebook.

There was a rush of cold air as the door suddenly flew open and Annie flopped back into the passenger seat.

"I thought I was going to explode I had to pee so bad," she gasped.

Nate had quickly tossed the notebook into the obscurity of the backseat before Annie noticed.

"I think nobody called for you while you were out," he said.

Annie picked up the phone and looked at the screen. "Yup, that's nobody all right," she said with a practiced eye roll.

"So, does nobody have a name?" Nate said, trying to pierce Annie's wall of camouflaging witticisms.

She pulled a CD book out of the backseat and began flipping through the pages. "Yes," she said without looking up. "Nobody does have a name." Rather than reveal Tyler's name, a brief but detailed description of Annie's music collection ensued, narrating the journey from cover to cover.

Nate, who knew little of such things, simply nodded whenever she asked if he had heard of a group rather than risk the disapproving end of her vocabulary for somehow failing to purchase the imported, first press, limited edition, B-sides and outtakes from a side project of the lead singer for the band whom the critics lauded as the most undeniable influence on modern pop music, despite never actually breaking into the Top 40 themselves. Then, as suddenly her dissertation had started, it ended. Annie squealed in delight at the CD she was looking for.

"What is it?" Nate asked.

Annie quickly shushed him with one hand as she silently slid the CD into the slot in the dashboard with the other. Then she reached across Nate's lap slowly, relishing the horrified look in his eyes as he instinctively sucked in his gut to avoid being brushed, which stopped his breathing momentarily. Smiling mischievously, she suddenly yanked the release latch causing his seat to recline violently and then reclined hers to match.

Nate took a deep, stuttering breath that pushed against the seat belt stretched across his chest and looked up through the windshield at the single patch of stars visible through the cloud cover. He wondered if this was how Frankenstein's monster felt: strapped to a gurney high atop the ramparts, terrified and alone, facing an angry grey sky in a situation that if survived, would only end in dealing with the entire world's complete misunderstanding of his existence. Shudders overtook Nate and for a second he was entirely convinced that they would be the end of him too. Then the music started.

Deep washed out organ faded in on the left; a hauntingly minor drone that soaked Nate down to the marrow with the beauty of its subtlety. Bass pulsed softly inside his rib cage, a cadence leading the delicate melody through an emotional battlefield. A guitar twinkled tastefully underneath the changes, then snarled at the other instruments like a cornered jungle cat. Nate wanted to curl up and live in the speaker—to become a science major so he could convert his consciousness to electricity and bond with the signal path, and weep with joy. But he felt paralyzed, as if moving might frighten the music away, scattering the sound waves into the atmosphere like getting too close to animals in the wild. He breathed cautiously, fearing a stampede.

Nate now understood why thousands of people greeted the Beatles at the airport in New York, why mothers were terrified of their children listening to Elvis, and why it was said that music was best on mountaintops. It was a siren's toxic call sans reef, audio heroin offering the unadulterated bliss of singular immersion for three and a half minutes, a safe harbor available simply by pressing play, a benevolent and nonjudgmental messiah, a lover's embrace. And then, in a mirror of its appearance, it faded out slowly.

Nate turned to Annie to ask the name of the band and found her soundly asleep, breathing softly. He wanted to kiss her, but instead, reached across the car and took one of her cigarettes. He sparked Annie's lighter and lit the smoke, inhaling deeply as he leaned back and unbuckled his safety belt. The hole in the clouds above him was getting larger. More and more stars were fulfilling their destiny to twinkle above the heads of young people looking to them for answers, the way he had looked to the dome light. The stars very well may have been screaming the answers the entire time but were too far away to hear. Nate pressed the repeat button on the CD player. He took another drag, letting the smoke linger in his mouth, warming his uvula. Then he blew the smoke skyward, watching it float lazily across the ceiling like clouds on a summer day as the organ faded back in and he slowly drifted off to sleep.

Nate awoke comfortably with the rising of the sun and carefully got out of the car so as not to wake Annie. He strolled about fifty feet from the car to a scrubby looking bush at the edge of the lot and unzipped his fly to pee on it. Throwing caution to the wind, he performed the act with no hands, stretching his arms wide and reveling in the stirrings of life in the valley below as he whistled a pop song he'd heard once. Today was going to be a good day.

Nate zipped up and returned to the car. The rocking of the suspension as Nate sat down awakened Annie.

"Hey there," he said cheerily.

Annie took a heavy breath and raised her head up to look around. "Where are we?" she said.

"On top of some mountain," Nate replied.

Annie made a grunting noise that roughly translated to "okay, whatever" and then reburied her face in the backrest.

"Do you still want to go to New York," Nate continued, "or are you ready to give up and go home? Perhaps we should consider Botswana instead."

"No Botswana," she groaned. "I wouldn't have a thing to wear anyway."

"Well, home then, I guess," Nate said and held the keys out to Annie. She waved them back at him and told him to drive. Nate started the car and pulled back onto the road down the hill. Moving again after being parked felt slightly off-kilter, like a rear-projected scene in an old movie. Halfway down the hill, Annie spoke again.

"Thanks for running away with me, Nate."

"Thanks for inviting me to run away with you," he said gleefully.

Face down, Annie's eyes rolled. "Don't be so difficult. Cheer in the morning is unnatural."

"Maybe..." Nate replied, slightly stung.

Fuzzyheaded, Nate drove down the hill and back to the freeway. He accelerated to takeoff speed down the on-ramp and merged into society, now plainly revealed in the glaring light of day. Pockets of rain came and went, leaving the freeway shiny like a glimmering mirage as they headed back towards Oregon. It was a dull-eyed commute that replaced their daring adventure north. Nate played the stereo softly to pass the time and imagined future conversations with Annie over dinner or drinks. He planned the right thing to say at goodbye time while she slept in a position that seemed destined for chiropractic intervention.

Annie's phone rang jarringly just as Nate was exiting the freeway back to the real world. She sat up with a jolt and dug madly for the phone, silenced the ringer and tossed it into the back seat in irritation.

"I'm moving to the rainforest," she said and lit a cigarette. "Rain, no phones, fresh tobacco, really living the in the shadow of impending disaster instead of just feeling like it. What more could a girl want?"

"I don't know," Nate replied.

"It was a rhetorical question," she said shortly. "Never mind."

Nate felt niceties were more in order than rhetorical questions to move things along properly. They were almost home after all. "Did you sleep well?" he asked.

"Yeah," she said dryly. "Thanks for driving."

"Thanks for letting me drive," Nate piped in. "I don't get a chance to very often since I moved here and I really enjoyed it." She gave Nate a look to remind him of her take on good cheer in the morning. "Well...I live just down this way, so I'm going to drive to my place and then you can drive home. Is that all right with you?" he asked delicately.

Annie looked straightforward in response, repositioning her razor from her wit to her tongue.

"It's fine." The words slithered. They were like poisoned air trapped in a tomb for a thousand years, seeping into consciousness instead of actually being conjugated by human speech. Ten-pound syllables. The remainder of the drive was spent in the uncomfortable silence of realization.

Nate pulled the car over in front of his apartment building,and turned off the engine. He got out of the door. Annie slid awkwardly over the stick shift and across the seats to take the driver's position.

"I guess this is goodbye," he said awkwardly.

"I guess…"

This was the moment he had planned to ask for her phone number, to tell her how alive he'd felt the night before, to say what a jerk Tyler must be, and to suavely offer to chauffeur for her whenever the need arose. Those weren't the words that came out of his mouth.

"I'm never going to see you again, am I, Annie?"

She looked at the steering wheel and said nothing.

Nate took a quick breath. "I see…" he said.

"Yeah," she whispered. "I think you do." She handed Nate a cigarette and looked him in the face when she did so. "Have one for the road."

"Thanks."

Nate closed the door and stepped away from the car as Annie started the engine. She pulled out into the street leaving Nate alone on the sidewalk. He watched the blue car fade into the distance and reintegrate with the collective static. Nate put the cigarette casually behind his ear and walked into his building and back to his life.

154

ECHOES

She asks me why I never write stories about her.

What kind of a question is that, I tell her.

You write about all your ex-girlfriends.

Not all.

Enough of them. Why them and not me?

They're not around. And I'd like for you to stay.

So you only have bad things to say then?

It doesn't matter if they're good or bad. It's the true parts people don't like. Even when they're fictional.

Don't I deserve to be written about?

That's a loaded question.

Well, don't I?

Yes. Psychology papers.

I'm serious.

Why does it have to be me? Shouldn't it be someone who doesn't have to answer to you?

I like your stories.

You have to say that.

Yes. But I still like them.

So you say.

That's why I want you to write one about me.

No.

Why?

I just told you. Who'd want to read it anyway? It'd be dull.

You're calling me dull?

No.

You are.

I'm saying you're nice.

Nice sounds like dull.

Would you rather be a total cunt?

I'd rather know how you really feel.

I tell you that all the time.

I'm not sure you do.

Stories are generally about horrible people's creative justifications for horrible actions. We don't even fight. It would be a dull story.

We're fighting right now.

Are we?

I think so.

Okay, then you tell me. What should I write about? Paying our bills on time? Going to the supermarket? The movie we saw last week?

How about this fight we're having?

About what? It would be fluff. The lack of drama even in our "fights" makes for a good relationship, but a boring story.

I cheated on you.

Did you?

Would that be story-worthy?

Would that somehow excuse it?

No.

Did you?

Yes.

Should I ask with whom or why?

Do you mean for background information?

No.

Ask if you like. I don't think it will help you for anything other than background though.

I can't believe you're telling me this. How are you being so cavalier?

Is it enough? Does it break my character out of being dull?

Are you serious?

Yes. I'm ice cold. I cheated on you and I'm playing it off like I'm more interested in my goals than your feelings. That should be an archetypal female lead. Does it make me worthy of being written about now?

Yes. Dear John letters should be written by the gross.

Why don't you take this seriously?

I think I could ask you the same question.

I'm being deadly serious here. Don't I deserve stories?

Why does it matter so much to you if I write a worthless, unpublishable dialogue about you to myself—something that no one else will ever see and will likely be lost or thrown away?

Because you do it for them, for her. Not for me.

It's not for them.

Well, who is it for then? You? To relive things you don't have with me?

To relive all that pain? What kind of masochist would do that?

A writer.

You give me too much credit.

And you don't give me enough.

Says the cheater.

Don't I deserve to be written about? Because if you don't think I do, what are you doing with me?

Is there a correct answer to this question?

Yes, obviously.

Will it make you happy?

For now.

Fine. You deserve sonnets, novels, plays, dictionary and encyclopedia entries, feature articles, reviews and histories. All varieties of writing imaginable in every language of the earth. Your actions should be narrated in Cyrillic, Hebrew, Arabic, and hieroglyphic languages. Helpless children should be forced to compose essays on your motivations and dialect. You should be panned by the critics, yet still make it onto the best-seller list. Happy?

Yes.

You deserve all of that. But not by me.

Why not you?

Because I'd have to answer to you for it.

No, you wouldn't.

That's what everyone says. Let someone who can embellish all the right things with impunity have the job.

What do you mean?

Helen of Troy was more proud of her lazy eye than anything else in the world. Thought it was a gift from the gods. That confidence gave her the beauty she was famed for. But now she's the face that launched a thousand ships. Eyes ahead. Just because of some blind asshole poet. Could you live with being betrayed like that?

Is that true?

Sure. Why not?

I don't think I believe you.

I'm not sure I believe you cheated on me.

I did.

I know. And I'll probably write about it someday.

When?

Someday.

Will I see it?

Never.

Why?

Because I'll be with someone else then.

ONE FRIDAY IN APRIL

It is Friday, 9 a.m. and our appointment is at noon.

It was only on Tuesday that Erin found out she was pregnant. The sun was out for the first time in weeks and our roommate Jessica and I were drinking mimosas in the front yard. Erin leaned out the front door with a puzzled look on her face.

"What's with you?" I asked. "Are you stoned or something?"

"No," she said, squirming just enough to confirm she likely was.

"Yeah, you look totally high," Jessica chided.

Erin sucked in a quick breath and grimaced slightly. "Jess, you're going to find out anyway," she said. "So, here it goes—I'm pregnant."

Without another word, she disappeared back inside.

"Well," I said, putting down my mimosa and standing up. "I should probably head in for a talk about now." Jessica nodded. She would later tell me my face had worn a look of complete panic, though I can't recall feeling anything at the time.

"Do you want to talk about this now, or forget about it for awhile to clear your head?" I asked Erin. She was pacing in and out of the bathroom.

"No, just don't worry," she said without looking at me. "I'll take care of it." Her phrasing stung, as if she was presupposing attitudes I would cop and demands I would make. More than that, it was clear she'd already made the decision. If discussed, we would likely have come to the same decision, but it would have been nice to be consulted.

"God…I don't know what to do with this," she said of the pregnancy test. "Should I keep it to show to them?"

I didn't know what to tell her.

Erin and I met two years ago on the Portland State University debate team. As such, we are very aware of the arguments for and against abortion—everything from the moral standards protesters rant about in front of abortion clinics and at Republican conventions, to the economic studies about the effects of unwanted children on crime rates and the costs of incarceration on taxpayers. We even know the argument that a baby is an invading parasite that steals nutrients from the mother so that it may live; Oxford won the world championships with that argument.

Erin and I dissected the issue for near an hour while walking our dog one day, both ending up in roughly the same place on the issue: that abortion is pretty awful for all involved, but a ban is far worse. Instead of trying to ban abortion, the focus should be on promotion of sex education, birth control and family planning to diminish the demand.

I once wrote an article for our school newspaper saying exactly that.

My guess is that this conversation was the basis for her decision. In it, we both agreed we lack the financial or emotional readiness to provide for a child. Neither of us even particularly like children. We often scowl at them in grocery stores and complain to one another about the menace of strollers. We call babies "the new purse dogs."

But now abortion is real, not an academic abstract. It is her body and her choice. I support that absolutely. Still, it hurt to be informed rather than consulted.

We are having breakfast like it is any other day. Pancakes. Coffee. We watch the *Daily Show with Jon Stewart* online and check the news headlines. Afterwards, we walk the dog.

Though we don't discuss it, we are both keeping one eye on the clock.

Truth is, this couldn't have happened at a worse time. Erin was just fired from her job and mine barely covers my share of the rent. Neither of us have any savings or promising job leads. Plus, our relationship has been rocky lately. Although Erin says the pregnancy explains her moodiness and lack of interest in sex for the last two months, I don't know if I believe her. Mostly I am concerned the trauma will push her further away from me. A previous relationship I was in ended from a pregnancy scare.

It's especially frustrating because my way of dealing with pressure has always been to make jokes, but I can't do that in this situation. It isn't funny.

With an issue like abortion, it is hard to find support. It is so politically and emotionally charged that it is difficult to know whom you can trust to confide in—if you're even comfortable speaking about it at all. Several of my closest friends have revealed their serious objections. I can't even imagine discussing it with my parents. They would likely view it as an assault on them personally.

Erin didn't expressly forbid me from talking about it, but I know she isn't comfortable with people knowing. Still, I couldn't bottle things up any longer. A relationship is about supporting one another. But in this scenario, she needs my full and unwavering support while being in no position to return the favor. And if not her, then I had to turn to someone else.

That's why on Wednesday after work, I went out to have a much-needed drink with Neil and Mara.

"So what's going on?" Neil asked.

"Oh, you know…" I said. "Have you ever just had one of those weeks where you really hate your job and are really generally frustrated and broke and then your girlfriend tells you she's pregnant?"

The look on Neil's face must have been the one Jessica described as being on mine when I found out.

"So you're going to be a papa?" Mara asked.

"No," I said. "She's doing the thing on Friday."

"The operation?" Neil asked.

"No, the pills."

"My friend Robin took those," said Neil. "She said it was

two days of sitting on the toilet feeling like her insides were falling out, but it was still better than the vacuum."

"I don't really think there's a good way," I said.

"Weren't you using birth control?" Neil asked.

"I thought we were," I said. "Erin says this ought to make her less forgetful about her pill in the future."

"Are you okay with this, Isaac?" Mara asked.

"Doesn't matter, does it? It's not my decision."

"But are you okay?"

"I have to watch her suffer, knowing that it's partially my fault and there's nothing I can do about it," I said. "That's just how it is."

"I know," Mara said quietly. "I have nothing but sympathy for that girl. This is going to be with her for the rest of her life."

I had strangely morbid thoughts as I rode my bike home that night.

Couples often refer to pregnancies in the group possessive. So if people say "we are pregnant" does that mean that "we are having an abortion"?

If going around the next corner I were hit by a car and died, would Erin decide to keep the baby to keep my memory alive? Would she give it a middle name in quotation marks like I would want?

If she weren't pregnant, I would have asked her those things when I got home. But odd philosophical musings lose their whimsy when they become immediate practical realities.

As if to highlight our destitution, we have to borrow Jessica's car to get to the clinic. Neither Erin or I can afford one and this is a situation in which neither bikes nor buses will suffice.

Thankfully, Jessica does not give us hard time about asking.

We are actually so broke that last night, when a friend called and asked me to be a ringer for his pubquiz trivia team, rather than stay home with Erin for the night before the big appointment, I went out and tried to win money to help pay for the abortion. The last time I'd done a bar trivia night, the pot was $600, which I tried to explain to Erin when she called me, wanting me to borrow Jessica's car to pick her up from work. She hung up on me when I told her where I was and why I couldn't come get her. Shortly after that, I found out that the prize was $20 worth of bar tokens, which we didn't win. I knew it was a stupid thing to do. Money shouldn't be a factor when staring down an issue as ethically, morally and emotionally gray as abortion. But it is. One of the many reasons we can't have a baby is we really are that broke. There is less than $100 in my bank account and I don't know how I will pay rent in two weeks. Sad, pathetic and failed an attempt as it may have been, pubquiz was the only potential way to raise money that presented itself and I wasn't in the position to be picky.

I change the radio stations constantly as we drive to the clinic, chattering about the music to avoid the awkward silence that allows contemplation of where we are headed and why.

The media has not been kind to me over the last several days. While washing the dishes yesterday, NPR broadcast a half-hour program on abortion and family planning within Somali immigrant communities.

Later, I watched a TV show about a vampire pregnant with a human child. She performed an emergency C-section by staking herself in the heart and crumbling to dust around her baby, saving it from being trapped in her dead womb.

I felt the same way about these shows that people do when they drive past car accidents.

I didn't tell Erin about either.

"It's admirable what they did with this place," I say to Erin when we arrive at the clinic. "But I don't think you can make a waiting room not feel tense. Not as long as you know what you're waiting for."

She nods, more to get me to shut up than from agreeing.

I don't tell her this is the same clinic I came to with a previous girlfriend so she could get an I.U.D. installed.

"What's our household size?" she asks me. "Three?"

I resist the urge to look at her stomach and say not for long.

"We're not married," I say, "so it's just you."

"But what about Bubba?" she smirks. "He's a dependent, isn't he?"

"Dogs don't count," I say.

She makes a face of disapproval, and in that moment I am so full of love for her I feel like I might pop.

The truth is I hate this place. I believe in its mission and am glad it exists, but I can't help but feel that within its walls, I am the enemy. I am the abuser. The impregnator. The carrier of disease and giver of emotional trauma. When I am here, I am the face of all the men that aren't. I feel the patients look at their magazines and stab their pens into paperwork—the scared young girls who come in pairs, clutching each others hands and trying to hide their tears, and the ones who sit alone. Even worse, though I am fully aware that most of this is in my head, I am angry with them. Shouldn't I get credit for being here, for trying to hold Erin's hand even though she pulls it away? I deserve better than icy glances and innuendoes.

I am not invited with Erin when her name is called. She will tell me later that I'm not allowed because of privacy laws, but I think she was more concerned that my inappropriate humor would further humiliate her. It's a reasonable concern.

The receptionist tells me it will be at least an hour, so rather than bathe in the tension of the waiting room, I leave the clinic and go to the coffee shop downstairs. And this is how I pass my visit to the abortion clinic: sipping a mocha at a sunlit window table and chatting with a friend who wanders by about her new apartment.

I am called back to the clinic to go over the details of Erin's outpatient care. A nurse leads me into a small back office where Erin is sipping a juice box and dabbing her puffy eyes. My insides ache to see her in this state, but it would be inappropriate to hold her and not let go in a doctor's office. I must stay strong for the both of us.

All that happened while I was gone was blood work and an ultrasound. Diagnostics. The nurse tells us that the real work is about to begin. She gives us a checklist of different pills that must be taken at different times over the next two days along with what to expect from each of them. Pain. Fever. Nausea. Vomiting. Diarrhea. Drowsiness. Lots of bleeding. Then she tells me that my job is to keep watch in case things go too far and Erin needs to go to the hospital. Based off what she told us to expect, I have no idea what would be considered a red flag.

"I'm intentionally making this seem much worse than it probably will be," she says. "Just, that way you're prepared."

We say we understand.

"Are you ready?" the nurse asks. She is holding a pill in her hand. "Once you take this, there's no going back."

"Just like *The Matrix*," I say, "with the red pill."

"I didn't see that movie," the nurse says.

Erin swallows it swiftly and without comment. I fear my pop culture reference may have embarrassed her.

Before we leave, the nurse asks if we'd like to see the ultrasound. Curiosity gets the better of me.

She opens up Erin's file on the desk in front of us and gestures with her pencil as she narrates the image in the center of the file.

The ultrasound is a gray blur with a small, dark, featureless oval. Realistically, it doesn't look like anything at all.

But in my head, it does. I see little fingers and toes. I see weird hair and an awkward childhood. I see a hole in my own life that I never would've wanted to impose on any other person. I see Erin quickly look away.

The nurse holds up her fingers to show how big the fetus is; I've seen larger peanuts.

We thank her for everything and make an appointment to come back to ensure that everything worked the way it was supposed to. Then we leave.

Prior to Tuesday, there was a lot on the agenda for the weekend: band practice, theater tickets, the annual Easter Beer Hunt at my friend Tara's house. Instead, on the way home we rent a lot of movies and get a selection of Erin's favorite snacks with my food stamp card, and settle in for the long haul.

Erin takes a series of pills and immediately goes to bed at 3 p.m. I leave shortly afterwards to go to my temp job loading freight at the airport.

People at work ask me how I am. Over the roar of jet engines, I lie, shouting that I am fine. There are not words or consistent, logical ways to state what I am really feeling. It would be inappropriate to do so anyhow, especially since there is a myriad of horrific ways to die if I divert my attention from work to sort out my emotional turmoil.

I feel anxious and worried; crushed by a cargo container.

I feel relieved; sucked into a jet engine.

I feel angry; chopped up in a propeller.

I feel sad and confused, unsure if we made the right decision and that maybe I might want a child after all, that it might have been possible for me to avoid inflicting the pitfalls of my own upbringing by cataloguing them and devising alternate rearing methods that didn't involve the forced eating of cottage cheese to cure the flu or spiritual boot camps to enforce Zen teachings on a first grader; hit by a forklift.

I feel hungry; my skin is melted off by chemical de-icer.

When I get home, Erin is asleep. So I watch TV in the living room to give her as much space to rest as possible.

It is Saturday and she is supposed to take the big pills at noon. We get up and have a light breakfast. Erin lambastes me for my snoring, then goes back to bed. Though we don't discuss it, we are both keeping one eye on the clock.

The pills must be taken in a specific sequence. First, she puts a nausea patch on the back of her neck several hours beforehand. Then, an antibiotic to prevent infection. Then several pain pills. And finally, the main event—the bringer of pain and nausea and bleeding and skeletons to be hidden away in closets. It must be placed in her cheek to dissolve for a half an hour.

The nurse recommended also sucking on hard candy to soften its bitter taste. Erin chose a cherry Life Saver. In her situation, I would have preferred a Werther's Original. A Life Saver seems too cheekily morbid.

All these pills so specifically ordered highlights the irony of this event beginning with a forgotten pill.

Staring at that last pill, Erin is scared; she's having second, third and fifteenth thoughts, not sure if she still wants to go through with things.

"I love you and don't want to see you in pain," I say, "but it's really too late."

"Why?"

"You took the red pill yesterday. Things have been set into motion. If you try to stop them now—"

"It will have birth defects. I know."

"It's your choice, Erin, and I'll back you. But you're choosing between discomfort and a retarded baby when neither of us can even take care of a normal one."

"I know," she says. "I'm just scared."

"Me too," I say, "but we'll get through it together."

She puts the pills in her mouth, both of us knowing full well that despite the best of rhetoric and intentions, she will be facing this alone. All I can really do is watch.

It is twenty minutes later and I am watching TV in the living room, trying let Erin sleep through as much of this nightmare as possible. Suddenly, I hear her shouting for me. I sprint through the kitchen and down the hall to our bedroom. She is sitting up in bed, thick white crud caked around her mouth. Panic is in her eyes.

"I threw up," she says.

I see more of the thick white goo all over the bedspread and floor. It looks like country gravy.

"It happened so quick," she said. "I don't know what to do."

"It's okay," I say. "The nurse told us to expect this. Just, go in the bathroom in case you have to barf again and I'll clean things up."

"No you don't understand," she insists, pounding her fists into the pillow. "The pills weren't dissolved yet. It's only been twenty minutes."

"And now they're…" I look at the barf and Erin nods.

"What if it doesn't work," she says. "I can't do this again. I just can't."

She is panicking, breathing quick and shallow, unable to think clearly. I'm not far behind her but have somehow managed to shift into autopilot.

"Go in the bathroom," I say. "I'll clean this up. We'll call the emergency number. Everything will be fine. All we can do is move forward." These are the words that come out of my mouth. The ones in my head are mostly synonyms for run and hide.

"But—"

"No buts. Just do it."

Erin gets out of bed and lurches into the bathroom. I quickly strip the sheets, the pool of barf wrapped up in them like a bindle stick. I carry them at arm's length to the basement where I set them on top of the washing machine to be dealt with later. I run back up the stairs to get the bed back together and find Bubba lapping up the vomit on the carpet. I shoo him, wipe it up and call Erin out of the bathroom.

It all took less than two minutes.

"I can't do this again," she repeats.

"We'll call the number. Everything will be fine."

I pick up the bright pink piece of paper listing the order in which the pills should be taken that the nurse gave us and dial the phone number she highlighted at the top of the page.

A machine picks up and I leave a message.

"What happened?" Erin demands.

"It was a machine," I say. "Just rest. There's nothing we can do until we talk to them and panicking will only make things worse. They'll call back." I wish there were someone to tell me the things I'm telling Erin.

"I can't do this again," she insists.

"I know," I say. "Just, please, rest."

The phone rings two minutes later. I explain the situation to the woman on the other end and she tells me that it's likely that the pills were in Erin's mouth long enough to be effective. But the only way to know for sure is if she starts bleeding sometime within the next twenty-four hours. We'll just have to wait and see.

Erin's reaction when I relay the information makes it clear she wanted something more concrete than wait and see. But that's what we got. She goes back to sleep and I go back to the living room to watch TV and await the next shouting of my name.

Four hours later, her vagina is bleeding heavily. She seems relieved in a nauseous sort of way.

Every half an hour or so, I go in to check on Erin. For most of these visits, she's asleep, so there's very little to see. But eventually I catch her awake, watching an internet video. I lay down next to her.

"Babe," she says firmly, "I can't handle you in here tonight."

"Fine," I say and get up.

"Because of the snoring, I mean," she says weakly when I am almost out the door. "That's all."

"It's fine," I say. "You need rest more than me."

A little while later, my friend Madeleine appears at the door bearing beer. She, Jessica and I sit around the kitchen table having a competition over whose day was the most trying. Jessica met new and irritating varieties of customers at her restaurant. Madeleine worked for the first shift since most of her coworkers were laid off and their responsibilities were transferred to her. I spent the day on call.

Erin calls me into our bedroom and asks if we can head down to the corner bar to keep it down.

"Sure," I say, "whatever you need."

I go back to the kitchen and suggest we head to the bar. The idea is not received well; bars are expensive. We are here.

"Erin's really sick," I say. "I just want to let her rest."

"You know, I live here too, and I don't appreciate being kicked out of my own house," Jessica snaps. "She seems fine to me. I don't see what the big deal is."

I am about to unleash all of the pent up rage and frustration at Jessica for her callousness, but just then Bubba trots gleefully out of the bathroom with an engorged and bloody maxi pad clutched in his jaws. It is like a Greek myth where my animal child is eating the ghost of my human child. His tail is wagging and he is looking at me proudly. I don't know whether to laugh or cry. So I take it from him and throw it in the garbage. Then we go to the bar where Madeline proceeds to lecture us about how cheap it is to build a log cabin.

I sleep on the couch that night. When Jessica leaves for work in the morning, she gives me a look asking how I screwed up as she passes through the living room.

It is Sunday and Erin has been sleeping on and off—and bleeding nonstop—for eighteen hours. Instead of being dead like I would be, she somehow feels better. However, better is far from good.

It is Monday. Erin just woke up, and she is smiling at me. What the future holds, I don't know. But right now, she looks genuinely happy for the first time in months. And that is enough.

We barely mention the experience until the next weekend when we go out to breakfast. Discussions of how to spend the sunny day turn into discussions of feelings for one another, then turn into me explaining my fear that she is emotionally isolating herself by refusing to talk about what happened. Eventually, she opens up a little.

"I'm one of *those* people now," she says. "It's not an abstract or something I support on principle or discuss academically. I was faced with the decision and I chose a side. I can't go back on that." But then the waiter comes and she clams up.

She orders a Belgian waffle and I have the eggs Benedict. Both taste like things left unsaid.

It is over a week later that Erin calls me in a panic to say that she has just passed an enormous clot at school and bled through her pants, that she doesn't know what to do, and wonders whether she should go to the emergency room or not.

"I'll come as quick as I can, but you need to call the emergency number," I say. "They'll know what to do."

"I threw the paper away," she says. "I didn't want to look at it anymore."

I suck in an angry breath. Not angry at her so much as fate or the world. "What can I do?" I ask.

"I don't know, I don't know, I don't know," she says. "I just… can you come here? Please?"

I ride my bike as fast as I can to get to her school, imagining the worst—Erin sitting in a puddle of blood, white pants stained red to the inside of the knee, like a scene from a movie we recently saw about a housewife in the fifties who dies from a home abortion. I see Erin's uterus dripping out of her. I see angry, deformed, horror movie babies crawling from her vagina seeking revenge. I see her classmates standing in a circle laughing and eating popcorn.

When I arrive Erin is wearing dark blue pants and I can see no stain, blood colored or otherwise. We go outside. She says she doesn't want to go to the hospital; it's too expensive. And since her follow-up appointment is for the next day, she insists she'll be fine. Then she gives me a hug and says she should get back to studying.

"Can you come pick me up when I'm done?" she asks.

"Sure," I say. Then I ride my bike home, borrow Jessica's keys and wait for Erin to call.

It is Friday and our appointment is at noon. We get up and watch *The Daily Show* online while eating breakfast. Though neither of us mention it, we are both keeping one eye on the clock. We borrow Jessica's car and go to the clinic. This time, instead of sipping a mocha, I do a crossword puzzle while Erin is being probed.

Half an hour later she is given the all clear. We are officially fetus-free.

So we get back in the car and go out to lunch to get on with our lives. I order a pepper bacon cheeseburger with no mayo or pickles. Erin has the same. This time the food tastes like normalcy.

But like most things, moving on isn't as easy as we believe it will be.

It is one month after the abortion and Erin is still bleeding. She has run out of tampons and neither of us have the money for her to buy more. Most of her time is spent in bed, listlessly reading comic books or perusing help wanted ads at fancy shoe stores. Bleeding. We cannot even have sex, the original free entertainment, because of the thick clots of blood still dripping from her. I beg her to make another appointment with the clinic and feel bad every time I do. My concern for her health and safety feels like I am callously griping about being horny.

And I can't deny my horniness. Even depressed and frumpy, I find her intoxicatingly attractive. Her dark hair and brown eyes are like mysteries I ache to unravel. Her breasts are the most perfect I've ever seen, in person or on film. I've mapped the moles and freckles that pepper her creamy pale skin. She is soft in all the right places, curved where one needs a handhold and topped off with a brain I'm frequently in awe of. But she will not even change in front of me because of the blood. To distract myself, I masturbate several times a day. Often while she is making coffee in the mornings, I will grab her hips from behind and mime sex, dry-humping over the kitchen counter as we both giggle at the absurdity our sex life has been reduced to. This is the only time I see her laugh anymore. So I do it a lot: in the kitchen, on the couch, in the front yard, and even in our bed at night. Three minutes of dry-humping and bad jokes and then I retreat to the living room where I watch internet porn while Erin goes to sleep.

Nonetheless, my first concern is her health. It just never seems to come out that way.

It is a Sunday. After a meal of soup, salad and freshly made bread that I hoped would cheer Erin up, we go to the theatre to see a play Erin is supposed to review for the school paper.

The play is a one-woman show by a local rock singer that focuses on her history of drug abuse, mental illness, family problems and sexual deviancy. A comedy. And just before the intermission, she is strutting up and down the aisles, bellowing a catchy sing-a-long called "My Vagina is Eight Miles Wide" and shoving the microphone into the faces of the middle-aged stuffed shirts who had no idea what they were in for. I am laughing so hard that tears are streaming down my face. Erin is not.

She grabs my arm, pulling me towards her, furious.

"Why are you crying," she hisses.

"What?"

"Why are you crying?"

"Because this is fucking hysterical?"

"You're an asshole," she snarls.

By now the people next to me are splitting their attention between the spectacles.

"What are you talking about?"

"I can't believe you'll cry at this, but not what I'm going through."

"What?" I try to grab Erin's arm, but she pulls it away violently. The singer is right there in front of us and I am terrified I will be put in charge of the chorus, but suddenly it is the end of the act. The instant the lights come up, Erin bolts for the door.

I grab my jacket and follow her. "What are you doing?" I say.

"Leaving," she snaps.

"Where?"

"I don't care. Home. Away from you." She ducks and weaves through the geriatric theater crowd.

"Stop following me," she hisses.

"What do you want me to do? Let you walk? You wanna go, we'll go." She tries to get around me, but it doesn't work so she stops at the stairs. "Can we please talk about this?"

"I just want to leave."

"Why are you so mad at me? Because I thought the song was funny?"

"Because you were crying."

"Because I was what?"

"You were crying. Because you cried at this."

"It wasn't a choice. It's an autonomous reaction."

"One you never have for me."

"That's bullshit."

"You cry at movies all the time, but never about real life. Why? Isn't what I'm going through real enough to evoke an autonomous reaction for you?"

I smile weakly and pause a moment to let an elderly couple pass through the eye of the storm.

"Real life isn't structured and constructed to evoke a deliberate and intense emotional reaction. There is no comparison to be made."

"I haven't seen you cry once over this," she says, shaking her head.

"Is that what you want? For me to bawl? To break down so you have to take care of me? I was trying to stay strong for you, and keep my crying private."

Erin squints at me, assessing if I'm just trying to appease her.

"I have to go to the bathroom," she says and turns back towards the theater. So I sit down on a bench to wait. When she comes out, she decides to go back in for the second act. And though her manner is glacial, she says I can still sit next to her.

Erin is laying in our bed with her head on a pillow while I am sitting on the floor. This is our fighting position. She wants to go to sleep. I don't want to her to do so angry, nor do I want to stay awake being angry at her because she refused to acknowledge how hurtful her comments were. I also don't want to sit in the bed with her because that feels like a romantic pose you hold over a sick loved one. Also, sitting there while fighting just puts you in a prime position to hold a pillow over their face.

"I wish you wouldn't lay down like you don't care," I say.

"But I don't," she says. "I don't feel anything anymore. Haven't you felt me pulling away from you?"

"Of course I have. I'm not stupid. I was trying to give you space to work through this."

"Work through what?"

"You know what."

"This has nothing to do with the abortion, Isaac."

We both know it does; we argue on anyhow. It is difficult to fight with Bubba whimpering and climbing into my lap to be petted. It makes everything either of us say, no matter how poignant or cutting, somewhat comical. Perhaps that levity is why we are able to patch things up. Perhaps Bubba is our mediator, our peacemaker, our savior.

That or the fact that I threaten to leave and Erin knows she is incapable of paying the rent without me.

It is Monday morning, 10:30 a.m. and Erin is shouting at me. Crying. My behavior is no better. The standard names and accusations are being tossed about with the standard waffles between venom, passive aggression and passionate pleading from both parties. Erin wants me to stay, though not as a couple. She says she cares. But now it's my turn not to. Eventually I demand Erin leave because I can't pack a bag with her watching me, though the truth is I can't pack a bag because I'm so flustered I can't find one.

"But this is the last time I'll see you," she says.

"If I have anything to do with it," I say. My voice is flat and cold. I don't even look at her when I speak. I witness her departure through my peripheral vision. She is pushing her bike away, sobbing. And I am glad.

That's when I look through my phone and realize I have nowhere to go: no friends that can have me, no family home to return to, not enough money to blow on a hotel, and no possibility of finding a room to rent without a steady job or a steady job without a place to live.

So when I finally find my backpack buried deep in the basement beneath Erin's old photos, the large fan from our old apartment and a box full of dishes, I go to sit in the park. Before I leave, I tear down the photo booth picture strip of us kissing that hung on our bedroom door and throw the flowers I brought her that morning into the garbage.

It is Monday afternoon and I have yet to hear back from any of the friends I called about a couch. Since I wished to adhere to the popular literature about being homeless, I am drinking cheap whiskey from a brown paper bag in the park. But the kitsch isn't making the whiskey any smoother or me any less bitter. I brought a book with me, but I can't pay attention for more than a paragraph or so before my internal monologue takes over—viciously ranting all the things I couldn't think to hurl at her earlier. I mulled over a hodgepodge of responses to the tirade she hurled at me that showcased her cruelty, her hypocrisy, her heartlessness and general physical repugnance. I hate her so much right now it feels like acid reflux.

I have no home or possessions. I can't see my dog, none of my friends are returning my phone calls and I have no real family. I have no appointments scheduled, no clubs I am a member of, and none of the things John Lennon listed in the song "Imagine." I don't even have any more tears to cry.

Hating Erin is all I have.

It is three days later and I tiptoe into the house to reach the anxiety pills in the bathroom before anyone sees me. I suck several down and beckon Bubba to come sit outside with me in the yard. But Erin spots him leaving and follows me.

"A supervised visit then is it?" I say.

"Are you coming home?"

"That's the first question you ask me?"

"Why? What should I ask?"

"Maybe something a little less self-serving. How are you, perhaps. Where have you been, maybe."

"I know the answers to those questions. You've been at Neil's."

"And how have I been?"

"Bad."

"Sometimes it's not about getting the answers as much as it is asking the questions," I say. "That's something you've never understood."

"Fine. Whatever. Are you coming back or not?" Her face says she is not interested in philosophical musings or communications techniques.

"I don't know," I say. "I need to think about it."

And then, we talk, the breadth of our relationship examined under a microscope. Indiscretions. Lies. Truths. Admissions. Whether or not it's possible for us to still live together. What the chances are of us reconciling. For better or worse, in sickness or in health, we talk about everything. Everything except the one thing that really matters.

"I'm just not ready to talk about it," she says.

"When will you be?"

"I don't know," she deadpans. "Maybe never. I don't know."

"Will you please come to me when you are?"

"No."

"What do you mean no?"

"I mean no. If I go to anyone, it will be a psychologist."

"Erin—"

"No, I don't owe you anything. Not anymore."

And then I am mad. "No, that is such bullshit," I growl. "You want to keep what you think about my personal habits or the thoughts you have on world affairs to yourself, that's fine. But this experience is half mine as well. And I've done everything you asked of me to get you through it while you've withheld everything. This you do fucking owe me."

Her mouth says nothing, but her face says plenty. She knows I'm right. She knows she is being mean, and she really hates agreeing with me. But she still isn't ready to talk about it, and she knows that by the time she is, the chances of me being in her life are slim to none. It's like dodging one bullet and being hit by another.

So she asks me if I'd like a sandwich. I say yes. We both have pastrami on rye with asiago cheese and yellow mustard. It tastes like ambiguity.

It is Friday and I begin a new job at noon. It was just nine weeks ago that we were relatively carefree and happy. Now we are taking turns on the couch, unsure if speaking, or hugging or even looking at each other is crossing some sort of line. She no longer poops while I am in the shower. I no longer make her breakfast. This is sad because I miss our talks and she cannot cook. Maybe one day things will change. Maybe one day she will be ready to talk about it, about the life we made and lost and about the baby that never was. Maybe one day I'll be ready to cry without the aid of the cinema. Maybe one day we will be together again and happy. But not today. Today is just another Friday, a little less painful than the last.

A LOVE OF HISTORY

Rachel was a skinny girl. But not plain skinny; she was the kind of skinny that the other girls at college described as disgusting, anorexic or walking death, though she was none of these. She ate when she was hungry and oftentimes more than what she considered her share. Still, her legs were two ice picks with softballs for kneecaps. She felt like a flamingo when she went wading in the summertime. Her skin was fleshy, factory shrink-wrap sealing her skeleton from the elements.

She had dropped out of anatomy class due to the heckling she'd endured about the teacher having plans to use her as a visual aid—not because it bothered her anymore, simply because it was taking away from the class. It wasn't her fault.

She was just a skinny girl and no manner or amount of junk food seemed to change that. So she endured, going from class to class, ignoring the condemning down-the-nose looks from 115-pound girls on diets and boys who asked each other if they'd seen the new photo spread of some supermodel in a men's magazine.

She closed her ears to the sermons of activists clucking at her in disapproval about the need to conform to the image perpetrated by such magazines and to the concerned voices who pushed her to seek counseling for her illness. She thought that they might as well have been advocating for people with asthma or congenital heart defects to seek their cures in Prozac and questions about their parents. What others thought didn't matter to Rachel anymore; her one and only success with weight gain had been a significant thickening of the skin over the last several years that had brought her to a grand total of ninety-three pounds.

Dan did not have the same problem. He was a slightly pudgy boy with hair like an electrical storm and a complexion like the glaze on a donut. He blended in with the furniture, camouflaged by banality, disregarded rather than reviled. Like Rachel, his skin had also grown thick, as had the stacks of history books he took home from the library each Saturday night as medication. His knowledge of World War II was as deep as his associates' desires not to hear about it.

"Quit bumming me out," his brother said to him over dinner one Thanksgiving. "That shit is depressing."

Considering the vigor Dan had been infusing into his analysis of American neutrality prior to the Pearl Harbor bombing, he was at a loss to understand his brother's sentiments. History was like cutting out all of the mundanity of day-to-day life and experiencing only the pertinent events, like the highlights after a sporting event, or the way films skipped over parts of the story where characters did things like going to the bathroom, washing dishes or reloading firearms. Dan often wished he could live in a history book rather than experience it firsthand with all the commercials and station identifications uncut.

That was why seeing Rachel walking between buildings startled him so much: she was the first thing in real time that he could recall having any interest in whatsoever. The visible joint motion of her hips moving side-to-side as she walked enthralled him, as did the perfect space between her thighs, which were thin cylinders jutting straight down from her pelvis. The bend of her knees was erotically familiar. Her shoulder blade jutted out from her shirt, a razor's edge threatening to rend the material in two. Her breasts were only a rumor and you could have juiced an orange on her cheekbones. He was smitten. A rush of primal, animalistic memory rose with his blood pressure. Dan couldn't explain it, only that he liked her. He wanted to approach her and profess his sudden and obscene desires to her with phrases plagiarized from the most lurid of publications. He closed his eyes and saw her naked body laid out on the ground, beckoning to him, a dark triangle of grainy coloration shading her thin frame, a spacer between femurs. It looked heavy enough to crack her bones in two from supporting it and yet she soldiered on.

He thought it was crazy, that it would never work. He charged after Rachel anyway, almost losing one of his books in his excitement to catch up to her, but recovering it in a move that would have made his football-loving family proud of him for a change.

Dan tapped Rachel on the shoulder awkwardly, his surprised lungs nearly exploding a blast of air on the back of her neck as he did so. She stopped and turned around, receiving him with the practiced skepticism of the butt of the joke.

"Yes?" she said.

Dan huffed in shock, not actually having planned a next step, or even the first one for that matter.

"Um…I'm Dan," he said extending his hand, this time returning shame to his family by fumbling his copy of *Selected Letter's of Winston Churchill*. Dan quickly dropped to one knee to recover his tome. He would need something to hide in later.

"Is there something I can help you with, Dan?" Rachel said impatiently.

"No, not really, well yes, I mean…"

Rachel recognized the classic inability to follow through on some sort of cruel joke he'd been put up to by a group of snickering meatheads hidden somewhere nearby.

"Well let me save you the trouble then. My finger doesn't taste like chicken."

"Excuse me?" Dan said, genuinely perplexed.

"Nor am I an albino Ethiopian," she continued, "or suffering from a gypsy curse or working in a cornfield to pay my way through school. So if you're done now, I'm going to be late for class."

"Actually," Dan said pathetically, "I was just wondering if you'd like to go out sometime…"

"Let me guess, for dinner?" Rachel snarled.

Dan looked at the ground and mumbled a barely audible affirmation. He continued to look at the ground as she whirled around and stomped down the hall, her bulk increased considerably by the fire shooting from her eyes. Rachel thought it was one thing to mutter things as she passed by, but addressing her directly was so childish and invasive. College was supposed to be different, but Rachel's experience was that the clucking was the same no matter the henhouse.

Rachel caught another glimpse of Dan as she rounded the corner to an adjoining hallway. He stood exactly where she'd left him with waves of hurried students flowing around him, like water smoothly circumventing an obstacle in the creek bed as if it wasn't really there but in reality gradually wearing it down. He looked from side to side dejectedly, trying to find an opening into the current. There were no high-fives or jeering faces of compatriots, only the crestfallen features of Dan; his one interest in the present was now history. Rachel's realization that she'd met his sincerity with the same venom generally sent her way only caused her to miss one beat before continuing on to class. It was the first beat she'd ever missed due to contemplating an apology—one for the history books.

Dan trudged home and decided he'd been right the first time. History was more accepting than the present. No matter how behind the times he might be, he'd always be ahead of history. Simply having heard of the Copernican system put him academically beyond Plato. It was an accomplishment to be heralded in all corners of his private dorm room. It deserved a celebration marking his return to his homeland, perhaps his favorite documentary. Dan put his love-worn video of *Night and Fog* into the VCR and hit play.

He settled back onto his cot to watch the delicate tracking shots between the abandoned buildings of Auschwitz, occasionally reciting the narration along with the video in perfect time, despite it being in French. He whispered grandly, imagining that he was giving a lecture on the subject while simultaneously terrified that his neighbor would once again take issue with his rehearsal.

"Who needs girls when I have you," he said to the television. Its tube glowed warmly in response. Dan smiled to himself, content to be back in his world. And then he saw Rachel.

Well, not Rachel specifically, but his image of her—a grainy black and white body on the ground, pale with death and emaciated from months of starvation. He recognized the tantalizing joint motion of her hips and saw her arm flop over limply beckoning to him as a bulldozer rolled her into a mass grave full of matted grays, the only coloration on the pale bodies were grainy dark triangles of pubic hair stacked thirty deep.

Dan's mental impulse was that he should run to the bathroom and vomit, punishment for his choice in pornography, but he stayed sitting where he was. Dan didn't feel sick at all.

Instead, he turned off the tape and sat in the dark at his window, watching people pass through the courtyard below for several hours until his eyes could no longer stand the strain of fending off sleep and he passed out sitting up. By sheer force of will alone, Dan didn't dream.

Rachel on the other hand, did dream. She dreamt of all of the cruel things people had said to her over the years and all of the jokes they'd played, and how she'd tried to rise above it and remain detached, letting her spirit float above her body to watch things play out rather than participate in the beating. They crowded in around her, a thick smog of disapproving glares and halfwitted commentary, forming a circle to block Rachel's escape to the world beyond their opinions. And watching the jeering crowds poke and prod at her delicate frame disapprovingly from the wings, was Dan, a solitary face of pained sincerity. He looked like he wanted to say something to Rachel, but the crowd was too thick for him to break through, so he was forced to wait on the sidelines for the world to finish their denigration of the way Rachel was born. Then he looked up and saw her floating above the fray.

"You're beautiful," he said sadly.

"I know," Rachel whimpered, "but no one's ever seen it before."

Dan looked down at his shoes. The color began draining from his face until he was just an ashen shadow steadily growing dimmer, being absorbed into the abyss beyond the crowd. Rachel shrieked and found herself awake, still surrounded by judgment, but spread out over the whole country instead of in a steadily tightening noose.

She got out of bed and walked to the window of her dorm room. Rachel looked across the courtyard and thought that she could just barely make out the dim image of someone sitting in a window looking right back. She stayed at the window for an hour, thinking about her history and her future, about how she had always wanted a boy to fumble his books over her and how pitifully she'd faced that moment when it came. She went to sleep knowing that the next day would be a difficult one, but that it held the promise of opportunity.

Rachel had never visited the cafeteria before. Her impression of lunchrooms from high school was that they were noisy affairs, rife with giggles and scrutiny about the contents of her tray. She much preferred to take her lunch from a food cart, then find a quiet spot beneath a tree or sit in the darkened back rows of the auditorium where she could hear the orchestra rehearsing from the comfort of obscurity. She was there today because she wanted to find Dan, whose path she'd never crossed prior to yesterday. A place that most students (other than herself) visited daily seemed a sensible place to start looking.

She scanned the area and thought that while it may not be the hotbed of pointing fingers and raised eyebrows she remembered, it certainly was drab. There was no music or foliage, just rows of identical molded plastic booths and the dull hum of air conditioners and florescent lights. Blending right in, was Dan.

He was sitting at a table in the back corner, hunched over both a tray and a thick hardcover book. There was a small dribble of red sauce unnoticed on his shirt. As she approached him, Rachel couldn't help but look at his segmented tray and observe the remnants of a slice of pizza. Dan's attention was so focused on the book that he didn't notice Rachel until she spoke.

"Hello," she said cautiously.

"Oh, hi," Dan replied without looking up.

"I'm Rachel," she said.

"Hi…" Dan was truly nervous now; one yesterday was enough for his lifetime.

"What are you reading?"

"Um, it's about, well, you know when the concentration camps were liberated in Germany?"

Rachel nodded, then said "yes." Nevertheless, Dan was still afraid to look up at her.

"Well, it's a book about the Jews trying to find their families afterwards," he continued, "when they were all scattered and a lot of them had changed their names and were pretending not to be Jews because they were still scared."

"Some of my family died in Auschwitz, actually."

"I'm sorry." Dan looked up at her for the first time and now noticed the polished silver Star of David pendent hung around her neck. He suddenly felt very sick.

"It's all right. I never knew them, obviously. But my grandfather talks about it sometimes. He says that the Americans should have bombed the gas chambers or the rail lines leading to the camps if they really cared about saving anyone."

Dan's illness faded and he had to control a sudden burst of excitement—this was the exact same thing he'd been trying to explain at family functions for the last year!

"They, I mean we, didn't, you know," he babbled. "The whole world knew about what was happening to the Jews in Europe, but we only got involved in the war after Pearl Harbor was attacked. It was self-interest, not humanitarianism."

Rachel looked at him, trying to pump her moxie reserves into active duty.

"So, I came to tell you that I'm sorry about the way I treated you yesterday."

"It's okay," Dan said, looking back down and starting to feel ill again.

"No. It's not. I just…" Rachel stopped, trying hard to pull out something sincere to match Dan's attempt the day before.

"I'm just used to expecting people to treat me a certain way because of my weight, and I was wrong to do that to you."

"I shouldn't have bothered you."

"No, Dan, you should have. I'm glad you did, and to step out on a limb, if you'd still like to, I'd very much like to go out with you sometime." The words were a pained liberation to Rachel, the release of a near-lifetime of normal feelings that had been locked away behind layers of torment for their own protection, but now free.

Dan didn't answer. He just focused on Rachel's pendant, staring at it for what felt like an eternity: thinking about what it meant to him and about her, its overreaching symbolism to the entire world, how something so elemental as metal had been forged into complex divisions across the whole world, how something so shiny had transmuted to the grainy black and white of historical record like reverse alchemy.

There was a sour, acrid heat bubbling in his stomach, a cold understanding of what had drawn him to Rachel in the first place. It dared him to open his mouth and give it a doorway to freedom, to drench her tiny frame in morally sound remnants of pizza, to bathe her in judgment against himself. He had to say something soon or else he was sure his insides would be crushed from the weight of his dilemma. Dan mentally recited the narration of *Night and Fog* over and over again as his eyes slowly traveled up her collarbones and the fragile lines of her neck all the way to her eyes.

"Yes," he said softly. "That would be nice."

Rachel smiled, her eyes sparkling like her necklace. "Let me give you my number," she said and pulled a pen out of her pocket. "Do you have anything to write on?"

Dan looked around and found nothing. His napkin was soiled and torn from the pizza that had never reached his mouth.

"No," he said.

"It's okay," Rachel said and grabbed his wrist.

She spoke her phone number out loud as she wrote it on the inside of his forearm, then walked away jubilantly. Dan's stomach churned rapturously as he watched Rachel's tiny hips happily wagging back and forth as she melted indistinguishably into the blur of other bodies crowding the hallway.

CANNED KEROUAC

Nick let off the throttle and pulled his motorcycle over to the side of Highway 101, easing it to a halt and killing the engine. He looked around drowsily and assessed the situation. The trees offered a bit of seclusion. It was miles from any sort of town or dwelling, so it seemed unlikely that he would be disturbed. It was probably quite idyllic and picturesque in the light of day—these were the California Redwoods after all. What else could he ask for? This place seemed as good as any of the others he'd come across and he was very tired.

His legs felt like they weighed a thousand pounds each as he dismounted his bike and pushed it off the highway to make camp. Sharp pains shot through the forearm of his throttle hand, a stiff, gnarled claw that continued vibrating as he unstrapped his backpack and sleeping bag from the motorcycle and deposited them in what seemed (after a hasty glance) like the most appropriate place. Nick set off in an awkward bowlegged lurch, gathering nearby sticks for a small fire to warm his wind-chilled body. He huddled close to the flame while snacking on trail mix and finishing the last of the water in his bottle.

This frugality wasn't comprised of choices made out of necessity. The salary of an Insurance Benefits and Rates Assessment Associate offered plenty of money for restaurant food or a hotel room. But that wasn't the point. He was out here to experience life unfiltered, to harness the freedom that Harley-Davidson ads talked about. He'd read the stories of throwing society and civilized travel to the wind and wanted them to be his own, having grown weary of living vicariously through them for the whole of his life. Setting off into the jungle of America's highways with only a backpack and a willingness to endure was a romantically alluring adventure, an industrial-age pilgrimage every man should take to better himself.

He'd heard the call a week earlier when a coworker moving overseas offered to sell him an old, yet sturdy, motorcycle for little more than a handshake. On the same day, his uncle died comfortably at home, surrounded by suburbs and armored by a white picket fence paid for by a lucrative career in insurance. His death was a brutal reminder of the temporary nature of all things. Travelling the several hundred miles to the memorial by motorcycle seemed like an opportunity to seize the moment, possibly cleansing himself in the process. Nick cashed in his vacation chips and hit the open road for an unspecified period of time with no real plan other than attending the funeral.

So far, the rash on his ass was the only notch added to his belt.

Nick curled up in his sleeping bag, still wearing his jeans and leather jacket to fight the chill blowing off the Pacific Ocean. He employed his boots as a pillow. This is July, he thought to himself—July and freezing. He closed his eyes tightly to drown out the scenery, eventually convincing his exhausted body to sleep against a lifetime of training that this was not the place to do so

Nick dreamt of Kerouac riding bitch on Peter Fonda's motorcycle, preaching poetry through a megaphone to roadside oglers as they tore through the countryside. He spoke in one run-on sentence, about madness and lust for life, thirsting for it like a man lost in the desert of the nine-to-five stiff and starched collars and sensible shoes of the middle-class masses—he alone, classless, through and through. Flames rocketed out of the tailpipes behind them, setting the fields lining the highway ablaze and their audience with them. They drove on anyway, oblivious. Heat pulsed off the towering walls of flame, becoming so intense that the riders caught fire and then the cycle. Poetry sang forth from Jack's mouth undeterred as the flesh melted off of his body and his bones charred black. His audience was enraptured. They drove on, words spewing forth from the tongueless mouth of a wilting skeleton holding a melting megaphone. They drove on, a force of nature burning too hot to touch. They drove on.

A forest ranger's boot shook Nick awake at dawn, informing him he wasn't allowed to camp there and needed to move on. Nick groggily stood up and pulled on his boots under the scathing glare of a man charged with the dubious task of keeping the public off of public land. He then stuffed his sleeping bag back into his backpack and remounted his bike. He winced slightly at the raw feeling in his butt as his weight settled in, but bore it silently as he kicked the engine to life and started down the highway once again for nowhere in particular.

Five days on the road had done nothing but sap his will and drain any desire to ride whatsoever. He realized now that the stories were just that—stories. They were embodiments of someone else's dreams, canned in novels and films that he thought he could open up and reap the benefits of if he so desired. But he now realized that wasn't the case. He was no Dean, no Dennis Hopper, and there was no real point to any of this adventure as it had never really meant anything to him. He just wanted it to. He didn't even like his uncle that much. His death was just another excuse in a lifetime of excuses to follow the path laid out for him.

Nick had no idea what mattered now, other than checking into the first motel he came across, showering, then pulling the shades down and sleeping until late in the morning. Dreams only mean something to the dreamer and Nick now understood that meant he would have to learn to dream for himself. Life-changing experience be damned, all he really wanted was to go home.

CUSTOMER SERVICE

The man approaching my coffee counter smelled awful, even from across the room. He was equally as oppressive and taxing on the eyes as he was on the nose. A latticework of greasy smears of black grime covered the red, crisped skin of his face. He had few teeth and his long hair appeared to be matted with clumps of the same grime layering his cheeks. A thin, bony neck led down into a filthy, one-piece, zip-up ski outfit that was at least twenty years old and must have been hell to wear in the heat of an LA summer. A ramshackle brace, likely salvaged from a hospital dumpster, reinforced one of his legs as he hobbled towards me on crutches probably found at the same time. There was no way to know how long he'd been homeless. A condition like this could only be reached after many years, but exactly how many was a mystery.

He reached the register and began slowly counting out change with one shaking hand.

"What can I do for you, sir?" I boomed cheerily, and followed with my best customer service, wide-mouthed grin.

Terrified, his eyes frantically darted back and forth between me and his pile of nickels and pennies as if I might attack at any second. I didn't. I changed to my waiting grin and watched as he continued cautiously counting until the mountain of change totaled the price of a small coffee. Then he spoke.

"One small coffee, please."

I'd never heard a more pitiful sound in my life. His voice was high, squeaky and hoarse, like a mouse on the tail end of a speaking tour. But underlying the tone was shattered confidence—real terror that his request might be denied or that I might prefer to light him on fire. Apparently the mouse's speaking tour wasn't going well.

"No problem, sir. Coming right up," I said, making sure to ramp my cheer down a notch or two for his comfort. I filled up a disposable cup from the machine behind the register. "Would you like some room for cream?"

He didn't respond, only continued eyeing me suspiciously, as if my friendly customer service was going to turn out to be a cruel joke.

I put the coffee down on the counter between us and fastened on a lid.

"Would you like me to carry this to a table for you?" I asked, thinking of the tremendous effort he'd expended trying to inch across the shop to order. Holding a coffee in one hand would certainly inhibit his crutching even more.

He wheezed, "no," and carefully cradled the cup in his fingers while keeping the heel of his palm on the handle of the crutch so he could slowly work his way out the front door. There were no other customers waiting to order so I watched his exit carefully, trying to note all the details of such a heroic effort. It took two minutes for him to get outside and set the cup down on one of our patio tables. He'd picked a table near the entrance shaded by a large palm tree, my favorite. It was a perfect people-watching spot because of the line of sight to view the passersby on the Walk of Fame and the café entrance. The man had good taste.

I smiled to myself as he awkwardly settled down to enjoy his well-earned cup of coffee. Even from inside, I could see the excitement on his face as he prepared to drink: the way his lips trembled as he lifted the cup to them, like they were reaching out to ensnare wild coffee as it passed by or a drink from a sacred waterfall. If there had been any doubt, the pleasure evident when he took a sip made it clear exactly how miserable this man's life was. I had just witnessed a spiritual event.

"That guy fucking stinks," Justine said as she emerged from the kitchen. She was carrying a fresh supply of cups and napkins to restock the counter. "I could smell him even in the back."

"Yup. It's pretty bad," I said disinterestedly. Justine seemed to be heading in a direction I didn't want to go.

"Pretty bad? That's it? Are you serious? We're lucky there aren't any other customers here right now."

"Yes, it's awful."

"No, I mean, like, really awful. Like he bathed in sewage or something—"

"Or like a skunk died in his armpits or he's curing road kill under that ski suit. I get it. Can we change the subject please?"

"Why?"

"Because I just…because. Okay? Don't you have work to do?"

Justine set the supplies down and looked me over skeptically. "Phil, I can't get through customer service on my own. I need an ally in the war against the customers."

"You have one," I said. "I am a patriotic, class warrior."

"Then why aren't you making fun of the easiest mark ever to walk into this place?"

"You're mad that I'm not picking on a hobo? That's kind of fucked up."

"Well, we're kind of fucked up. This whole place is kind of fucked up. The only way to survive is to be more fucked up than everyone else so you come out on top. That's Hollywood, and that's the service industry."

"Well, if he comes back for a refill, you can light him on fire then. Happy?"

"Phil, dammit—"

"No, Justine, look, The Guru is a loon who makes my life difficult. The actors from the school upstairs are vapid hacks who would be lucky to peak in a detergent commercial. You want to crank up the music to interfere with their improv games? I don't care. I'll help out even. But picking on a homeless dude is crossing the line."

"Why this guy? Why protect a medieval beggar crawling in here with leprosy?"

"Respect."

"Oh," she said, setting down the cups and studying me up and down. "I'm lost here, Phil."

"Dude smells like a tire fire and spends his time begging pity change from people while sitting in a pool of his own filth, and yet, when he wants a cup of coffee he chooses to come here, an upscale coffee shop on Hollywood Boulevard rather than to the convenience store across the street. He's absolutely aware that he doesn't fit in here. And it's not about proximity because he hasn't been begging nearby or I'd have seen him before, and I haven't. Don't you find any of that the least bit curious?"

"No, our coffee is better."

"You know a lot of culinarily snobbish hobos then?"

"I don't know any hobos," she said with a set jaw.

"Quit being like that. I just think his coming here was a deliberate decision made on pure moxie, like he just decided he liked the ambiance of the place and felt like thumbing his nose at perception. I respect that."

"He still stinks," she said indifferently.

"Justine, do you really want to piss off the other customers?"

"What possible reason could I have to please them? They only tip because they think it makes them look affluent to whomever they're trying to butter up at the time."

"Can you think of something that would piss them off more than trying to have a business lunch with that dude wafting over?"

"So this is a new guerilla tactic?"

"Sure," I tried.

Justine shook her head. "Nope," she said. "You're just saying that to appease me. I don't buy it for a second and I'm kicking him out." She started towards the door.

"Why?" I called at her.

"Because I think it would be funny," she said over her shoulder. "Because I don't want to smell him. Because you need to get your head straight. Take your pick."

"Seriously, don't," I said sternly. Her hand was on the doorknob.

Justine let go of the door and turned to me. "Seriously Phil," she said. "What other choice do I have? Forget our customer-bashing dispute for a moment and ask yourself what would happen if Frank came in now? We'd get fired on the spot. I need this job just as much as you do."

"No, we wouldn't," I said. "He's a paying customer."

"Phil, don't be an asshole. You know that doesn't mean a thing."

"Famous Java is a *business*. Paying means everything."

"No, Phil. People pay to come here so they don't have to smell people like him. We choose to work here so we can afford to live in a neighborhood where we don't have to see people like him. And Frank started a café like this one so he wouldn't have to serve people like him. Paying doesn't mean a damned thing unless we say it does."

"We say it does for The China Doll, or The Guru or the stuck up douchebags from the acting school."

"This is Hollywood, Phil. Weirdos are fine, as long as they have money."

"He has money."

"Money that doesn't get counted out of a paper cup," she sneered.

"I see," I said. "Well, you've made your position clear."

"Good." Justine took hold of the door handle again.

"Now let me make mine clear. If you kick him out, I'll tell

Frank about your habit of pocketing exact change."

"You wouldn't!"

"That man stays."

Justine looked wild-eyed and furious. But before she could act on it, a group of chattering vapid-looking attendees of the acting college upstairs came through the door, theatrically overplaying their reactions to the hobo's stench. If their plugging their noses and doubling over as they passed by bothered him, it didn't show. He just kept dreamily sipping his coffee while they filed past Justine and through the door. The moment they were inside, they leapt up on tables and dropped to one knee, bombastically hollering out sandwich orders in Shakespearean English. Justine glared at me as she retreated back to the kitchen for the next half-hour, filling their orders and the orders that came shortly after when the next class got out. By the time she returned to the counter, the homeless man was gone and the dispute turned to which actor specifically was the most obnoxious and whether or not he had been the guy in the used car commercial with the giraffe.

Justine and I were the lunch crew again the next day. It was shortly before eleven and The Guru was standing in his usual spot several yards back from the counter, holding his arms open wide and proclaiming his order with messianic zeal. He refused to get too close to the cash register as it had "negative energy."

"Let it be written that Chai was a gift from heaven, and that all people of true spirit should drink it on Tuesdays," he said.

Someone told me The Guru had been a tabloid news anchor until he'd fallen in with whatever sort of drugs and mysticism fitness program had been hot at the time and reinvented himself. He'd been coming in twice a day for as long as I'd worked here and his only tips were on the path to true enlightenment. Some days it involved enemas, others intensive rerun therapy. From what I could tell, he spent most of the interims between his visits here dancing on the street corner.

"Right, Chai," I said, "on Tuesdays."

The Guru then lofted a five that he'd twisted into a gyrocopter at me. "Lincoln was an angel," he said. It flew off-course and landed in the bleach bucket behind the counter. I plunged my hand into the water to retrieve it, mentally cursing the concept of rent for leading me to this end.

When I returned to the register, The Hobo was there, counting change out of the cup I'd served him coffee in yesterday. Though the bleach was still burning my nostrils, I could smell him.

"Liked our coffee, I take it?" I asked. He ignored me and continued counting until he reached exact change.

"One small coffee, please," he squeaked without looking up.

"No one's a conversationalist anymore," I grumbled, and filled up a cup for him. The Guru could wait.

"I can carry this for you, if you like," I said as I set the coffee down on the counter.

The Hobo said nothing. He weakly picked up his coffee like he had the day before and again started his slow march to the patio.

"What is that smell?" Justine said stepping out of the kitchen. "Oh…"

"Don't even think about it," I said.

"Fine," Justine snapped and went back into the kitchen.

I started making The Guru's chai, but went about it slowly as I was far more interested in watching The Hobo's shuffle and lurch through the café.

"Just don't ask me to cover any shifts for you," Justine said through the window.

"Does this really have to be a show-stopper?" I responded. "Aren't we still united in everything else?"

"Yeah, I suppose," Justine said. "But you threatened me and that changes things."

"You didn't give me any choice," I said. "Just leave the poor guy alone."

"I still don't get why you care so much."

"Just Hollywood, this place, it's getting to me. I want to do something…good I guess?"

"What does that even mean?"

"I don't know."

"That should be a sign," Justine scolded.

"Yeah, probably," I sighed.

"Oh shit," Justine said and gestured at the door. "This place is turning into a sideshow."

I turned around and saw the tightly stretched alabaster-pale face of The China Doll walking through the door. She was dressed in her standard black stretchpants and turtleneck, her teeth bared in a frightening smile ringed by savagely bright crimson lipstick.

"I'll take care of her," I said. "Just come out here and finish this chai for The Guru."

"The path to enlightenment begins with purification," The Guru thundered upon hearing his title. The China Doll skittered sideways a little, her eyes slightly panicked, but her face frozen as always.

"Damned right," Justine shouted through the window. "Racial purification."

"Intestinal purification is the new racial purification," The Guru announced. "You heard it here first."

Justine exited the kitchen and went to work on The Guru's chai. It was a delicate process, for he was quite particular about how it was made and had on one occasion thrown an offending beverage through the order window leading to the kitchen, proclaiming us heretics undeserving of his teachings. Justine and I had been unable to ban him for life as we were told he constituted "local color" which Frank said was what tourists wanted when they came to Hollywood.

The China Doll reached the counter and leaned over it towards me as far as she could. "A white chocolate mocha," she hissed. Her face didn't move when she spoke. It never did. It remained a garishly painted, frozen mask.

Over her shoulder, I could see The Hobo settling into the same seat as yesterday. It really was the best one in the place, and for one of the strangest shows in town. Alcohol attracted lowlifes, but coffee attracted weirdos and we were serving coffee in the epicenter of weirdos for the whole world. We had so many that whole industries had arisen around broadcasting their behavior to the rest of the world as entertainment. From that seat, you could watch it all live. What a life.

"A white chocolate mocha," The China Doll hissed again. I wondered if her jaw was wired shut or if that was just part of her shtick.

"Right, I'm on it," I said, and picked up the money she'd left on the counter. I rang the mocha into the register and opened it to make change, but as I did, I looked over The

China Doll's shoulder and through the windows. Two cops were picking up The Hobo underneath his arms and hauling him out of his prize seat.

There was a sudden hot flash in my chest. I dropped the money into the open cash drawer and vaulted over the counter, pushing past The China Doll and sprinting across the café and out the door.

"What the fuck are you doing?" I shouted and blocked the cops from hauling The Hobo away.

"You're going to need to step back, sir," one of the cops said, "unless you want to get tasered and hauled down to the station."

"Leave this man alone," I shouted. "He is a paying customer!"

One cop leered and the other laughed a deep belly laugh. "This piece of shit?" he cackled.

The Hobo looked terrified. His eyes were darting back and forth between the three of us, clearly not sure who to be more scared of. A noise halfway between whimpering and hyperventilating was coming from his mouth.

"You're trying to tell me this waste is a paying customer? Get out of the way."

"He paid," I said, my feet firm but my voice wavering. "I'll show you the receipt if you want, but you leave him alone."

"What's it to you?" the cop said.

"What's it to you?" I threw right back.

"Someone called in a complaint," the cop leered. "Said the smell was driving off the customers. That's what it is to me. My job."

A small crowd of people from in and outside the café had gathered, no doubt attracted to the fiasco by my uncontrolled shouting. I felt a hand on my shoulder and jerked away roughly.

Justine was hissing in my ear for me to knock it off, that I was going to get the shit kicked out of me by the LA-fucking-PD, but I didn't care.

"This man is a paying customer and it is never our policy to arrest our customers," I said. "That's my job. Do you understand me, or do I need to call your supervisor?" My heart was a jackhammer against my sternum, but I was not going to let this man who only wanted to enjoy a cup of coffee be hauled off by these scrubbed Neanderthals just because he smelled putrid.

The cop looked me up and down with angry sneer on his face and one hand on his nightstick. Then he laughed.

"Whatever you say, chief," he said, and roughly released The Hobo. His mangled leg was useless in catching himself and he fell to the ground.

My fingernails dug into my palms as the cops left our patio. I'd never been so mad before and it was terrifying. What if they hadn't left?

"Anger is not the way," The Guru said.

"FUCK YOU!" I whirled and shouted at him. "Just get a fucking clue already you fucking loon. Goddamnit!" I waved my arms to shoo him. "Beat it already." I turned back to The Hobo cowering on the ground and saw that his coffee had been spilled during the scuffle. The cup lay on its side on the table, the precious dark brown liquid pooled on the glass tabletop, spoiled.

"I'm so sorry," I babbled. "I'll get you another. Just, hold on. I'll be right back. Just, give me one second."

I ran in the door and back behind the counter, possessed with the need to get this horribly smelly man a fresh cup of coffee.

"Are you insane?" Justine said. "What are you doing?"

"Was it you? Did you do it?"

"Do what?"

"Call the cops. You did it, I know you did."

"I didn't call the cops."

"I just can't believe you'd sink that low, attacking a man with that little, when we're surrounded by real assholes who have it coming."

"I said, I didn't call the cops."

"Oh bullshit, Justine! After all you said yesterday—"

"It was me," said a deep voice. I turned and saw Frank in the office doorway. "Man smelled like piss. Can't have that around when I'm trying to run a business."

"He paid for his coffee," I pleaded.

"I don't care," Frank said. "He can pay for it at the liquor store across the street just the same as here."

I looked to Justine for support, but she just gave me an angry I-told-you-so look.

"Now," Frank continued, "go get rid of him."

"What?"

"I called the cops and you got rid of them like a fucking idiot, so now we still have a stinking pile of garbage scaring people off the patio, in addition to the scene you caused. So if you want to have even the slightest hope of keeping your job, you go outside and get that man the fuck off my patio and make sure he NEVER comes back."

I opened my mouth to respond, but Frank shook his head to intimate "don't even fucking think about it." Gritting my teeth silently, I took a paper cup from the stack by the register and filled it with fresh coffee. I picked the highest quality blend.

"NOW!" Frank shouted.

"I'm fucking going," I shouted back. I took the coffee and went outside, glaring hate back at Frank and Justine. I should just walk out, I thought. Let them do their own dirty work. There were other jobs, probably better jobs. The instant I handed off this cup of coffee, made things right, I'd find one. I swore it.

But when I got outside, The Hobo was gone. Only the pool of spilt coffee marked that he had ever been there. I pulled a rag from the pocket of my apron and wiped the table off, then threw the fresh coffee into the garbage and went back inside. I hadn't made The China Doll's white chocolate mocha. She got antsy if it took too long.

TOOTHPASTE AND BUMPER STICKERS

Before Ned had been crushed by a drunk driver last month, Dexter had been able to perform surveys with ease. He almost liked it, the way you could knock on a total stranger's door and get a tiny window into their life through their answers to simple questions: Do you have a job? Kids? Who are you voting for? What brand of toothpaste do you feel best represents you as a person? Now those simple questions drilled into his head during training were gone. In their place—pain.

No matter how hard Dexter tried to think of anything else, it seemed to inevitably drift to images of Ned alone on a darkened street fully aware that his guts were dripping out of his ass and even if anyone could hear his panicked whimpering, there wasn't a thing they could do to help him.

Dexter found that any sort of conversation had become impossible. A supermarket cashier had asked him how he was that day and he'd almost told her. In fact, that was the worst part: Dexter wanted to tell people. He wanted to walk up to strangers on the street and shout that Ned was a great guy, the best, and now he was fucking dead, and then sob on their shoulders. But he couldn't; he was just composed enough to realize that would be insane. And it would be even worse to knock on someone's door to shout at them about the death of some teenager they'd never met, definitely a fireable offense. That wasn't something Dexter could risk. It had been months since his last job and his landlord wasn't the type for charity. He and Ned had planned to move to the coast and look for work on a boat. Obviously, that wasn't going to happen now. This job was all Dexter had, even though the act of doing it made him physically sick.

The first day back, terrified he would be fired, Dexter had filled in the survey cards on his own as he hyperventilated in an alley. Then he did it again the next day, and the next. Though he'd gotten out of the alley, he hadn't knocked on a single door since. Instead he used the available clues every house displayed to fill in the answers. Minivan in the driveway? Kids. Volkswagen van? Liked natural soap. Manicured yards meant career professionals and unkempt ones indicated academics. Apartment-dwellers worked in the service industry. Then there was the wealth of data available from bumper stickers. They almost did his market surveys for him. Dexter justified it to himself; at least he was making educated guesses. His answers were based on his observations from the time when he actually did his job properly. And though it would have been easy for him to fill in extra cards to boost his numbers, he never did. He wasn't a crook, he was hanging on by a very thin thread, one that he could suddenly see was about to unravel.

"Did you hear me?" Roddy said.

"Yeah," Dexter mumbled. "You're going to do evaluations during rounds tomorrow."

"Right, so fair warning and all that," he grunted.

Dexter agreed. It was fair. That was probably more than he deserved.

The van ride to the turf the next day was torture, primarily because no one else seemed remotely concerned. Tina gabbed about a club she'd hit over the weekend while Diane put on sunscreen and Jim restlessly scanned through radio stations. Michelle didn't say a thing, but she never had; she just sat in the back listening to a set of oversized headphones. Roddy was going over routes on his clipboard in the shotgun seat.

It was the first time anyone had sat there since Ned's last day.

Dexter was trying to silently rehearse his rap, but instead he found himself staring at the seat for blocks at a time. Next thing he knew they were at the drop point and he felt ready to vomit.

"I'm gonna start with Tina," Roddy said, slamming the van door shut. He wriggled his mustache as he checked something off on his clipboard. "You all know what to do. I'll catch up with you when it's your turn." Then he hitched up his pants and started off in the direction of Tina's turf. Tina shrugged to Diane and hurried to catch up.

"What a miserable fuckwad," Jim chuckled. "Wants to follow us around being all serious. A monkey could do this job, you know. A retarded monkey even. With a gimpy leg."

"Right," Dexter offered halfheartedly.

"I should be a doing carpentry. But whatcha gonna do, right? I got kids to feed."

Dexter just nodded, standing still as Jim started off in the direction of his turf. Michelle's back was already vanishing into the distance. Dexter stood still, pretending to get his paperwork in order until Jim was out of sight as well. Then he sat down on the curb, sucking in breath after useless breath. He couldn't do this. And yet he had to, that was all there was to it.

"Just stand up, start walking," he said to himself. "And quit talking to yourself," he hissed. He sucked in a few more breaths, then stood and forced himself to walk in the direction of his turf for the day.

He found the first house after ten minutes or so. It towered three stories above the ground with trees positioned around the grounds like sentries. Dexter felt his chest tighten up at the thought of laying siege to a castle like this and kept walking, cussing under his breath. He reached the end of the block, then turned around and came back determined to give it a go. He knew he couldn't hide any more. But the house looked no less imposing on second glance, Dexter's breathing was no less labored, and Ned was no more alive.

Ned wouldn't have had this problem, Dexter thought. He could've charmed the pants off a nun in the middle of an earthquake. I can't even keep it together enough to ask them about bath products.

"Okay, okay, okay, okay," he wheezed. "What you need is a

nice start. Get things going easy until you get your groove and then get back on the horse." Dexter knew this was a bullshit cop-out, but at least it was a sensible one.

He looked the house over a few times and decided it was clearly owned by a contractor, one who'd built an extra floor on his place for practice, and who'd been able to afford it because of the savings provided by his aggressive use of generic dish soaps. Three kids. Easy as pie, Dexter thought. He strolled to the next house where a pair of childless lesbian architects insisted on recycled packaging, and the next where a widower preferred spearmint toothpaste for his two prized show bull-dogs. There was actually a bumper sticker claiming registry in the AKC, so Dexter didn't feel this was too absurd.

He was cooking along but still didn't feel ready, although that didn't really matter anymore. He had to get it together before Roddy came along or he'd be fired for sure. As bad as he felt now, that would be worse. The next house would be the point where he turned it all around.

It was a white Tudor surrounded by a picket fence and a lush green lawn, like something out of a '50s sitcom. The elderly woman who lived inside probably baked cookies and threw the neighborhood Christmas party. This was the kind of house he could handle. Dexter stepped through the gate feeling confident that even if he broke down, a kindly soul like that would probably invite him in for hot chocolate.

The giant Doberman that suddenly appeared was a whole different matter. Dexter sprinted back out the gate to what he thought would be safety, however, the Doberman seemed to think of the fence as little more than a formality and hurdled it with ease. Dexter sprinted down the sidewalk for dear life and desperately scrambled up a tree in front of the next house with the Doberman close behind. He'd gotten a good hold of the lowest branch, but struggled to hoist himself all the way up. Instead he clung to the bottom of the branch with the snarling dog's impossibly large mouth nipping at his bum.

With a tremendous effort, Dexter hooked his heel onto the next branch and pulled himself to safety—though in the process he felt something in his calf strain and stretch in a way he knew it wasn't prepared for.

The dog wasn't snarling anymore. Instead it was sitting perfectly still, staring at him, ears and eyes as sharp as its teeth. Dexter's clipboard and survey forms lay scattered around the dog like a nest.

Dexter chuckled to himself. So long as the dog stayed put, he'd just gotten a reprieve.

It had been dark for at least a half-hour when Dexter heard someone calling his name.

"Over here," he said. "But be careful of the—"

"What are you doing up there?" Michelle asked, suddenly appearing beneath the tree. She patted the Doberman on the head. It nuzzled up against her, then wandered off.

"Nothing," Dexter said. He lowered himself down cautiously.

"Everyone's been waiting for you."

"Sorry." Dexter gathered the scattered forms. "I'm ready now," he said.

Michelle lead the way back to the van through the darkened neighborhood.

"What were you doing out here anyway?" Dexter asked.

"Roddy sent me to find you," she said. "After what happened to Ned…"

"Right." Dexter just realized that in the panic of running from a mad (and apparently sexist) dog, he'd forgotten all about Ned. He felt a brief pang of guilt and choked up.

"Are you all right?" Michelle asked.

"Yeah, just, I've never known anyone who died before. It's a lot to process."

They walked the next block in silence, then Michelle suddenly stopped.

"Look, I wasn't going to say anything because I know you think Ned was your friend and all, but I can see you're really broken up about this and you have to know, he's not worth it. Not worth a single tear."

"What do you mean?" Dexter felt a little hole burning in his chest.

"Fuck it, I don't mean anything," Michelle said and started walking again.

"Wait, no stop…Clearly you mean something, so what is it?"

"He just wasn't such a stellar guy, that's all." She kept walking.

"What do you mean?"

"I don't want to talk about this."

"Then you shouldn't have brought it up."

"Fine," she snapped. "You ever wonder why he took this job?"

"It's a tough market. Everyone's gotta get by."

"Yeah, but did you ever notice how while we're just getting by, he never seemed to be short on cash?"

Dexter tried to remember who'd picked up the majority of the lunch tabs, but this was all happening too quickly for him to think clearly. "I don't know, maybe."

"Yeah, well, trust me, he did. And that's because he was a mule."

"A what?"

"A mule. A delivery man for drugs."

Though she'd said it of Ned, it felt like a personal accusation against Dexter. "That's not true," he stammered.

"Fine, it's not true." She started walking again and Dexter trotted after her.

"How do you know?"

Michelle kept walking.

"How do you know?"

"I just do, all right," she said. "Just like I know that's why he wanted to go work on a boat and why he wanted to take you with him. I used to think he was my friend too."

"Why did he want those things?"

Michelle didn't answer. She put on her headphones and grunted for him to hurry up.

When they got back to the van a few minutes later, Roddy asked where he'd been. Not knowing what else to say, Dexter told him the truth.

"I was in a tree hiding from a giant dog."

Roddy chuckled. "You must have been over on 35th Street today, right?"

"Yeah."

"Probably shoulda warned you about Cujo. He goes after someone nearly every time we're working this neighborhood. Doesn't seem to mind women though."

"Yup," Dexter said, feeling his skin bristle. "You probably should have said something."

"It's all right," Roddy said. "I guess we'll just have to do your evaluation tomorrow."

"Fantastic," Dexter said. He didn't speak for the rest of the drive.

The next day's turf was the kind of sub-development where every third house is exactly the same, along with every resident. It was exactly the kind of place where Dexter's strategy to avoid human contact would have worked flawlessly, were he allowed to use it. The instant the van was parked, Roddy got out and down to business.

Roddy made the standard mark on his clipboard and hitched up his pants. "Let's get this over with," he said gruffly. Dexter thought he looked the tiniest bit like a walrus.

Regardless, he followed behind in silent dread. On top of the anxiety over actually talking to anyone today, Dexter no longer knew what to think about Ned, who had brought it on in the first place. Since Ned was gone, there was no way to confirm or deny anything Michelle had said. Even if he could, would it matter? Ned had shown Dexter what ropes weren't plainly visible in this job and offered him a friendly ear after their shifts ended. Then he had died miserable, scared and alone. The image was so real to Dexter he felt as if he'd been there, as if he was the one whose bones and innards were crushed beneath a set of Goodyears, whose blood trailed for half a block and who the papers has said was still conscious for an hour after being hit.

"All right, first house on your list. Here it is," Roddy grunted. "Ready?"

"Yes," Dexter said weakly.

It wasn't just that he didn't want to be here. He didn't want to be anywhere, here least of all.

He opened the gate.

His lungs seemed to shrink a little bit with each step to make room for the rest of his insides to vibrate violently.

He walked up the stairs.

And then on the doorjamb he saw a Mezuzah. Wasn't Ned Jewish? Was this his parents' house? Dexter knew they lived around here and there weren't that many Jewish families in the area.

He knocked on the door.

His heart pounded harder and harder with each of the three knocks. His lungs shriveled down to singularities. His skin crawled. They would open the door, know who he was, that he had switches routes with Ned the day that he'd died, know that it should have been Dexter walking on that street. They might even forgive him, tell him there was no way he could know about the car, that it wasn't his fault. Dexter could hear the creaking inside and knew it was going to happen any second.

"Aw, there ain't no one here," Roddy grunted, shifting around on the wooden stairs that lead up to the door. "Let's hit up the next one so I can get back to my route."

So they did, and two more after it, all the while Dexter's panic seemed to run in a loop. No one was home at those houses either.

"These fucking early start times," Roddy said. "I keep telling corporate no one's home at three in the afternoon. People got jobs you know."

"Right," Dexter said.

Roddy shifted around from foot to foot and grimaced. "Look man, I'll be frank with you. This evaluation B.S. is a waste of time. Crackheads can do this gig you know."

"I do."

"You barely even need to talk to these people to know what they're gonna say half the time, just read their bumper stickers." Roddy snorted. "Look, point is, this was all supposed to be done yesterday and I gotta get back to my turf, which is way the hell in the opposite direction. Ya understand?"

"Yeah."

"So I'll just mark down that I saw you and you did great and you're a fucking model employee and a testament to the company training strategies and all that, and you'll buy me a beer on Friday. Deal?"

Dexter could feel the air scraping the dryness of his throat. "Uh, yeah," he said. "You got your own work to do."

"Right, right," he said and hitched up his pants again. "I'll see you back at the van then."

Dexter watched Roddy disappear around the corner and then slumped down on the curb.

The house across the street from him was plain, neither imposing or inviting. The people who lived in it were also probably plain. He couldn't be sure of course, but he also couldn't say which was better or worse.

He bit into his lip, knowing this would all go away if he'd just knock on their door. The panic would subside and he would remain gainfully employed. But now that the evaluation was past, he didn't even have to bother. He could go back to filling in the cards, turning them in and collecting a paycheck without concern. Roddy and Jim were both right. A retarded, crack-addicted, crippled monkey could do this job. So long as the cards came in, no one cared. He should feel happy, relieved. He didn't. Dexter wanted to cry except that he felt too angry.

Across the street, a car pulled into the driveway and a man stepped out. He opened the trunk and began to unload several bags of groceries. He was exposed and vulnerable; the time was right.

Dexter stood up, dusted himself off and threw his clipboard in the first trash can he saw. His apartment sucked as much as his landlord, and he knew few people outside of work. He'd take the check due to him on Friday and make his way to the coast. It didn't matter what Ned was or wasn't. Dexter was going to find a job on a boat.

CONTRAST

It was the best of times; it was the worst of times. But it all depends on how you look at it and who's doing the looking.

While Tom and Zoe irreverently pulled Tom's battered compact up to Montmartre Chez-Soi, Joel sauntered up the steps to Sarah's house, greeted by a chorus of hollering drunks.

While Tom and Zoe sipped from a bottle of wine made more than five years ago from a list they chose not to look at for fear of losing their nerve at the prices, Joel victoriously smashed a beer can on his forehead to show he was the first to drain its contents and was hoisted in the air like a true champion.

While Tom and Zoe giggled as they both ate escargot at the same time, neither of them willing to go first, Joel caught a piece of watermelon in his mouth that had been thrown across the room by his rival in the chugging contest. Distracted by his achievement, a second piece of watermelon hit Joel in the eye.

While Tom and Zoe reached the moment in the evening in which they both stared deeply into each other's eyes, partly from enduring affection and partly from their full bellies temporarily lulling their conversational skills, Joel held back Sarah's hair and tried to help her aim at the cars of people she didn't like as she vomited off her balcony.

While Tom and Zoe shared the kind of kiss that fairy tales are written about, Joel took a pillow to the kisser, swung by a beautiful face in a half-naked crowd. And later that night, when Tom slipped the words *I love you* into Zoe's ear, Joel slipped his penis into the beautiful girl who had bested him in pillow-fighting and of whose name he was unclear.

Best friends inseparable until Zoe, both Tom and Joel thought that they had never had it better and that the other had never been further from sanity. Years of machinations laid on bar-tops, blood oaths thinned far beyond the legal limit, travel plans not involving "the sights," half-cocked business ideas, fully cocked business ideas, debt, revenge, redemption, hunger, cold, finals and the special kind of intimate sincerity that only arises over your team losing the Super Bowl—were now all second fiddle to a mere girl. That was the true meaning of the worst of times, though neither Tom nor Joel was able to apply that label to the situation as a whole, rather than intimate that it was the other's fault.

Still, it was the best of times.

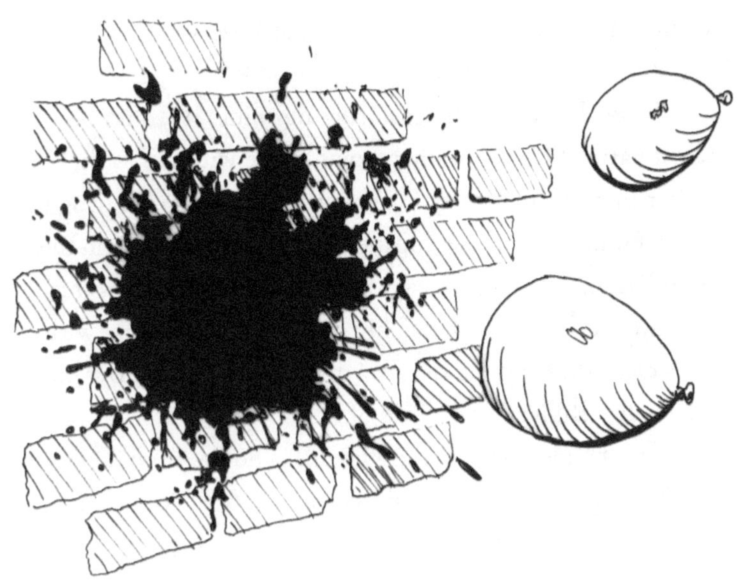

KILLING A ZEITGEIST

It was Seth, Marc, Allison, Charlie and I, and not one of us were fooling ourselves by thinking this mission was about anything other than revenge. It was just that we didn't see revenge as an illegitimate motivation. Revenge was balance, and no system or element within a system can function out of balance. Lacking revenge—every beating, every crass slur shouted from the window of a moving car, every hassle, shake-down and look down the nose for our clothes not fitting right or walking slowly to enjoy the fresh air—would remain on the books, tilting the balance, hindering our function.

There was nothing lowly or dishonorable about seeking revenge. What was lowly was deliberately inflicting the kind of pain and misery on others that precipitated it. And as we'd spent years at the receiving end of that misery, our eyes were dry about returning the favor.

When I left for college in the morning, it would be the worst parts of Cranston that would come with me to the city, rather than the parts worth keeping. I wouldn't be moving up, but running away. Those staying wouldn't be building on their foundation, but trapped. My car was packed and I was ready to leave. A full-ride scholarship and a whole new life with a truly clean slate awaited me an eight-hour drive away. But there were a few things to take care of first.

Seth handed out the supplies at his house. Booze. Gloves. Booze. Superglue. Booze. Paintbombs. Booze. Compost.

"Ew, you can carry that bag," Allison said, wrinkling up her heart-shaped face. "It smells."

Generally, Seth had the unique ability to wrap almost everything the average person had to say over the course of an entire evening into one sentence, yet still have his guns loaded. He somehow managed to contain his irritation as he silently took the plastic-lined duffel bag full of stinking garbage back from Allison's outstretched hand. The pale, sharp angles of his thin face and shaved head didn't even twitch. Considering the typical additional depth and volume of specific opinions Seth professed on the mannerisms of my now ex-girlfriend, this was a near superhuman feat. Especially, since in his worldview, offering her the most potent albeit most disgusting weapon in our arsenal was an attempt to make peace, one she had spurned. Seth handed the bag to Marc, who opened it up and took a gleefully deep whiff, marveling that such an abomination even existed.

"What's in this?" Though partially obscured by the chin-length brown hair tucked behind his ears, a slightly queasy look passed over Marc's round face. "It's terrible," he said.

"Little bit of everything," Seth said. "Rotten food, dogshit, medical waste."

"A crap cocktail," Marc smiled. "All right." He picked up the whiskey bottle from the middle of the circle and took a drink.

"Where did you get medical waste?" Allison questioned.

"Please tell me it's from an abortion clinic," Marc chirped. "The thought of slinging baby jello all over town is just too good."

"There isn't even one in the county, Marc," I said, "let alone in town."

"Why does it matter?" Seth sneered at Allison.

"Because it could be infectious," she snapped.

"Well, you're not carrying it, so what do you care."

"Don't you care, Marc?"

"Seth gave me gloves," he shrugged. Though it was a barely perceptible difference from his standard scowl, Seth beamed at Marc for shutting Allison down. No one could have caught it but me. I felt a tinge of sadness knowing that so intimate an understanding of another person would be tossed away with my departure.

"Well, I still want to know," Allison demanded.

Seth now glared at me, once again silently demanding to know why Allison was even here since we'd broken up. Of course, it was the same glare he used to give me demanding to know why she was places just because we were dating. Though he'd never have admitted it, I'd always suspected he had a bizarre crush on her. Allison always claimed the crush was on me.

"It's tampons," Marc said pulling one out barehanded and

waggling it Allison's direction. "Probably from a women's room."

"You went rooting around in the tampon bin?" Allison gasped.

"Only the best for Tripod's going away party," Seth said, taking a drink of the generic brand whiskey for himself.

"That's disgusting," she said.

"And the rest of it isn't?" Seth snarled. "That's the fucking point, to fuck shit up and coat it in a layer of rotten filth that won't ever wash out. Jesus. The door's right over there if you're even the tiniest bit uncomfortable, princess. But perhaps if we carried you on a chair so you could toss candy at our enemies that would be better for you?"

"Fuck you, Seth," Allison snapped. "Just cause I don't want to give people fucking AIDS—"

"Whoever caught AIDS from a tampon?"

"Who fucking throws them at people? It's blood. Where do you think AIDS comes from you fucking retard?"

"The people on our list would deserve it—"

"Children, children, children," I said. "Let's bring it down a notch so we don't get the cops called on us before we even get out of the house. Watching you two bicker is not how I want to spend my last night. Okay?"

Seth and Allison's faces made it clear things weren't remotely okay, but they both shut up.

Only Marc, the big puppy, the mass of energy just waiting to be focused, was unaffected. His grin was trademark wide, and as always, he was raring to go.

"And Seth," I added, "don't call me Tripod anymore. I broke my leg six years ago. The nickname never caught on."

"Says you," he chuckled. "I think it's hilarious. And since you aren't going to be around, I can call you whatever the fuck

I want, fucko. Soon as you're gone I'm gonna put up a three-legged billboard in your memory. Yearbook photo and all."

"So, what's this bag then?" Marc asked, pointing to small satchel on the floor. "Needles?"

"Nothing," Seth said, kicking it out of the way. "It's mine."

Allison was still glaring at me, furious at being shut down. So I grabbed the whiskey bottle back from Seth and took a quick pull. "Soothing," I gagged, and offered it to Allison. "Really, they oughta call it the peacemaker."

Allison kept glaring at me, but she took the bottle, wiped the mouth off on her shirt and silently took a drink.

"Why are we still here?" Charlie cut in disinterestedly. "I thought we were ready to go." He was the only member of our raiding party that wasn't part of my inner circle. I'd only met him a few days earlier when Seth introduced him as a guy from work who was "down with the mission." So far, I didn't like him or his acne-scarred face. But I don't think I was supposed to; he was slotted to be the new me.

"One second." Marc got up and went into the kitchen, returning with beers for each of us. "First," he said, "a toast."

Charlie snorted in boredom, but a sharp look from Seth cut it short. He accepted the beer sourly as Marc went around the circle.

Allison moved to open her beer, but Marc stopped her. "Shotgun toast," he said.

"Wouldn't be right to run damage like this without one," Seth agreed. "To shotgun toasts!"

"No," Marc said. "To the end of an era." He hoisted his drink high in my direction and nodded sincerely.

"To the end of an era," I echoed, touched. I popped the top

off of my beer for the corresponding drink but got a super-charged spray of foam in the eye and a double-dose of Marc's laughter in the ear. "You motherfucker," I grunted. I quickly snatched the beer from Allison's hand and leapt to my feet to douse Marc with its discharge. He squirmed with laughter, trying to escape the foamy justice, then switched strategies and started to return fire with his own beer. We leapt to our feet and crashed through the room and out the front door, hollering battle cries at one another as Seth, Allison and Charlie snatched up the supplies and chased after us gleefully, not caring how much attention we drew.

We'd been a gang for years, seen each other through the best and worst times of our lives with absolute loyalty and unbreakable bonds. And though no one would say it, we all knew that after this night, nothing would ever be the same. Life would move on and the next time we met, we may talk about the old days or possibly try to relive them with some sort of harebrained scheme involving theft of lawn ornaments or tipping over livestock, but it would be a lost cause.

We'd seen it happen to others and sworn it would never be us more times than we could count. Crossed hearts. Spit-soaked handshakes. Pinky swears. All manner of verbal contracts dressed up with arbitrary ritual. It didn't matter. Oaths can't change destiny. There was no way off the road we were headed down and we knew it. Which meant that right now, all that mattered was that we were a team. United until death or dawn, whichever came first. The game was on. There was no going back.

I met Allison when I was working graveyard at an all-night

gas station the previous summer. Her car got a flat two miles outside of town and we were the only place open.

"I'm not sure what good I'd be," I said ruefully, as my job had never presented me with the opportunity to save a damsel in distress before. It barely even presented me with a paycheck. Mostly, I did it because the lack of customers gave me time to write entrance essays and draft samples for my endless applications to architecture programs. "I just work the register," I continued. "I don't actually know how to change a tire."

"I can change it on my own," she snorted contemptuously, green eyes fierce and bright behind curtains of dark hair. "I didn't bring my jack is all."

"Sorry, I didn't mean…What happened to your jack?"

"It's holding up my house."

"Oh…That would cut down on its mobility I suppose."

"There was a broken pipe and a sinkhole and I don't know why I'm telling you this," she said. "Just, do you have one I can borrow?"

"Probably," I said. But I couldn't seem to picture what a jack looked like, not with the image of Allison in the forefront. So I told her she could have a look around on her own.

After she smirked briefly at my ignorance, she rooted around and found one in the garage, then thanked me and started walking back to her car.

"Wait!" I cried out as she reached the sidewalk.

"What?"

"How do I know you'll bring it back? Shouldn't you leave your ID or something?"

"I don't have it with me."

"Holding up your house too?"

"The kitchen table, actually," she smiled.

"Oh…"

She turned and walked a few more steps, then stopped. "I know," she said, turning back. "Why don't you just come with me. Then, when I'm done with it, you can have it back."

"What about the station?" I asked, stunned.

"Do you really care that much?"

I took a quick glance around and realized I didn't. The chances of there being another customer were negligible, and it didn't remotely matter to me if there were. Potentially losing the privilege of spending three nights a week in a gas station didn't worry me much. My concern over her returning the jack was more based in a desire to see her again. This was even better. So I locked the door, turned out the lights and began the hike back to Allison's car with her and the jack.

"You know, the irony of this," I said on the walk, "is that I like the graveyard shift because it generally requires the least work."

"Well, we'll do our best to keep it from feeling like work then," she smirked.

For the next year, the only part of it that had, was mediating between her and Seth. We liked all the same movies, hated all the same actors, both wanted to live in a loft apartment with a spiral staircase and a bookshelf with a ladder that stored nothing but trashy paperbacks. We both liked to eat pasta every night, and we both laughed so hard when we tried to make a home porno that we had to look up on the internet if there was some sort of giggling sexual disorder. That was why I'd asked her to move with me and why I was so taken aback when she declined.

"I don't want to break up," she'd said. "I just don't want to go with you." Somehow, that had never made the sense to me that it did to her. But I knew her well enough to know that she was done talking about it.

I also knew her well enough to know that she wasn't fully engaged in the true spirit of the evening. By the second block, we'd given up the running and shouting to adhere more closely to Seth's master plan, which he'd detailed earlier along with his complete list of those who'd wronged us—democratically compiled, ranked in order of importance and impact of retribution as well as plotted out on a map for maximum efficiency. We were now in a steady and boisterous march complete with songs and toasts. And while Allison had joined in, there was a skittishness to her movements, a nervousness to her voice that betrayed skepticism. However, she'd made it clear she no longer wished such things to be my concern. So they weren't. She was on her own.

I marched on. This was too good a moment to waste with contemplation anyhow. It needed to be fully absorbed. Our procession looked somewhere between a gang of coffeehouse pseudo-intellectuals gone bad and an army of hobos. Marc led the way bouncing off rocks and trees, hurdling over parked cars whenever they happened into his path. Seth smoked with the fury of his manner of verbal assault. He was a tiny volcano, walking down the street threatening to erupt a molten hot stream of cuss words and tirades against the machine. Charlie, the new me, patrolled the flanks, happily strolling along and pretending to fire a machine gun at anything that moved and a few things that didn't. In order to avoid being hit by non-existent return fire, he took evasive action similar to Marc's chaotic waltz back and forth across the sidewalk, but with less frequency. Allison took up the rear so no one could see her fret while I walked smack in the middle of the whole ordeal with a smile on my face like I had just crapped out a large supply of winning lottery tickets. Despite whatever images of stealth we may have had in our minds, we were about as inconspicuous as a sasquatch in a nudist colony.

Block after block we marched, until Seth suddenly held up a clenched fist. "Hold up a second," he commanded, and pulled a map from his back pocket. We stopped as he checked an address he had circled on the map. "This is the place," he said. Marc and Charlie immediately dropped into slightly comical attack crouch positions in nearby shadows.

"What is?" Allison sneered.

"Brown house on the next corner." He pointed to the end of the block. "Casey Meek. 1359 Browning Street."

"That cornfed loser from chem class?" she gasped.

"Yes."

"But why?"

"Keep your fucking voice down," Seth hissed, and pulled her into the shadows. Allison looked ready to kill, but I shook my head no and she swallowed it down.

"Losing your nerve on the boat ride to Normandy?" Marc snickered. "Here, this should help." He once again offered her the whiskey bottle, from which she took an angry sip. "Don't worry, Private," Marc chided. "We'll get you back to your mama without a scratch."

Allison took another drink, thoroughly humorless.

"Everyone clear on the plan?" Seth said. Everyone but Allison nodded. Seth turned and glared right at Allison. "I said, is everyone clear on the plan?" This time, she nodded contemptuously. "Good," he said, then motioned to Marc to start the first wave.

Marc crept in low, keeping to the shadows of bushes and trees, brandishing his tube of superglue like a spy pistol. Once he'd made it up to the front door, he filled the locks with glue and coated the knob, then did the same to Casey's car parked in front of the house. He crept back out of sight and gave the all clear.

Seth, Charlie and I burst from hiding whooping and hollering, flinging tight barrages of our latex paint bombs and small burst-on-impact sacks of compost at the Meek stronghold. Allison, our lookout, wiggled the stick in her butt deeper into the mud.

Our artillery burst loud splotches of pink and hunter safety orange across the house and yard, peppered with black rotting chunks of garbage. It looked hysterical and smelled worse. It was like the yard was reverting to a primordial stew rife with primitive and brightly colored sea life.

Lights flipped on in the house and voices shouted. Allison whistled sharply, the agreed upon signal, and we loosed our final barrage as the Meeks cussed and wrestled with the useless doorknob. We heard an angry snarl as a foot broke the door down to escape, but by then we were near a block away in a full sprint, leaving our terrorist work of abstract art behind us. Ahead lay redemption. With grins on our faces and malice in our hearts, our little army dashed on into the night, ever closer to the societal fringe guidance counselors warned of.

The adrenaline wore off by the time we reached the next house on our list. But after it had fallen, and the two after it, and the fast food palace that had imprisoned the three of us two summers back, and the diner we'd been disinvited from for "lookin' funny" the same summer, adrenaline had given way to an intoxicating confidence that stretched far beyond chemistry; it was righteousness. The Meeks, the Aldens, the Turnhills—the bullies, the thieves and the hatemongers—they were the sinners and we were the flaming sword of a God we could finally get behind, dishing out smitings like they were going out of style, and leaving a trail of beer cans in our wake.

Predictably, the only one not ecstatic was Allison, code-named Agent Wet Blanket. We'd expected her to stay at the lookout post for the duration of the mission, but she was calling things early just so they'd end and we could go on to the next house. And she was growing surlier as the night went on. That's why I was less than thrilled to feel a light tug on my elbow, holding me back for a council as our gang skipped through an alley.

"How many more houses are there?" she whispered.

"Why do you care?"

"How many?"

"I don't know. What does it matter?"

"It matters because at a certain point, the cops are going to catch on that something is going on. Seeing as how we're the only people wandering around dressed like low-rent cat burglars, we're probably going to get stopped on principle."

"Well, I wouldn't want to get you in any trouble," I sneered.

"It has nothing to do with me, you asshole."

"Great. Thanks for the information and the personal critique. Glad to have you on the project."

"Oh, come on Tyler, come back," she said.

"No, no, no, just…" I stopped. "All right. You know what? I didn't want to say it at first, but Seth's right. What are you even doing here? Aside from trying to ruin things I mean?"

"Look, you know how Seth talks. I didn't think we would actually…" She stabbed her finger towards my face, but stopped it short and clamped her eyes closed tight. Then she took a big breath and softly exhaled, "Do you love me or not?"

"What kind of bullshit question is that?" I snorted, and started back down the alley.

Allison trotted behind me, talking at the back of my head. "The only one that matters. Do you?"

"You're making it hard."

"But do you?"

"Yes." I grumbled. "Mostly."

"Then don't do this."

"What?"

"Run away with me right now."

"You don't know what you're saying."

"I do. We can just turn and head the other way. Marc's too drunk to notice. Charlie doesn't give a shit. And Seth—"

"Don't—"

"You're already gone to him, Tyler. The way he sees things you sold him out already just by leaving at all."

"You don't know the first thing about me and Seth."

"Fine. I don't. But please, let's go right now."

"Why? So we can have one last night together and you get to feel like you saved me? Fuck that."

"No, Tyler, that's not it at all."

"Please, explain it to me then, since I'm too stupid to figure it out on my own."

"You're being such an asshole."

"Oh, you're right, I see that now. Thanks for the update. Later."

"I'm saying I was wrong before."

"Well, I'll mark the occasion in history."

"No, not that I was wrong, that I changed my mind."

"About what?"

"Going with you."

"You mean, to the city?"

"Yeah."

"But I thought—"

"I was scared. But I don't care anymore. I want to go with you. That's what I meant before. I already packed everything I need at my house even. We can be on the road in fifteen minutes. Let's run away. Right now. And keep running until we get somewhere worth stopping."

I had no idea what to say.

"You do still want me to go, don't you?" she asked.

"Yeah. More than anything, I just…I just never thought you would is all. Independent woman and all that."

"Going with you doesn't mean being your slave. It means being in your life."

"Pasta every night. That sort of thing?"

"Yeah."

I paused for a moment, unsure of how to say what I needed to. "You love me, right?"

"I do."

"Then don't ask me to run out on my friends like this."

"I'm trying to protect you."

"That's fucking touching, but I don't need protecting. What I need is closure. Running away just leaves more things open. I'll do anything for you, like I'd do anything for them. If you haven't noticed yet, no matter what they think of you, they'd never make me choose. If you do, then…I don't know really.

It's just the kind of thing that would stick with me. I wouldn't want that. Not if you're serious."

"I'm just getting a really bad feeling here."

"That's cause you started with a bad attitude."

"Yeah, I suppose I did. But that doesn't change my bad feeling."

"Just one more. Then I'll say I'm tired or something."

"Promise?"

"Yeah," I whispered. Allison clenched her hand tightly to mine.

Just then, Seth held his fist up signaling that we'd once again reached a target.

Marc and I had been friends since the first grade, both of us sharing a penchant for the same back table in the lunchroom and weekly close-up examinations of Casey Meek's knuckles. But Seth didn't move to Cranston until the 7th grade, which was the year that Marc's older brother took to threatening us if we didn't do whatever he wanted. We'd fought back the first time, but a black eye apiece, as well as a prolonged fit of laughing from Marc's dad who thought we could use a little toughening up at the hands of his favorite pituitary giant, put a stop to our insurrection real quick. So we carried Richie's stuff. We embarrassed ourselves for his amusement. Sometimes we had to pay for his lunch, meaning we couldn't afford our own. Things like that.

That is until Seth, new in town and oblivious to the danger, mouthed off in the locker room and Richie conscripted us into an ad hoc gang with Deek and Simon, the only other guys in town big and dumb enough for Ritchie to call friends. They saw Marc and I as a mercenary first wave who could drive Seth to the ambush point: the closed down lumberyard behind the school. The way Richie told it, Deek and Simon were going to beat something bloody, but it was our choice whether it was Seth or us. Since we didn't know or care about him, Marc and I quickly agreed Seth was on his own.

He ran good. A skinny kid like him with a bad attitude and a taste for all black had lots of experience. But the only thing Richie's mind was any good for was battlefield strategy and the plan he'd given us drove Seth against the back fence, where there was only one route of escape: through the kicked down gate that led into the lumberyard.

Seth ran through the cratered wasteland, dodging around wrecked machinery and tarred up slag piles. We would have lost him, except that he'd run right into the narrow corridor of slag piles and rusting buildings that Richie wanted us to maneuver him into, the one that ran straight into a deep gulley at the edge of the yard.

We were too far behind to see how it started. But by the time we got there, Seth had a bloody nose and a drawn knife that he whipped through the air in wide arcs as he cussed and spit like an angry viper. Deek, Simon and Richie had him surrounded and they were all inching closer, jerking back when the knife whizzed past, but not stopping their advance. Deek was easily twice Seth's size, and after a few dodges, he darted in catching Seth's wrist in his mitts as Simon and Richie pounced. The knife dropped to the ground, as did Seth a moment later. The three gorillas kicked and punched the sad little heap curled into a ball in the dirt. All Marc and I could do was watch.

But then Richie picked up the knife.

Marc jumped on him from behind, clinging to Richie's knife arm, kicking and screaming wildly, landing blow after blow to his brother's ribs and legs and splitting the assault on Seth. Then suddenly, not really aware of how, I too was in the fight, swinging like mad and fighting for our collective lives. The last thing I remembered was a straight blow to the face knocking me backwards.

"You don't know where we are, do you?" Seth smirked.

"Should I?" I said.

"This is my goodbye gift to you," he said gesturing grandly. "Sure, there's a few more on the list, but this is the big show."

I looked down the street but couldn't see what Seth was going on about. We were standing in the grown-over mouth of an alley on a nondescript block lined with average one and two-story houses. The one closest to us had a sagging fence corralling a broken-down Chevy Nova. Another had a tree with a hammock. I was reasonably sure I'd never even seen this street before.

"I know where we are," Marc said quietly. He tucked his hair back behind his ears, making it obvious his trademark big puppy grin was MIA.

"You do?" I exclaimed. "Where? What am I supposed to be looking at?"

"It's that one," Marc said, pointing to a sky blue ranch house with a tiny, dead-looking front yard. "That's Richie's place."

"What?" It was a name I'd never expected to cross paths with again.

"Aw shit," Charlie laughed. "Him? Really? That's fucking great. Well done Seth. He's a genuine fuckwad."

"Moved back about a month ago," Seth said. "Just in time too."

"I don't get it," Allison said. "Who's Richie?"

"Nobody," Marc grunted. "Just another jerk that has it coming."

"Yeah, but this jerk gets something special," Seth smiled. He opened up his backpack and pulled out a package of M-80s and a long coil of extension fuses. "More than just the artillery. He gets to actually wake up in a warzone."

"What the fuck are you going to do with those?" Allison said.

"Just scare the shit out of him like he did to us," Seth fired back. "What the fuck do you think we're going to do?"

"Yeah, him and everyone else on the block. What happened to your bullshit code of nobility, only going for revenge? What happens when one of those neighbors calls the cops or something? We can't glue down every house on the block. You're going to get us all arrested or shot or who knows what."

"I told you before princess, you don't like it, scram. But drop the superiority act 'cause you don't get me, or any of this and you never will. As much as you think might think you do, you don't even get Tripod."

"I'm not doing this one," she said firmly. "I'm done."

"Good. Who needs you, Yoko," Seth said.

Allison grabbed my arm. "Tyler, don't do this," she said. "Let's just go, right now, like we talked about. You don't have to go through with this."

"AAAAAGH!" I said, shaking my arm free. "I'm so fucking done with you two. Just, fuck it!" I ran at the house not caring if anyone followed.

They did, and quicker than I would have expected. Paint and garbage bombs flew in swarms past me as I ran. I didn't even bother with mine. I kicked over the fence, then scooped up a rake and started pounding on Richie's car, knocking off a mirror and cracking a side-window, screaming and paying no attention to the lights clicking on up and down the street or the artillery strikes surrounding me. This was the big one. This was where balance was truly restored. I was chipping bits of paint and glass away to reach redemption underneath and be done with this place. Put it behind me and never look back. It was the only thing that mattered. I barely even heard the gunshot.

After our brawl in the lumberyard, I woke up in the bottom of the gulley. I didn't know how long I'd been there, but it was starting to get dark. Seth, his face all bloody tatters, was shaking me.

"Wake up you fuckhead," he growled. "We can't wait any longer."

"Huh?" I said. "Wait for what?"

"Good," he said. "You're awake."

"I was asleep?" Suddenly I recognized Seth as the kid I'd been chasing and cringed, sure his boot would be arriving on my face promptly.

"What the fuck else would you be if I just said you're awake," he fumed. "Come on, we got to get you outta here."

"What happened?"

"Your fucking retarded friends beat the shit out of me, stabbed your pal who was chasing me and left you down here for dead is what happened."

"Richie stabbed Marc?"

"In the arm. Barely. I'm sure he'll be fine. They sure ran like hell once it happened. Hell of a town you got here."

"They're not my friends," I said. "I'm sorry. They told us it was either you or us."

"Look how that worked out for everyone," Seth laughed. "Now come on, we gotta get you up and to a hospital." He put my arm around his neck and tried to hoist me up, but I screamed in pain and he stopped.

"I think my leg is broken," I whimpered.

"Yeah. I know," Seth said, "but since none of those apes are going to ever mention what they just did, there ain't no one coming to find us. Which is why we have to get you out of here."

"Can't you go to a phone?"

"You want me to leave you here alone?"

"No."

"Doesn't matter. I wouldn't know where a phone was anyhow. I'm new remember?"

"It really hurts," I said.

"Yeah. And it's probably going to hurt a whole lot worse once we get moving," Seth said. "So let's just get it over with."

I took a few quick breaths to ready myself, then nodded that I was ready. He pulled up hard, swiftly dragging me upright and causing pain I'd never imagined, like someone was routing out a cavern in my shin. Then it was over. Just the panting, tears and knowledge that lots more pain was coming remained.

"Ready?" he said.

I took a few deep breaths, then nodded. He shifted his arm around my shoulders, then put mine around his neck and we started the agonizing lurch through the gulley to get back to the road. It was slow going and painful, but I couldn't escape the awkward comedy of our movements.

"This is a ridiculous way to travel," I grunted.

"Sorry I don't have any crutches on me, kid," he laughed.

We limped on a few more steps in silence. The mouth out of the gulley was close, but we'd still have to cross a field and then go around a fence, since there was no way I could climb one.

"Why did you stay?" I panted. "You could have ran too. I certainly don't deserve your help."

"Let's not make a big thing of it, okay," Seth said. "Word gets out about us playing paramedic and everyone will want me to haul them out of a ditch."

"Okay," I grunted. We lurched forward a few more steps and then chuckled. "How could I tell anyone. I don't even know your name."

"It's Seth."

I nodded. "I'm Tyler, not that it matters. I'm sure the crutches will get me saddled with some sort of stupid nickname. Tripod or something like that."

"Tripod?" Seth mused. "That'll never catch."

"We'll see," I said.

"Guess so."

"Really though, why did you stay?"

"You kidding?" Seth laughed. "Someone's gotta help me get back at those fucks, and who's going to be more motivated than you?"

The terrible trio were all shipped off to out of state relatives or military schools before I was even out of the hospital. Marc got some stitches and another beating from his father when no one would tell him what happened. Seth loaned me a book on architecture to pass the time while I recovered. The three of us had stood together ever since.

There was tugging on my arm and a slush of words that mixed with the sounds of cracking glass. Threats, demands, all manner of curses—then there was another shot. This one I heard clearly, because after it, all the other noises were replaced with flashing beams of red and white light. Then we were running. First back to the alley, and then anywhere and everywhere. Marc's face had a blurry grin, Seth's angry righteousness, Charlie's a flushed pained grimace. I couldn't see Allison's, but I could hear her huffing and swearing behind me. Houses and cars flew by, some doused in neon splotches of color, some in the strobing psychedelic of a pursuing police siren. A retrospective: the house I'd been born in, the corner where I'd fallen from my bike when I was six, the bleachers I'd sat out on at gym classes, the place where Allison's car had broken down and the site of our—my—first kiss. I ran and ran and ran, though bushes and over fences, with no regard my safety or to the safety of anything that got in my way. All that mattered was getting back to Seth's house where my car was parked. I crashed through his back fence and through the yard, fishing my keys out as I ran. I hadn't seen either the cops or my friends for blocks, but I could hear the sirens and knew that they couldn't ever be far enough behind me.

The keys slid roughly into the door lock, turning agonizingly slowly to the left. I threw the door open and leapt into the driver's seat, quickly starting the engine and slamming it into gear. I peeled out into the street and tore down the road, my eyes fixed on the rearview mirror. I had no idea what had happened to my friends, but I didn't care. They were the past. My shiny new future lay ahead. It was just a hundred miles to the state line, then straight on till morning. After tonight, there was nothing left for me here.

TRYING ON HATS

"We can't tell anyone about this," Tyler said as she stood up with her pants still down around her ankles. In the rush to take advantage of the moment, her shirt and sweater had stayed on, keeping her breasts a mystery. "I don't want it getting back to Jared."

James was staring at her still exposed lower half, even post coitus, unable to comprehend its mythical status. Still, he wished she had said something else first, rather than jumping straight to the subject of her boyfriend.

"What about when our children ask how we got together?"

"Jokes about kids right after sex aren't funny," she said reproachfully.

"Sorry. I don't understand these sort of things."

"Seriously though, I don't want this getting around," Tyler lectured.

"Don't worry," James said somewhat sourly. He was still sitting down and the damp ground was cold on his butt now that the warmth of physical activity and contact were waning in tandem with Tyler's demeanor. That combination was pushing his mood into a decline as well.

Tyler placed her hands on her still bare hips and fired back. "I have a reputation to uphold." She said it as if he didn't.

"I get it. It's fine." James was annoyed now.

Tyler hitched her pants up. "Not that it wasn't fun, or that I don't like you, just…" Her voice trailed off as she fiddled with her zipper.

"I know. You have a reputation." His tone was an especially genuine tone of sarcasm.

Zippering complete, Tyler crouched down, grabbing James by the crotch, making a noise of satisfaction as she slid her fingers slowly down the length of his penis, squeezing ever so slightly as if she was milking it.

James looked at her in confusion. "What are you doing?" Five seconds ago Tyler's shoulders had been as cold as arctic wind.

"Just saying goodbye," Tyler smirked back. "You know that's an amazing piece of equipment down there, right?"

"I have been in a locker room before."

"You're not planning anything for it are you?"

"What do you mean?"

"I know you people are into surgery, but I think that sometimes its better to leave well enough alone, if you know what I mean." Her eyes glimmered in a way that made James the slightest bit uncomfortable.

"I'll keep that in mind."

Tyler's eyes glimmered again. "It's a shame we can't tell anyone about this. It'd be fucking great to just walk up to people and say, hey, we just fucked in the bushes…if we were a couple I mean."

"Just tell people. They won't believe it anyway." Tyler took in James's idea with the same disdain in which he presented it. The honeymoon appeared to be ending. After several seconds of awkward silence, Tyler cashed in the IRA as well.

"Would you mind waiting here for a few minutes? I don't want people to see us coming back together."

James let out a heavy breath signifying his dissatisfied compliance. He knew Tyler had a boyfriend, but there was a part of him that thought she was more concerned with people finding out she had slept with him than that she had cheated, as if he personally was some sort of social crime or carried a communicable disease. Sex with a girl was a disturbingly unusual complication, and he didn't have the slightest clue as to why he'd done it, other than perhaps it seemed like an interesting idea at the time—not that James thought Tyler gave any heed to the subject's weight for him. She might, but Tyler was gone before James collected his thoughts enough to quiz her on the subject or remind her to check her hair for sticks and leaves.

He laid back on the ground, looking up at the stars and letting the night air caress his exposed, postcoital skin, the way Tyler wouldn't. From outside of the bushes and across the lawn, he could hear alcoholically amplified voices welcoming Tyler back to the party. A loud *where ya been?* and *now it's a party!* cut through the din and were answered with a flimsy excuse about smoking a cigarette. It was partially true. Cigarettes had been smoked. That was how things had started: a smoke and a chat, then one thing led to another, as things are wont to do.

But now, bullshit was the operative word. It permeated James's cognition of voices and the fleeting emotions drizzling out a leak in his left ventricle. Who did she think she was? He was the one who'd stepped out on a limb with no clue as to why. Fuck her boyfriend. How convenient James was. He made up his mind to hate Tyler for using him and thought how much he'd enjoy watching her suffer pain and humiliation beyond the psychologically healthy amount to wish on others. He hoped that her perfume would attract a swarm of killer bees or that a chandelier would fall on her, even though there weren't any chandeliers on the premises.

James reached into the pocket of his jeans lying in a crumpled pile on the ground beside him and pulled out a cigarette and his lighter. A gentle wisp of flame brought his cigarette to life. James inhaled deeply, wishing to feel every single toxin individually entering his mood, lulling him gently towards a slow and satisfied death.

"What a bitch," he whispered to Gemini, circling silently overhead. The rest of James's cigarette passed without editorial comment.

Satisfied enough time had passed, James gathered his clothes off the ground and put them on. He tied his shoes and worked his way through the bushes so as to go around to the front of the house, pulling twigs from his hair and brushing himself off as he walked.

James emerged from the bushes and walked straight into the broad chest of Tyler's boyfriend, Jared.

"Hey, easy there James," Jared said jovially. He held up his hands in surrender. Each finger looked thick enough to wrestle a python. "No need to get rough with me. I'll let you by."

"Sorry," James mumbled. "I was going to get some beer, but I forgot my wallet here."

Jared's smile cracked open to release a warm-hearted laugh as he gave James a rough, good-natured clap on the back from a Christmas ham mounted at his wrist. "Don't worry. I'll grab you a few out of the car."

"Thanks," James replied weakly.

"No problem." Jared made a weaving beeline for his car, and James for the front door. If he got his bag from inside, then he could leave, an option preferable to getting the star treatment from Jared ten minutes after fucking his girlfriend. Correction: after *being fucked* by his girlfriend.

Gabriel, the reason James had gone to smoke in the bushes in the first place, spotted him the moment he walked through the door. He beckoned James with a martini glass and a wink. James ignored him and started looking around for his bag. It wasn't in the closet where he left it, so James walked from room to room, eyes scouring the floor, searching behind every piece of furniture that could possibly conceal his bag. It seemed to have vanished without a trace. James found himself in front of the closet again, without a clue, and oblivious to the noises surrounding him. He wondered what had happened.

Like creeping jungle vines, Jared's mammoth arm shot out, wrapping around James's shoulders, taking him hostage, pulling him in.

"There you are buddy! Have a drink," Jared beamed, handing James a half-empty, six-pack ring of Coors with John Wayne's picture on the cans. James accepted the beer with a weak smile and asked Jared if he had seen the missing bag.

"You aren't leaving are you?"

"No. I just thought I had a beer in there."

"Well then, problem solved." Jared's smile showed more teeth than an attacking shark. James thought considering the circumstances, he might be better off in the water.

"Yeah...I guess so," he said, faking a laugh.

Maintaining his social-death grip on James, Jared walked towards the kitchen and its waiting crowd of party-guests.

"Look who I found trying to leave!" Jared thundered, tightening his grip as they entered so that the hold was nearing a headlock. The crowd thundered assorted rally cries right back. "Sell-out! Keg-stand! Take his shoes!" James realized escape was hopeless. His arms were hairless, slender and delicate looking. They seemed to bend in a smooth curve sans elbows, while Jared's bent at sharp, vicious looking angles blurred by dark hair. He was a Gumby doll in the hands of Sasquatch.

A beer was roughly put to James mouth and a drink administered. He faked another chuckle and imagined acid rain pouring down from the fire-control system on the ceiling, watching the faces of his entire graduating class melt off in unison.

Twenty pounds of arm lifted from James's shoulders and was redeposited on Tyler as she entered the room. She snuck a menacing smile at James and kissed Jared on the mouth, lingering for dramatic effect. James could taste Jared's breath from across the room, a thick sour musk that could melt any material but the human heart.

At that moment, James couldn't decide which one of them he hated more. He wanted to feel the bones of Tyler's face crumble to powder on his knuckles, to feel the soft flesh of her face mold itself around his hand. He wanted Jared to watch and jack off.

So dedicated to his irritation was James, that he didn't notice pipe-cleaners like his own wrapping around his waist, until their owner whispered into his ear with the same rotten stench.

"Hey there, sexy." The words slithered from Gabriel's mouth like they were returning to nest on Medusa's head.

James squirmed only slightly less than his insides, but stopped when he got another glimpse of Tyler's coy smile, secure in a fortress of Jared.

The snake rode again. "Where have you been?"

"Just now, or all your life?" James whispered back, his eyes on Tyler.

"All my life."

"Out of my mind," he hinted and let Gabriel do the math from there.

James made a smile creep across his face as he felt the warm moisture of Gabriel kissing his neck, coupled with the exfoliation of evening stubble. He didn't care who else stared as long as Tyler was on the list. Gabriel caressed James's stomach lightly, eliciting a chorus of catcalls and whooping from the kitchen. James was not typically an exhibitionist, but this was definitely a performance for the benefit of one, and his evening had already been anything but typical. James let his fingers intertwine with Gabriel's, as they moved gently across his navel. He smiled deeper as he did so, taking the time to stretch his face out so that the casual observer could observe every phase of emotion he was faking as he swiveled his neck towards the rotten breath warming it.

James was so wrapped up in his performance he barely noticed Tyler's livid expression as she slunk out of the room unnoticed amidst the whooping and flashbulbs. He opened his mouth and let Gabriel's tongue greedily push inside like it wanted to annex James's tonsils.

Jared put a drink to his mouth and shook his head in disbelief at the scene unfolding before his eyes. "That's actually pretty fucking hot." His admission was delivered with the volume of a passing train.

James felt a sense of satisfaction Jared had stayed to watch rather than attend to Tyler, whom he guessed was now headed for the bushes to cry for the second time this evening. But this time, James fancied himself the cause, and not the remedy. He'd already tried on that hat, and like girls in general, the role of do-gooder was a poor fit.

Gabriel continued his sloppy assault on James's virtue to little physical resistance, but the mind was another matter altogether. James was remembering the feeling of that gorilla arm around his shoulders and wondering exactly how mean he really was.

SECOND CHANCES

People think it's hard to fake your own death, but it isn't. It's basically just a matter of purchasing a new identity, something illegal immigrants have been doing with little difficulty for years. You can generally do so on public transportation lines that go through the urban sprawl sections of any major city. You'll presumably end up with some ridiculous name like they handed out at Ellis Island—mine is Rob Ert—but it's not likely to set you back more than two hundred dollars. Once you've got your new ID, then you make a brief (but noteworthy) appearance at a bar, toss a few alcohol canisters around your car, and then run it off a cliff or bridge into the ocean or a large river. Basically any place where your death can be inferred by the condition of the car, but the lack of body can be easily explained away by strong currents or being eaten by animals. If you do it in a small town, then you will also ensure your death will be quickly ratified as impossible-to-disprove-gospel-truth-gossip in the local sewing circles.

The only really difficult part is leaving everything behind, and it does have to be everything. The fact that your precious stamp collection isn't in your house or your car, or that your spouse doesn't seem genuinely bereaved—possibly because they're supposed to rendezvous with you and the insurance money in Rio—are known as red flags. Big ones. You shouldn't even have insurance if you want to succeed.

The key, better than leaving everything behind, is not having anything to leave behind. 'Cause if you do, no matter what it is or how small or unimportant it may be, eventually you start to wonder how it's doing and if you should go back to check on it. Maybe wear a disguise or send a letter to a trusted friend. Next thing you know, you're back up to your neck in whatever it was you faked your death to get away from in the first place. If you don't have anything, those issues never come up.

I knew I wouldn't be coming back from South America for anything because there was nothing to come back for. My parents were dead, along with theirs. There was a time when I'd had friends, but we'd grown so far apart that when I ran into one of them in the supermarket a few weeks ago, he didn't even recognize me. I worked at a gas station and didn't even do well there. To date, I had accomplished absolutely nothing with my life. I hadn't even dated anyone since the second year of high school, and even that wasn't much more than a blip. By the time Daisy and I had found each other, her parents moved her away never to be heard from again.

The only noteworthy possession I had was debt. First from student loans and then from my parent's medical bills. Hundreds of thousands of dollars of debt complete with spiraling interest rates and no possibility of ever paying it off. It was nothing I was going to miss.

Oh sure, I know what you're thinking: faking your own death is more of a plot device for cheap literature than a legitimate financial plan. But my life, being me, wasn't worth saving. I was overweight, undereducated and dull. I wasn't stupid, but nothing ever seemed to come out of my mouth the way I intended it to. Consequently, I really wasn't anyone worth looking at or talking to. All I'd ever done was make bad decisions that had lead to a failed and boring existence. I needed a way out. The emergency cash I took from my boss's desk when he went on a hunting trip and the murder of my '83 Pontiac had provided one.

At first I was sure I'd be found out, but the newspaper report I read in the airport several days later made the whole thing seem downright understandable. Crushed by debt, without any career to speak of and with no real support mechanisms, I'd gone to the Blue Moon Tavern for a well-deserved drink.

"It was a genuine tragedy," said Eunice Waller, a local resident who'd been in the Blue Moon that night. "That young man had a real rough run of luck and won't ever get the chance to turn it around."

"Other than being real down, he seemed okay to me, otherwise I would have called him a cab from over in Benson," said Horace Johnson, the bartender at the Blue Moon that night. "He must have had more booze in the car or something."

Of course, Horace had to say that to avoid getting himself in trouble. I didn't hold it against him. He was an integral part of my drama. Sure he'd overserved me—or the potted plant I'd dumped most of my drinks into depending on how you looked at things—but the more he denied it, the more it solidified the truth of my death. I didn't want to see Horace in jail, but I certainly wouldn't have minded a manslaughter trial. Because while authorities were busy bickering over whose fault it was, I was quietly boarding a plane to Argentina. And I was never coming back. There wasn't anything to come back for.

After landing, I caught a bus from the airport to a sketchy looking used car lot to peruse my options. My cash had to last. I was sure Rob Ert would find work sooner or later, but he had to get by until then, and a car was a wise investment as it doubled as a place to sleep should things get really rough.

I decided on a beat up little pickup truck with a camper shell. It was ugly and smelled like it had been flooded at some point, but the shocks were good and it started right up. The salesman tried to charge me the gringo rate, but I tossed around some of my first-year Spanish and got him down to the price written on the cracked windshield with soap.

I tossed my luggage into the back and then consulted the water-stained map in the glove box while I let the engine warm. My intention was to head south into Patagonia, maybe find some medium sized village where I could live like a king with the associate degree I'd very nearly completed.

Satisfied on my route, I put my truck into gear and carefully nudged out into the anarchy of South American traffic. But before I even fully cleared the parking lot, my head snapped forward violently and all forward motion stopped as an inbound jeep crumpled the little truck's front end like paper mache.

Dazed, I stepped outside to survey the damage. Steam was shooting out from under the hood and the bumper was sticking out like a metallic tentacle. I was no mechanic, but it looked totaled. And since the front right tire had technically left the car lot, I suspected that meant the warranty would be void. The jeep, with its high clearance and reinforced bumper, was undamaged. This was a metaphor for my life.

"Oh my God! Are you all right?" a woman's voice called through the steam. "Do you need help? A doctor?"

"No, just...no," I grumbled, still a little dazed.

"I'm so sorry," she insisted. "I didn't see you, and someone was tailgating...Are you sure you're okay?"

"It's fine, really. I'm okay," I said sourly. "I had my seat belt on. Just stunned is all."

"You're American?" she said, pleasantly shocked. It sounded like she was trying to maneuver around the wreck.

"Yeah," I said. "Just arrived." Until now, I hadn't even noticed her accent through the traffic noise.

"Oh God... And this is the welcome you get. I'm so sorry."

"Yeah, you mentioned that," I said.

"Can I do anything for you?"

"I, just...I think I need to sit down for a second," I said, feeling a little woozy and really not wanting to continue our little chat.

"Here, let me help," she said and extended a hand. I looked up at her for the first time and saw the genuine concern and surprise on her face, which eased a little of the irritation I felt. But more than that, I noticed her. A friendly pudgy face surrounded by chestnut curls. If I'd had a type, she'd have been it. But awkward losers, on the lam like myself, don't get such luxuries.

"Well, don't worry, 'cause it's completely my fault and I'm insured," she said. "Just let me get the paperwork." She walked back around to her jeep and started ruffling through the papers in the glove box. "What's your name?" she said.

"Uh, Leonard," I said, quickly cursing myself for accidentally using my real name. Either the girl or the accident had distracted me. It didn't really matter which. That was the kind of slip-up I needed to avoid.

"Leonard what?" she called out.

"You know, it's really not that bad," I said, quickly coming to my senses. "We don't really need to bother with the insurance." Insurance meant paperwork, which meant problems. Leonard needed to stay as dead as my truck.

"It's not Leonard Harrison, is it?" she said, reappearing with insurance paperwork. "I knew a Leonard Harrison, and it's been a while but…"

Panic washed over me, told me to get up, to run, but a dumbfounded, "I, uh," was all I could muster.

"It is you, isn't it?" she laughed. " Oh God, Leonard…"

"Yes?"

"You don't recognize me, do you?" she prodded.

"Er, no, sorry," I mumbled.

"It's Daisy," she said. "Daisy Copeland."

And that's when I really started to panic.

"So, what are you doing here? Tell me everything," she said excitedly. Daisy had paid off the car dealer to take the truck back for scrap and then offered me a ride. She seemed completely at ease in the killing floor avenues, probably because her jeep had just proven itself collision worthy. Not that it put me at all at ease.

"I, um, I'm just…Well forget me, what are you doing here?"I said, gripping the door tightly. "You're the one who left without a word of warning. You never even wrote." Deflection was crucial as I'd only just now realized I didn't have answers to the kind of questions she was asking. I was supposed to be dead and Rob Ert's history was still a work in progress.

"Yeah, sorry about that," she said. "Really, it's sort of a long story and I'd rather not get into it."

"Sounds mysterious."

"Ridiculous is more like it," she said. "But really, I'd rather not. Not right now, anyhow. Maybe later? Over dinner?"

"Dinner?"The world was clinging dearly to the memory of Leonard Harrison. But I couldn't just leave. Who knew how that would end up? "Uh, yeah, sure. Dinner,"I said as if it had been my plan. Dinner with Daisy Copeland—this was a terrible idea.

"It's the least I can do after totaling your car," she said with a violent swerve.

"Well, yeah."

"Though, with the way people drive down here, you may be able to chalk it up as callus building."

"Emm, I see."

"Not that it makes it okay. Trust me, I'm going to make it up to you."

"Great."The combined fear of being found out and being in a second wreck in less than an hour was taking a serious toll on my vocabulary.

"Plus, I totally want to catch up, but I've got to run some errands first."

"Right. Errands. Great." Anything that would stop this car.

"Oh good. Where are you staying? I'll drop you off there and then pick you up around seven?"

"Actually, I—"

"Of course, what am I thinking? You just got here. You don't have a hotel yet, do you?"

"No."

"Well, I'm at The Continental, near the airport. Why don't you stay there? You can just use my room until I get back if you like."

I did not like. I did not like at all. In fact, that was the worst possible idea one could have considering the current situation and I wanted no part of it whatsoever. "Sure," I said.

"Great," Daisy chirped. "I know this great place in town, really authentic food. My parents were friends with the owners, used to take me there all the time. You're just going to love it. Fantastic empanadas."

"Mmm," I said, as my stomach acid sloshed the slalom. "Empanadas."

The Continental had been a nice hotel in the 1920s. It had the arches and balconies and scrollwork that had been hallmarks of post-colonial South American architecture. What it didn't have was a capable handyman to maintain it. The brightly painted plaster was cracked, both inside and out, and the floor wasn't entirely even. But if there was a place more suited to clandestine liaisons and keeping secrets, I couldn't dream it up. It was perfect for my purposes. It was comfortable and stylish, yet not the kind of place tourists would seek out. The staff seemed both sharp and disinterested, depending on what they were being paid for at the time. There was no room service.

Daisy had dropped me off here and gone off to do her errands. I'd decided to use the time to work on my backstory.

"Tired of empty American culture," I said to the wall. "Wanted to find real life, real people." No, too new-agey. "Double-major in Spanish and anthropology," I tried, but decided it was too temporary, too snooty, and too smart. I was skeptical I could single-major, or even minor in anything. I wasn't that smart, being here was proof of that. Truthfully, I wasn't even entirely sure what anthropologists studied that was different from archeologists. If the story was going to stick, I needed to expand my boundaries, really find the right fit. Peace Corps reject? Deadbeat dad? Fugitive Nazi? Nothing seemed right. There were too many loose ends. Too many unanswered questions. And even though I'd constructed an elaborate system of lies to orchestrate the illusion of my demise, I'd never really uttered them out loud or actively pushed them onto real people. I'd just let strangers believe what they wanted, which happened to best match my purposes. Lying to Daisy seemed somehow wrong.

No.

That wasn't it.

I realized I actually wanted to confess to her, tell her the whole thing, to have a single sympathetic ear, a genuine emotional connection to the world. I wanted someone that cared and it was her. We hadn't had much time together, but it had been meaningful. At least I thought it had, and it seemed like it had been to her as well. I wanted that back.

"Is it so wrong?" I asked the wall.

I realized that no, it wasn't. She was here in the archaic outlands of South America, so far off the parade route it didn't matter what I told her. Yes, I was a confirmed pauper, wanted for felony theft and presumed dead, a presumption that would likely result in fraud charges, should it be corrected. But so what? As long as my secret was here, it was still under wraps. I'd said there was nothing for me to go back for, but maybe it was more than that. Maybe there was something for me to stay here for as well. How many second chances do you get? Maybe I was just on a roll.

The rest of the city, which I saw out the window as we rocketed to the restaurant, had a feel similar to that of The Continental: glamour in decay. Everything was brightly painted oranges and blues, reds and yellows. Some streets were still cobbled, some were still muck. Strings of lights hung between buildings, illuminating sidewalk cafés where tuxedo clad servers meandered to and fro, occasionally serving, but mostly chatting. I couldn't deny the energy seeping from the warm night air in this place and it saddened me to think that unlike the glamorous decline of old Europe, the ruination of Argentina would not be slow and stylish. South American buildings lacked the staying power of marble construction.

"Is this your first time out of the states?" Daisy asked as we got out of the car.

"Yes."

"What do you think so far?"

"That we, Americans, don't really give the DMV enough credit for the services it provides."

"Oh, sorry," Daisy giggled. "The traffic must come as something of a shock. I probably should have slowed down a little. I was just so giddy. It's just, it's been so long."

"Yeah, I know. Ten years."

"You probably have so many questions," Daisy said sheepishly.

"Menu recommendations and such."

"You're funny," Daisy smiled, making me remember why I'd liked her so much.

I held open the gate to a café similar to those we'd passed on the drive. "After you."

She entered and waived at a waiter across the patio, who pointed to an open table. We sat at a corner table with a good view of the street.

The waiter set two menus on the table. I picked mine up, but Daisy didn't bother. "*Pupusas y empanadas para dos personas,*" she said. "You're not a vegetarian, are you, Leonard?"

"No."

"*Carne y puerco.*"

"Okey-dokey," he said in perfect English, scribbling it down and sauntering away lazily.

"You didn't order us squirrel or anything, did you?" I asked.

"Double portions. It's a specialty de la casa. Casa means house."

"I know what casa means," I said. "Just not much else."

"Sorry," Daisy smiled. "Just, this is weird isn't it?"

"You have no idea."

"Well, tell me then."

"Yeah…" I drawled, scrutinizing my place setting. "Uh, I've been, uh, thinking about that. About how to say some things. About what to say." Crap. I was having trouble even looking at her. My thumbs had started a wrestling match of their own free will and it was proving even more compelling a distraction than my paper placemat detailing the timeline of the Incan Empire. Explaining the whole thing about the debt, the faked death and being in hiding, it was a bit much for a second date. Third, if you count the time we bumped into each other at the corner store and I offered her some of my Slurpee, which I did for purposes of padding the books. Even though the vaunted third date is by reputation the one where it's generally perceived as acceptable to go "all the way," I felt that wasn't a reference to potentially incriminating yourself. Lacking any sort of baseball analogy to adapt the unabridged, sordid details of recent criminal enterprises into popular lore and dirty jokes, I was flying blind. Fifth date maybe?

"Actually, I think I better go first," Daisy said, interrupting me as I pondered the appropriate etiquette. "'Cause it's going to be weird and I don't want to lose my steam here. I haven't talked about this yet and I think I need to get used to it."

"Uh, okay," I said, relieved that she was concerned about having the weirder of our stories.

"Just do it, go right ahead and…" she mumbled, trying to psych herself up. "This is really hard to say. I'm so afraid of…"

"Daisy?" I reached out to touch her shoulder to make sure she was all right. Her head snapped up the instant I made contact.

"Right, sorry," I said, recoiling. "I shouldn't have done—"

"My parent were drug dealers," she spit out. "There, I said it."

"Oh, that's? Huh…" Certainly didn't see that one coming. "So, what are you telling me here?" I asked. Daisy didn't say anything, just blanked out for a few seconds. "Daisy?" I almost reached for her shoulder again, but didn't have the nerve.

"God…" she said, coming around. "I can't believe how easy that was to say."

"It didn't seem that way," I said. "You kind of freaked me out there, with the hand and the shoulder, and the—"

"Just opened up and said it. Drug dealers," she rolled on.

"They were drug dealers and we had to skip town." She wasn't even really talking to me, just letting it go. "And God, how I hated them for it. For making me leave home, you. Jesus. It just keeps flowing. I'm afraid to stop since I've never told anyone before. You couldn't know." Daisy trailed off. "Sorry. It sort of petered out there. But I was really cooking for a minute or so."

"Yeah, you were." She understood having to go on the run. Maybe this wouldn't work out so bad after all.

"What kind of drugs are we talking about?"

"Why? Do you not want to talk to me anymore? 'Cause I'm not them, I swear." She was babbling, terrified.

I leaned forward and spoke gently. "I was just asking. It seemed like the right thing to do. I'm sort of lost here."

"Yeah, me too."

I reached out slowly and took Daisy's hand. More importantly, she let me. And she smiled. God how I'd loved that smile. Even when it had been sandwiched by younger, pudgier cheeks. Now was the time to lay it all out. Everything. Fraud. Theft. Improperly disposing of motor oil. Secrets laid bare. There wouldn't be a better opportunity.

"I—"

"It was just pot you know," she said. "It was barely anything. I mean, pot, outside of the government, who really cares?"

"The anti-pot people, I suppose."

"But you don't, right?"

"No."

"I was so mad at them for so long. The way they tore me away from everything, forced me on the road. They probably could have turned evidence and gotten off on probation. Maybe a tiny little jail sentence. They were such cowards. Instead, we came here and got stuck."

"Huh?"

"It's hard being a fugitive, you know," she said.

"I couldn't imagine." Or at least, I hadn't.

"And doing that to your child…Oh well. It's done now."

"What do you mean?"

"Leonard, are you sure you're not going to judge me?" Daisy looked genuinely worried and I couldn't fathom why.

"Does my opinion really matter that much?" I asked. "I mean, we haven't even seen each other in ten years. Surely—"

"I haven't really seen anyone in ten years, Leonard," she interrupted.

"Really?"

"We came into the city occasionally for supplies but mostly, we've been in the mountains on a ranch. No one else around but farmhands. I mean, I learned Spanish, but there wasn't much to talk about. It was so dull. I just…I just couldn't take it anymore. I wanted a normal life."

"There's nothing wrong with that," I said, trying to sound consoling through my growing confusion.

"So I turned them in."

"Huh."

"But I had to," she pleaded. "I mean, there were so many reasons. There's the damage it did to their lives, the money problems, health risks…No one should live on the run like that. It was really just about pride for them." I mumbled something in exclamation, but having built a verbal head of steam, Daisy just plowed over it unconcerned. "They're probably not even going to get in that much trouble. Misdemeanor charges and expired statutes of limitations and all. It was never that serious. I think maybe, they just wanted to run away."

"Imagine that."

"I know. Cowards." She was starting to sound bitter. Angry. Vindictive.

"Totally," I mumbled. "Cowards."

"They're mad at me now, but it won't last. Doesn't matter anyhow. It's done. They're in jail waiting to be extradited. And I can finally go home."

And that's when it hit. Panic. Dread. Horror. All manner of words used to advertise Vincent Price movies. "You're going home?" I stammered.

"Yeah, it's so weird. I was going to look you up, and then there you were. I ran into you as I was going to sell my jeep. Since I'm heading back to the states in a few days, I don't need it anymore."

"Isn't that funny?" I coughed.

"I know. Just imagine what everyone back home will think when I tell them."

"They'll never believe it." I had to get out of this ASAP.

"Do you see the old gang much anymore? Jenny? Shawn?"

"I think Shawn went to school at Dartmouth, but I don't really know. I'm sort of dead to them."

"I guess you'd grow apart in ten years. I'm sort of frozen in that time and all."

Now is a good time. Insult her and disappear into the night. "Yeah. But here we are."

"God, it feels good to get this all out, to talk like this. I hate secrets so much."

Now. Call her fat. Whorish. Diseased. Anything to make her hate you so much she'll never think of you again. "Yeah," I said. "Totally. Secrets are way out."

"I wouldn't know," Daisy laughed, looking at me in a way that made me feel equal parts tingly and panicked. "We weren't really up on the latest trends on the ranch.

"I suppose you wouldn't be," I said awkwardly.

"Oh God," she laughed. "Here I am babbling about me. I'm so excited about seeing someone I know, and speaking English no less, I'm being rude. What about you? It's been ten years, tell me everything." Daisy's chin was on her hands, elbows on the table, poised for listening.

Why was I still here? Why fake your death and then commit suicide? Was I really that lonely and pathetic? I was about to open my mouth and explain that, in fact, I was. But that's when the food arrived. I hadn't seen deus ex machina on menu, but apparently it too was a specialty de la casa.

Eating would give me a few extra minutes to plot, and I did it slowly to give myself extra time, mostly just pushing the food around on my plate, eventually abandoning it altogether and letting Daisy pick off my plate, her last South American empanadas. But afterwards, I told her the truth about what I was doing in Argentina: earning a double major in Spanish and anthropology.

After dinner, we drove through the Argentine streets to a beautifully dilapidated promenade aglow with lamps and children's fireworks. Drummers and guitarists busked as we strolled past, soaking up every bit of South American nightlife, me for the first time and Daisy for the last. Just past the bead stand, near a trio of hand drummers, Daisy grabbed my hand to keep me from getting run down by a passing bicyclist. My heart didn't skip a beat so much as accent one when he whizzed past, melting into the darkened jumble as swiftly as he had emerged from it. And even though he was gone and I was safe, I didn't let go of her hand. I clenched it tighter and guided it to her side.

I didn't want to let go because I knew as soon as I did, she would be gone and this wonderful feeling of wholeness, of being worthwhile, the one I'd gone to such lengths to find, would also vanish. And with it, my cover and my freedom should I ever emerge from the middle of nowhere to see what was playing at the movies at the edge of nowhere. It wasn't fair. Not only had we been torn apart the first time, setting us both on our course to misery, but the odds us being reunited like we had bordered on fate. I'd never been religious, but even I knew that this wasn't the kind of thing to be approached lightly, to squander. And just then, as the first bead of sweat passed from my palm to hers, I knew the solution.

"Stay here," I said to Daisy.

"What?" she laughed, then tugged on my hand to urge me along. "Come on, I want to see the dancers down the street."

"I'm serious. Don't go. Stay here with me. Be my research assistant. There's nothing for you there."

Now she stopped, solemnly looking me in the face. "Don't you think that's for me to decide?"

"I didn't mean anything by it, just…"

"Just what?"

"Just, well, it's been a long time. America's gone downhill," I offered. "That's why I'm here."

"I thought it was for school."

Fuck…That's right. "Well, yeah, but I could have studied at home," I quickly lied, still unaware of what my faux-anthropological focus was. "Study was an excuse for escape."

"Why do people always need an excuse? Can't we just decide that we want to do something and do it? Do we really need to create elaborate deceptions to justify it? Isn't it okay just to want something?"

"Like how you want to go home?"

"Yes." Daisy's face suddenly darkened. "I suddenly don't feel so well," she said. "I'd think I'd like to go…"

This time, my heart really did stop. "Why?" I blurted out. "Just because I want you to stay? Because I don't want to lose you again?"

"No, just—"

"It's so damned unfair, you have no idea—"

"No, Leonard, that's not it—"

But it was pointless for her to try. Words were pouring out that were only embarrassing, not awkward and self-destructive. But they were bare and raw and real, about feelings and second chances and taking back what life had taken from us. I was determined she would hear every word of it, rather than undermine it with minutiae and protestations. This was a rant that could bring the world to its knees.

But right as it reached its apex, when my eloquence was at a career high and polysyllabic gems were gushing to freedom in glorious grammatically correct spurts of poetry, she doubled over and barfed, heaving up chunks of empanadas and Argentine side dishes all over my shoes and the surrounding area. I was stunned, but as soon as I realized what was happening, I grabbed Daisy's chestnut curls and held them back from her face while she finished filling up the cracks in the cobbled streets for a three-foot radius around me—a barf shadow.

"God, I'm sorry, you were actually sick," I groaned. "I'm so stupid, I didn't know, I thought…"

"It's okay," she huffed. "It's…" And then a brief encore, followed by a series of heavy breaths aimed at the street.

I squeezed her hands for support. "Are you okay now?" It seemed like her stomach had exhausted its ammunition.

"Did you really mean all that stuff you said?" she said quietly.

"Are you kidding?" I laughed. "You ruined my shoes. But look where it happened." I gestured towards the shoe stand not twenty feet away. "What is that, if not fate?"

"I really missed you, Leonard," Daisy said quietly.

"I really missed you too."

"But, can we just go back to the hotel please? I really don't feel well."

"Sure," I said and put my arm around her to help her back to the car, not caring one bit that everyone else on the promenade was staring at the two fat, waddling gringos covered in vomit. It was the best moment of my life.

The elation lasted through the ride home, the trip up the stairs and into the room, through brushing our teeth and helping Daisy to bed. It magnified when I realized I'd never actually booked a room and she told me to just stay in hers. Even more when I climbed into bed with her and she squirmed into position in my arms, her fever sweat mixing with its nervous cousin seeping from my every pore. It was an all-consuming happiness that any clearheaded person could see wasn't sustainable. But being there, experiencing it firsthand was like moving so fast that nothing was real, an abstract blur of colors that couldn't be understood as real or logical or imminent. Only as garbled slush that wasn't worth examining. It transcended reality, so long as it didn't crash into it headlong anyhow.

That happened just after Daisy fell asleep and I realized I'd asked her to stay, but she'd never agreed to it. Meaning she was still leaving tomorrow. And even if she wasn't, my tapestry of lies was poorly woven and itching to unravel. I wasn't enrolled in the university and hadn't specified what exactly I was going to be researching in order to fake it. As I didn't know the first thing about Spanish or anthropology and wouldn't be able to learn enough about either quick enough to maintain the ruse, the truth was primed for its big, second act appearance. I loved her. At least, I was pretty sure that was what this feeling was. But I was a liar, a thief, a renegade and not even in any sort of romantic Errol Flynn kind of way. I was every bit as much a failure in my attempts at being an outlaw as I was at being a square—and every bit the coward on top.

The thoughts running through my head weren't of baring my soul to the woman I was pretty sure I loved and hoping that we in fact had a strong enough connection for her to accept me with all my flaws; they were of breaking her parents out of jail, of calling bomb threats into the airport, or once again orchestrating the illusion of my demise. I even considered smothering her in her sleep, though only for an instant. But that instant was enough to make it clear that I didn't deserve her.

My pathetic attempts to save my own neck were another example of the life that had lead me to this end, the one I'd thought I could shed simply by running away. I'd made the mistake of thinking the things in my life, the ones I was so adamant about leaving behind, or not even having in the first place, could actually be discarded. But I'd made the error of not understanding that they weren't necessarily external, that it wasn't just parents or baseball cards, or villas in the south of

France that you abandoned, so much as the feelings you get from those things. As long I cared about the taste of cheap diner coffee, or the warm spring breeze that graced my back porch in April, about the sound a needle makes when it touches down on a turntable, or the ache in my chest when I thought of Daisy—Leonard Harrison would be alive and kicking, no matter what name he went by. Clothes did not make the man, they only marketed him to others.

The thought that I could choose to leave myself behind was beyond arrogance, and Daisy's furor with her parents was now vividly clear. I could never make this right. Staying here with her would certainly result in the loss of my skin, which is what I deserved for such being such a damned fool. But worse, it would just bring more pain into her life, the pain she'd just taken such drastic steps to heal. I thought I loved her and I wanted to suck her back into a life on the run? No. It was wrong. There was only one course of action to be taken. Leave, right now. Get up and walk out the door, never look back. Maybe join a monastery. I'd almost believed in fate, or God, or something for a few minutes in front of the shoe stand, so why not?

Why not.

Why not…

The answer was because I'd have to go through the physical act of doing it. I was too weak, too cowardly, to run away.

I wrapped my arms tightly around Daisy's plump middle, lamenting the wonderfully soft comfort of her skin as I cried myself to sleep.

I woke with a jolt. Something was wrong; I was still here. I'd hoped to wake up somewhere else, that sleep would wipe the slate clean and my life would be the dream. Given recent events, it was debatable which state was more logically disorienting anyhow.

No, that wasn't it. It was a scratching noise at the door, like someone was messing with the lock, potentially breaking in. Should have expected it in a classy joint like this. I slipped quietly out of bed, leaving my pants off for maximum effect, and snuck to the door, dramatically throwing it open and yelling, "Ah-HAH!" to confront the aspiring bandits.

A member of the hotel cleaning staff stared back at me, my maniac's grin and my pasty white skin and underpants, clearly terrified. It was possible that *ah-hah* translated into something truly fearsome in Spanish, as his eyes were wide with panic. He blubbered something in Spanish and backed away from the door, pulling his cart behind him. For a moment, he almost looked familiar, but then he was gone. I hadn't even realized a hotel like this had staff.

Though the rest of the day was destined to go poorly and I'd woken up feeling off, this was too funny not to share. I closed the door and hopped back to the bed to relate the whole story to Daisy. Oh sure, it had probably woken her up and she'd seen the whole thing, but still, I'd never had a funny story to share with someone in bed before and I didn't know if that opportunity would ever present itself again. So it was now or never.

I clumsily flopped down next to Daisy giggling, and shook her shoulder to get her attention. "Oh my God, Daisy, wake up," I said. But she didn't move. So I shook her again, harder, this time noticing her shoulder felt cold. "Daisy? Hey, are you all right?"

Nothing.

Panic hit me like a taser, a dense paralyzing fear pumping out from my heart in waves.

Already knowing what to expect, but in no way ready for it, I cautiously reached out to her face and turned it towards me. Daisy's head flopped over limply, eyes glassy and a small dried stain of muck on her chin.

"FUCK!" I shouted, leaping up. "Fuck, fuck, fuck, fuck FUCK!" Through no intent of my own, I found was doing mad laps across the room, an emotional slash and burn. Thoughts, implications, questions and consequences were all flashing through my mind, a jigsawed mess. Only one thing was clear— this was very, very bad.

I had to go. Now. The rest was details.

Go, but first get dressed. Then go, but first grab my things and stuff them back into my bag. Go now, but what about fingerprints? Go now, stop wiping things clean; someone will notice the toilet paper. Don't flush it, just get out, get out, get out. Can't you hear me, Leonard, GET OUT!

Yes, yes, yes, I'm going.

I'm out the door and down the hall, one foot at the top of the stairs, walking calmly not running, though panting heavily, my shirt untucked.

If only there had been time to kiss her goodbye.

I'm going, going, going. Stopping for nothing. All I had to do was get through the lobby without freaking out and I'd be fine. South America was chaos incarnate and once I was out of the controlled environment I could run down the street screaming and pulling my hair out and no one would care. Gringos had to be crazy to come here.

I took a moment to compose myself and catch my breath,

then stepped cautiously out of the stairwell and into the lobby, walking as swiftly as I dared.

The cleaner who'd woken me up was at the lobby desk, talking to the clerk, both of them eyeballing me. I could feel it.

"*Señor*," the clerk called, waving me over. "*Uno momento.*"

I broke into a run, a mad dash for the door and freedom.

The cleaner sprinted after me and the clerk vaulted over the desk to do the same, both of them following me out into the heat of the Argentine midday. We bumped and weaved in and out of the crowds, breathing heavy and holding nothing back, because I knew where I'd seen that cleaner before. He'd been our waiter the night before, at the restaurant Daisy's parents had frequented. Where I'd given up my portion of the food that had poisoned her. How could I have been so stupid to think this was about love?

It was destiny that I encountered Daisy. Not to reunite us, but to complete my isolation from the world. Sure, I was running for my life now. But when I got away, it wasn't just that I had nothing to return to Argentina for, it was that without Daisy I had nothing to return anywhere for and I could truly start fresh. Daisy was dead and I was now truly free.

Lungs taxed, lacquered in sweat, I turned a corner and ran through an alley to the next boulevard where I merged anonymously with a bustling crowd on their way here or there—the cleaner, the clerk and Leonard Harrison all left in the alley behind me.

THE SANDWICH CLUB

My feet hurt, which is a good thing, since the pain keeps me from noticing the headache I'm sure is buried in there somewhere, subtly drilling a hole in my brain, waiting for the proper moment to hit me with a stroke and kill me instantly. I may die, but at least I won't notice it coming.

"Enrique, do you have that sandwich ready for table four yet?" I'm not even speaking at this point. It's just exasperation venting out of my mouth.

"Call me Franz."

"I am not going to call you Franz."

"But it has such a nice ring to it…It would be much better for my film career."

"Enrique—"

"Franz," he interrupts.

"Do you have the order or not?"

"Nope. Still waiting on fries."

I walk away quickly, hoping to jump-start the pain in my feet again. I need something to distract me from Enrique's perpetual good cheer. Pain will have to do. There must be someone in this place that needs a drink or something, some sort of time-killer. Anything that will give my throbbing feet enough time to wrest control of my irritation with Enrique and make it their own. I just don't get it. He's worked here for long enough now, he should be able to do his job in a timely fashion and be miserable about it like the rest of us. Some people just like to work against the grain, I guess.

Table four—the loud ones. They want that sandwich and I have no real explanation for its tardiness. Better to steer clear of them. They seem like ass-pinchers anyhow, a bunch of fuck-ing throwbacks to the '20s just out from the bar on the corner. But in this joint, what are you gonna do?

Number nine—a happy looking couple. That's definitely not what I want to deal with right now. I'd give them the old internationally recognized, long distance, diner gesture of holding the coffeepot up in their general direction, but they wouldn't notice. I may actually have to go over there, but not yet. I'm just not ready to face bliss.

Instead, I turn towards table one—much more my style. She's been here for a half-hour now, fondling that menu and nursing her refills so she won't get too wired. Too much coffee will just keep her up to stew tonight. She's checked her watch more than I check the clock. At this point we both know he's not coming, but we both also have the tact not to bring it up. I know that's the table for me. Misery loves company. But number four's not having it; wild arm motions and hollers beckon me over. I know I have to go. It's is my penance for Enrique messing up their order. That's one more thing I can hold against him tonight.

I try to posture myself in a way that dissuades chattiness, a way that says I am in a hurry without me actually having to say that I just don't want to talk to them. Weight on the left leg, right foot pointing out, coffee-holding elbow resting on my hip and my chin on my chest, slightly cocked to the side so I have to roll my eyes to look at them.

"You guys need some more coffee?"

The answers come quickly, like they have been rehearsing.

"No."

"I'm fine."

"None for me, thanks."

The last one shakes his head. Apparently I'm someone you gesture at, not talk to.

"Say there, Dollface," I'm Fine, says to me. "What's your name?" He appears to be body-language-illiterate in addition to being a jerk.

"Well," I say pointing at my breast pocket, "my nametag says Dottie, but most folks just call me Frank."

No and None For Me Thanks snicker at I'm Fine. That should teach him to call me Dollface. But he just eats it up that I can play the game.

"All right Frank, it's good to meet you." A hand is extended. "My name is Benny."

I switch the coffeepot to my left hand and limply shake his.

"All right! We have hand shake!" No says, punctuating the comment by thrusting his fist in the air.

They seem ecstatic, like they just finished blowing each other in the bathroom. That would explain the slightly disheveled-looking good cheer anyhow. But not the hunger…

"We like to be acquainted with the staff of a place, ya know? Greases palms, helps to get you regular status," Benny continues.

"Right…" If I were smart, I would walk away right now. I just know this is going to end with him trying to give me a hotel key or something lame like that.

"We're doing research right now," None For Me Thanks says. "We need to make sure we find the right place to become regulars at. It's easy to find a place you like, but when trying to attain regular status, it is key to make sure that they like you as well."

"So…any tips?" Benny says. "Comments? You're the expert, how are we doing as customers?"

Benny, No and None For Me Thanks are all staring at me intently. Head Shaker is more interested in scowling at his dry white toast.

"Well, I'll go in back and cross the extra spit off that sandwich you ordered," I say. "Is that a good start?"

"We have achieved no spit status!" No hollers with the fist once again in the air. They love it. I don't.

"Works for us," Benny says, apparently releasing me from my servitude as court jester.

I back away. During that brief period when my dad insisted I play sports, he told me to always keep your eye on the ball.

"That sandwich will be up for you in a minute."

Table two still looks like they are all sugar and no coffee, and therefore, not in need of my services. So I stroll over to number one. She seems like a kindred spirit.

"More coffee, hon?" Nothing butters up a mark like calling 'em hon. Show a little empathy at the right time and the tips roll in.

She leans forward over the table and looks down into her cup. Her short black hair reaches down towards the table and forms a protective umbrella over the mug. It's like she's moving in slow motion. That is fine. There's no rush. As long as she can stay there pondering the water line, both of us will have a distraction from the reality of this diner: he's not coming and I'm never leaving.

Apparently satisfied with the assessment that more coffee is needed, big soft eyes peer up at me as if they are asking permission. I feel hypnotized and suddenly long to shrink down and crawl into her eyes to live in the pupils. Suddenly, I feel very silly standing there, like the cover of a Supertramp album or something. I really wish she'd say something. Calling her hon was a dirty thing to do on my part. I really am a monster.

Luckily progress is the enemy of enlightenment. The moment is shattered by the air-splitting tone of the order bell.

"Sandwich for number four," Enrique bellows.

A sarcastic round of applause erupts from Benny and company.

"They're playing my song," I say, immediately regretting it.

Looking down at the ground, I quickly fill her cup with coffee and make my escape.

I swoop down on the order window to pick up the plate. There's about an hour left on this shift. But if Enrique starts again, it could seem more like three. The squeak of my shoes gives me away.

"Dottie," Enrique calls out. Walk away. Pretend you didn't hear him. He's just talking to the back of your head. "Hey, Dottie."

That was close. But he'll be back, no doubt of that. I have other worries now. Into the lion's den, so they say.

"All right guys, here you go. One grilled cheese, add peanut butter and bananas."

I put it on the table and get out as quickly as possible. Unfortunately though, I have to go somewhere. Number one's out. Just escaped number four. All right nine, you thorn in my ass, here I come.

Wielding my coffeepot like a shield, I make my approach.

They each have one elbow resting on the table. Looking directly at each other as they chat away. Their forearms arch over the table, meeting with intertwined fingertips. He has one hand in his coat pocket. They don't see me approach.

"How is everything over here?" I ask. They stop talking and turn to me. I suddenly know what comedians mean when they talk about a tough room.

"I'm fine," she says.

"Some more coffee would be great," he says, humoring me. I hear the words and get the message. I'm an outsider at this table. A rabble-rouser. An invading horde. Call it what you like, I shouldn't be there.

I start to pour. He gives me the *that's enough* hand signal almost immediately.

"Club sandwich, side salad for number nine," Enrique announces. All right Dottie, you're on.

"Well, that's for you," I say with a smile. "I guess I'll be right back then." Good news feet, you're not alone anymore. Now my face hurts too.

He's waiting for me this time. A small part of me wants to believe that the order was really just a trap. But the plate in the window would seem to point in the direction of irrational paranoia. It doesn't matter. My soul has been rented for fifty more minutes and I have to deal with it.

"Dottie," Enrique says. "How about Pierre?"

"Who?"

"Me. For me, Pierre."

"What are you talking about?"

"How, about, Pierre? You know, for my film name. You know, I am starting school next month and I'm trying to plan ahead. The name's the most important thing. It's people's first judgement of you. So, what do you think?"

I pick up the order and hold the sandwich out at arms length, pointing at "Pierre" as if this somehow will give my words more impact. "I hate it," I say as I walk away. I don't even know why. There isn't really anywhere to go.

Number nine is empty. A twenty dollar bill and a small black jewelry box are sitting on the table. One of these is a hell of a tip. And now I have a club sandwich.

I drop the salad off at number two and try not to look. "On the house," I say. She thanks me, but I wonder if she meant it.

I want to go eat this sandwich, or at least wrap it up for later. That might manage to kill anywhere from five to twenty minutes depending on how I work things. But Benny seems to have other plans for me. Once again, the wild arm motions are calling.

"What do you need Benny?" The sandwich I brought them

is sitting untouched in the middle of the table with a meticulous arrangement of sugar packets surrounding the plate.

"We have first name recognition!" No blubbers. "This is very good. We don't actually need anything per se, except perhaps answers."

"Well, it's good to have goals, Benny," I say.

"That's a repeat of the first name clause. Looking good," No says to nobody in particular. I imagine seeing him get run down by a car.

I try to make the segue to my escape. "But, I have to—"

"Frank, do you realize the historical significance of this sandwich?" Benny cuts me off at the pass.

A moment of clarity, the truth comes into perspective: this table is the point of no return. It is now easier to go through to the end than it is to escape. And worse, I'm starting to feel the same way about my entire life. Chin up kid, you can get through this.

"Only that this is the first time someone has rearranged the menu in this particular way," I say, hoping to avoid the explanation that I know is coming anyway.

"According to legend," Benny says, "it was Elvis's favorite food." He gestures with his hands as if he were conjuring up spirits and leans forward over the table like there might be enemy spies in the vicinity. I half expect him to hold a flashlight up to his chin and tell everyone to gather close. "Some say he ate one after every performance. And if the promoter didn't agree to provide one, then he wouldn't play."

And some say, on a stormy night, you can still hear him rummaging through the fridge at Graceland.

"Well, except for the cheese part," No added. "That was our personal touch."

"You have to tie it in to a normal menu somehow," None For Me Thanks says.

Benny looks at me very seriously as he takes a bite of the sandwich. Then he passes it and each one takes a bite until it reaches Head Shaker who puts it down on the plate, without sampling it's gooey innards. I'm starting to like him. More so when I notice Benny's irritation.

"Now, Greg here," Benny says, pointing at Head Shaker, "has an order of dry white toast, just like Elwood Blues. And Scott," (The artist previously known as No, I thought to myself) "has fried chicken and a Coke, like Joliet Jake."

This is worse than I thought. I'm almost wishing he would pull out a hotel key so this would be over with.

"It took awhile to find a place with the right menu to fit our needs. But, we think that…"

"You forgot the burger." I want to clap my hands over my mouth. God help me, why did I just say that?

"Well, actually," Benny says sheepishly (he thought I wouldn't notice I guess), "Jack just wanted a burger. But we figured that probably covers Ted Nugent. Which is better than the original plan of biting the head off of a dove like Ozzy." He pauses for laughter. When none comes, his eyes dart quickly around the table to see if there is even a glimmer of support for his failed joke. There isn't. "The thing is, Frank, I want you to look around this table and remember what you see. Look around and remember these faces. 'Cause one day, you're going to be—"

"Just shut up Benny," Greg interrupts. Head Shaker finally speaks. It's something of a historic occasion. "This is so fucking stupid."

No and None For Me Thanks turn their heads. Suddenly, the table has turned into a political hotbed.

"Leave this poor girl alone. She's just trying to earn a living and you're acting like she's here for your amusement."

"That is so not true! I just want to establish an identity for The Groove Pigeons, Greg. The four of us coming to the same place after every gig, to eat like our heroes? This is the kind of stuff that people will be interested in for interviews. You know? We're not upsetting her. This is the human angle behind the fame, stuff that people can relate to about being fans ourselves. She can understand that. It's so sad you can't see the bigger picture."

"The bigger picture? There isn't even a small picture to enlarge yet! Jack is still learning minor scales and Scott doesn't even own a matching pair of drumsticks! What the fuck are you talking about?"

"You just don't have any faith. That's your problem Greg. I know everything will work out."

"Oh, grow up," Greg says. "The only thing eating this crap will do for us is a maybe an endorsement deal with Rolaids. I told you this was a stupid idea and I'm fucking done with it."

Now this is getting interesting. But if I don't use the launch window provided, I may not be able to escape. So I start backing away, slowly at first, but then up to full speed. The argument has consumed their attentions. They don't notice me. Truth be told, I barely even notice me. I keep getting farther away until I find myself in the walk-in fridge, sitting on the floor and gripping my club sandwich with both hands, slightly fearful it may float free of gravity if I let go.

Breathing deep, I cautiously loosen my stranglehold until the food rests lightly on my finger tips. They delicately caress my treasure. It's all I really have in this place. I'm twenty-nine years old. I live alone in a shitty apartment in a lousy neighborhood. I slave away here daily, not knowing why I don't just walk out the door and never come back. This is my sad solitary life, laid out on the shelves in front of me: boxes of cabbage, frozen hamburger patties, industrial sized containers of yellow mustard and buckets full of tapioca pudding. Singular, low quality food items filed away in a giant cooler in a lousy diner. Their only hope in life that someone might notice them on the menu and draft them into service; that they be brought together with other ingredients to be part of something, something with order and purpose. Something that people desired enough to actually order and pay for, not just another unwanted carrot to be tossed into the compost bin and rot. This sandwich is to be my salvation. It's like a picture on an ad, perfectly sliced and layered, but heavy with purpose. I open wide and slide the club inside of my mouth, biting slowly, feeling every pore of the bread with my tongue, feeling the lettuce snap and the bacon crunch. I am in control of my own life. This sandwich is at my mercy.

Then, the door opens and Enrique pokes his head in. My mouth opens back up, releasing my prey to be recaptured at a later date. It just wasn't meant to be.

"All right, I've got it, Dottie. How about Bjorn?"

"How about not?"

"I don't get it, Dottie. You haven't liked any of the names."

"So? Why does it matter if I like them or not? It doesn't involve me."

"I just wanted your input and all. This is a big decision and I value your opinion."

"You want my opinion?"

"Yes."

"Okay…Enrique."

"Bjorn."

"ENRIQUE! You're fucking Hispanic!"

"Yeah…"

"How many Hispanics have you ever known named Bjorn or Franz or Pierre?"

"Well…but…it's film you know. Maybe that's what could make it work, the ambiguity. People would look at me on TV and say, 'I don't get it. He looks kind of brown, but his name is Bjorn. Where is he from?' There could be a whole *People Magazine* article about trying to guess my nationality…which my agent will keep a closely guarded secret. Wouldn't that be great?"

I grit my teeth and say nothing.

"Well, I need to pick one and those are the choices, so if you had to pick between those three, even though you don't like them very much, which one would it be?"

I exhale loudly. It is all I can muster right now. I wish I had the ability to actually blow steam out of my nose, like a cartoon bull about to charge. Or a smoke bomb. Hell, I'd settle for a button or a bumper sticker. Anything that might make people steer clear and let me stew in my own misery instead of theirs for a change. Somehow my half-assed, outdated weaponry of heavy breathing and biting sarcasm doesn't seem up to par.

"Okay, well, just think about it and tell me later okay?" Enrique says, backing out of the door.

The click of the latch on the door resonates off the metal walls. A thud so powerful it almost seems like a divine act. It hits me like a gunshot, right through the heart. And I know, really know, that I am alone in here. I throw my sandwich as hard as I can against the wall. It can't even save me now.

Running—the first refuge of a coward. Color me yellow, the door is calling. I know that leaving won't actually help anything. I'll just be out on the street tomorrow begging for another job no better than this one, and there won't be any money coming in for that humiliation. It's not escape; it's deferment. But if I don't do something, I will have to look myself in the mirror every morning and know that once again, I was too cowardly to chicken out. If I don't go now, I never will. I know that. Visions of myself thirty years from now play in my head. Shuffling from table to table in the same rumpled uniform, telling the customers that Bjorn Hernandez used to work here, and wishing that some man here from out of town on "business" might flash a hotel key my way. The first step will be the hardest. But it's like quitting smoking; if you can make it over that first hurdle, you can go the distance.

The shelves in the walk-in are cold to the touch. I worry that my finger might frost to the surface as I pull myself up. Even a little obstacle like that could be enough to break my resolve. Now standing, I take a step forward and my fingers break loose from the food-laden shelves. That was supposed to be the hard part. But I find that the second step is no easier, or the third or fourth.

By the time I have my coat on and I walk into the dining room things are a little smoother. I attribute it to my growing sense of detachment. Watching yourself do something is much less compromising than actually taking part in the act.

Bjorn is yelling at me from the kitchen. Benny is looking sour, as are No and None For Me Thanks. Greg is gone. That black jewelry box is still on the table.

I stop at her table but make sure not to look at her. I'm already a monster. What does it matter anymore?

"He's not coming, hon."

"Excuse me?"

"He's not coming. We're closing in half an hour. It's just time to accept it." I say it with a sense of finality and turn to the door. There's no way back now.

I walk out the door and feel the cool night air wash over my face and the first inklings of goosebumps seeding on the back of my neck.

A cab pulls up to the diner as I raise the collar on my coat. An older looking man gets out in a hurry and pays the cabby, telling him to keep the change so he won't have to wait. The cabby yells, "Good luck!" as the man rushes inside to Hon's table and picks her up in a grandiose sweeping hug.

Good call, Dottie. You're really batting a thousand tonight.

Greg is standing on one foot, leaning against the building and smoking a cigarette. He looks a little like a poster of James Dean I saw once.

He pulls the cigarette out of his mouth and turns it around, pointing it in my direction. I walk over and take the cigarette from him, inhaling slowly and deeply, trying to feel every single harmful chemical doing its separate damage as it winds its way through my airways.

"I'm really sorry about those guys," Greg says. "Just sometimes Benny doesn't realize what an ass he can be."

I hand the cigarette back to Greg and let the smoke wisp lazily out of my nose.

"They're really good guys at heart you know, just…They can be really insensitive sometimes." He takes another drag to give himself time to ponder his next statement. Right as he is at the climax of his inhalation, his lungs full of death and his mind pregnant with dialogue, before he has the chance to release either—I grab him by the collar and lunge forward pressing my lips hard into his. He stands awkwardly balanced, holding his breath as I keep him hostage under liplock and key. I hold him until he can take it no longer and the smoke starts to leak out the unsealed corners of our kiss. It travels down my cheeks and around my neck, warming both.

I open my eyes and take one last good look before letting go. His eyes are closed, his face pale and relaxed. My fingers release him from bondage, then straighten his jacket and collar, repairing the dishevelment they caused. Satisfied with my work, I turn and walk away. There is a diner down the street and I could really use a club sandwich.

DEBATE IS A
MANY-SPLENDORED THING

We are dead people. Ironic, since most debaters will speak unprompted at length about how alive the sport makes them feel. But as per their training, they aren't looking at the whole picture, only cherry-picking the details that support their case. They omit the way we purge our emotions and personal truths to slip more effectively into whatever position we are handed, no matter how repugnant. We tell each other proud stories about the time we defended child sweatshop labor to a packed house and dream of the day we get to defend Nazi eugenics programs just for the thrill, the dare, the challenge. If all we have to do is cast off silly, societal, preconceived notions of humanity or morality to do it, then good riddance. Empty shells are available to be filled with whatever the case requires. Hollowing ourselves out completely only means more available space, thereby increasing the likelihood of victory, the only thing that matters. Debate is life, and outside of it, we are inert wooden puppets without masters.

This is why I'm so thrown that Sofie just said she loved me. I truthfully don't know if either of us is even capable of genuinely feeling anything—let alone something so impractical as love—or if this is just the logical position for her to take in the circumstances. In the same way that she would insist that for-profit HMOs are essentially blackmail of the sick and dying when on the side of universal health care, and that any universal plan will inevitably lead to rationing of health care when against, she now says she loves me because she has snuggled her head into my arm pit, because the soft strands of light from the window play across our naked bodies in a way that could be described as romantic, because we are thick with musky sweat and our sexual exploits have knocked over half the contents of our hotel room, and because we have been doing this dance for the last six tournaments. Saturday mornings we glare at one another across the briefing, a power-point presentation backlighting the host coach as they drone the rules we all know and ignore. Saturday afternoons, we meet in a basement lecture hall to cite statistics, quote philosophers and call each other hypocrites. Saturday nights we stay at the catered tournament dinner just long enough to find out who will be advancing to the elimination rounds the next day, then feign tiredness to our classmates and sneak away to my hotel room.

Emotional attachments are verboten. We are intellectual soldiers defending the flags of rival universities and everything that we do falls under that umbrella of values. Debate is life. Without it, we are nothing.

And though it lacks three clearly outlined points with evidence supporting a thesis, *I love you* is every bit the proposition case.

Now I must somehow respond.

It should be easy. I've spent years training myself to be able to respond to anything instantly, to be an intellectual boy scout: always prepared. My mind is already racing. Preparing refutation. Opposition lines. Counterproposals.

One: That you say you love me is an unsupported claim. No evidence was presented to establish its accuracy, especially as love is an unprovable, intangible concept and there is no conclusive proof that it even exists.

Two: Love is an ambiguous term that comes in many varieties. And as you've failed to define love, how can you be sure that you actually do love me?

Three: You clearly don't love me because you slept with Dave at the Yale tournament.

But all these options carry the potential for violent blowback. As do their less confrontational, standardized counterparts.

Thanks! would only prolong the issue.

And I can't echo because *I love you* is by far the most dangerous, provocative phrase in any language. It's practically a formal declaration of war. Sofie and I have faced each other down dozens of times already. But what sets this moment apart from all our previous conflicts is there is no judge to moderate, no formalized structure, no partner to turn to in moments of crisis. There is only she, I, and the radical first strike attack she has just launched. The Caroline Standard of Pre-Emption no longer applies. Battle lines have already been drawn. I must somehow respond. And the clock is ticking.

Tick.

I first saw Sofie sitting with her partner waiting for the topic announcement at University of Southern California last year. She wore a dark blue pantsuit over a silk, button-down blouse with black buttons; it was an excellent ensemble that straddled the line between professional credibility and modern style effectively. It also perfectly complimented her dark, straightened hair and fair skin. A suit like that meant either a fierce competitor or a posing wallflower wanting desperately to be taken seriously at her first tournament. She and her partner were reading last month's Times article on the lack of electrical infrastructure in Africa, indicating a transition between those two phases. But I wasn't worried. I'd already found an article from an economics journal that refuted it on environmental and human rights grounds. Not to mention that the coach from her university was reputed for pushing his students to focus on arguments that were easy to characterize as overly idealistic. If Bill and I hit her in a round on Africa or energy subsidies, all it would take is a little hard-targeted pragmatism to knock her down into the bins with the freshman and the ESL students.

But it turned out to be a round on banning plastic surgery when we bared our teeth to cross tongues. She said surgically altering one's body to meet unrealistic standards of beauty was a dangerous standard to set. I responded that it was ironic to hear that argumentation from a girl with pierced ears and that our side believed that you own your body and whatever you choose to do with it, be that filling it with silicone or stabbing a metal bar through it, was your business and not the government's. The judge gave us the round, but gave me a warning about toeing the line of sexual harassment that I ignored. Winning was all that mattered.

Besides, the judge was Canadian and no one ever paid attention to their moralizing. No matter how much they insisted, debate was not a polite affair to be conducted civilly and it never would be. Tempers ran too hot and hormones too bold. Debate was the spice of life after all, dished out in seven-minute increments. And as evidenced by their plethora of boiled cuisine, Canadians preferred life bland.

Tick.

The round continued out into the hall and all the way back to the briefing room with her partner insisting that we should have been disqualified for my comment and Sofie continuing to argue her case to the back of the judge's head, citing statistics about breast implants in Los Angeles and Miami. But Bill and I had won. The runners had taken the judgment back to the tab room already. Nothing anyone said now would change that. Eventually she and her partner retreated to their corner with the rest of their team, and Bill and I to ours.

"What a piece of work," Bill snorted.

"I know," I said dryly.

"The way she kept going on about soft palette repair not being an example of surgically altering your appearance. Totally inconsistent. A big ol' knife."

"I know," I repeated disinterestedly.

The points from that round were enough to slingshot Bill and I into the semi-finals, leaving Sofie behind. And as I spoke for seven minutes the next morning on the perils of exporting nuclear waste to third world countries, she sat front row center in the audience so I would be unable to escape her evil eye. Bill and I did not advance. To the finals, she wore a smile. How could that possibly equal love?

Tick.

Within the fields of biology and evolutionary psychology, love is seen as a device to bond people together for purposes of child rearing. It is generally purported to last two to three years, the time it would take to birth a child and raise it to the point of semi-self-sufficiency in the wild. A child may not have been able to hunt or gather for itself at two, but it was no longer dependent on breast milk and would be capable of communicating enough to garner assistance. At that point, the bond was broken and the parents could move on to other partners to ensure a wide genetic pool within the tribe. Birth control of course threw off this entire schedule, generally pushing the child's appearance beyond the time frame of love's bond. Which, if you accept that analysis, could arguably make the creation of birth control a major contributing factor to the origins of the modern dysfunctional family.

But that doesn't matter. Sofie is applying to law school and I am pursuing a PhD. Neither of us has the time or inclination for children, making that analysis of love irrelevant to the current context.

Plato had a different view. He wrote that humans were originally binary creatures like conjoined twins until they were split apart by a lightning bolt from Zeus. Love is the desire to rejoin with our severed other half. Sex, popularly referred to as making love, is the attempt to physically reattach to one another.

By this analysis, Sofie and I are meant for each other; what could be referred to as soulmates.

While Plato is one of the most important thinkers in recorded history, a man whose political treatises are still being studied thousands of years later, he also believed that the sun was pulled across the sky by a man in a chariot. Therefore, it should be safe to say that his assessment of biology and psychology by lighting bolt is equally archaic. Especially as the socialization and gender roles of ancient Greece are not remotely applicable to modern first world liberal democracies in the midst of sexual and technological revolutions.

Besides, when Sofie and I debated the legalization of polygamy in Chicago last year, she countered my position that fracturing emotional devotion amongst multiple partners inevitably results in emotional trauma unless the partnership is not based on an emotional connection but on religious oppression and victimization of women in a telling fashion. She posited that the existence of and desire for polygamy in even a small percentage of the population undermines the entire notion of true love as a whole, that marriages were in effect business partnerships and that polygamy was analogous to expanding a privately held company into the public sector; selling stock to expand service. We won that round, but only because she argued the position on a surface level, lacking a strong philosophical framework, a sure sign she believed every word of it. If she didn't already have a blanket acceptance of love as an irrelevant, superfluous myth employed to sugarcoat the realities of survival, she would have done some research to back it up.

So even if I accepted Plato's position on love, it's clear that Sofie and I are not soulmates and that this analysis should also be rejected.

So what are we then?

Tick.

Marriage counselors have identified four kinds of modern first world relationships.

First is the traditional relationship, the kind that leads to marriage, children and a second mortgage. Its primary appeal is in its effective division of labor; one partner provides resources and the other maintains the home and cares for the children. But that doesn't seem like love so much as vertical integration. Plus the thought of either Sofie or I having, let alone staying home to care for children or a house is a satire worthy of Aeschylus. So clearly, this isn't the case.

Next is the romantic relationship, commonly thought of as true love. Though it can come in many forms, I'm reasonably confident that ignoring one another in public until called upon to publicly trash talk your partner does not fall under the definition of true love.

Then there is the open companionate relationship, in which both partners live their own lives with their own careers and often other partners on the side. To quote Fleetwood Mac, "you can go your own way." But that doesn't sound like the love I've heard described in literature or the kind that you'd whisper across a pillow like Sofie did. It sounds more like a mutual appreciation.

And finally, the Rescue Relationship, in which the participants help each other recover from a mutual childhood trauma that no other partner could possibly understand. But neither of us were abused or poor. We didn't witness a horrific accident firsthand or fall into a well at any point. So I don't see how we could fit into this definition either.

Tick.

We didn't speak outside of a round for the rest of that season, though what we said to each other in-round led us to speak volumes about one another to our teams, mostly in the form of venomous slander. We called each other ideologues, hypocrites and sophists. We called each other candidates for negative eugenics programs and future prospectors in snake oil. We claimed one another had only been admitted to school because of legacies, the only possible explanation for such blatant ignorance. No blow was too low, no slur too crass, no shot too cheap—until the opening banquet at Yale late in the year.

Dinner that night was formal. Assigned seats, tuxedos and catered chicken dinners. But in the spirit of camaraderie, each table had one debater from each participating school. That way, according to the tournament director, we'd get a chance to meet and talk with people from other schools in a non-combative way. Never mind the vicious ideological clashes that arose over dinner, the snarled theological implications of dinner rolls passed from secular to religiously educated hands, or that Sofie and I were seated next to one another.

We both sat, chewing silently and taking care to avoid anything that might be construed as eye contact. However the coach from Saint John's had taken it upon himself to moderate a table-wide "getting-to-know-each-other" session. Name. Major. Dream case you've always wanted to run. With the exception of one guy who wanted to use the flood in the Bible as evidence of the morality of genocide, the response was practically a Greek chorus: Law and eugenics. So when it was my turn, I went with requiring all elected officials to wear orange jumpsuits like race car drivers that advertised who'd given them campaign contributions.

Juice squirted out of Sofie's nose and she started violently hacking. Megan—NYU, law, eugenics—sitting to her left, clapped her hard on the back until the coughing stopped.

"Excuse me," Sofie groaned and got up from the table. She never came back.

Tick.

When I went to get Bill in the morning, I found him hunched over the toilet, bile dribbling from his chin. He was still in last night's pants.

"Just get my stuff," he said. "I'll be fine." He punctuated fine by hiccupping up another spray of stomach acid. He wobbled to his feet as I fetched his yellow legal pad, sticky notes and tri-color pen. But when I returned to the bathroom, he was back down on the floor. "I can do it," he said. "Just give me a second."

"You heard Chris last night," I said. "The van is leaving at 8:30 a.m. sharp. That's ten minutes from now and you aren't even dressed."

"Are you pulling utilitarianism on me?"

"Bill, you look like hell."

"It was that fucking chicken, man. Something was off about it."

"Really, hell. Just stay here. Sleep it off. You're no use to me like this anyhow."

"I can do it."

"Bill, you can't."

"I know," he sighed and slumped back over the toilet. "But it's Yale."

"I know," I said. "We'll get it next year."

I left Bill in his room and made it to the lobby just in time to catch the van, explaining the situation to Chris on the ride. He seemed more upset that the team had put out travel expenses on Bill and that there was no way to recoup them.

The plan was to have me debate with a swing partner from the tournament running pool. There were always a few squirreled away for just this kind of situation. But when we arrived, it turned out that Bill wasn't the only person whose partner had woken up on the wrong side of the chicken.

Sofie needed a partner as well.

Tick.

Prep time was tense. In-between–rounds-time was tense. Lunchtime was tense. But when we hit the podium, the dam broke and we unleashed a maelstrom of argumentation nearly mystical in its intensity.

We won the tournament by running a holocaust denial case study in a round on home schooling. Between dissecting freedom of religion, inferring but not outright stating a slippery slope, and explicating society's moral imperative to protect children…it was poetry.

Neither of us had won a whole tournament before. We were so happy, we smiled at each other for the first time ever. And for a moment, I actually thought she might hug me. But then her team picked her up on their shoulders and she was gone.

Tick.

Collette had gone to six colleges in three years and competed for all of them. She was also known for sleeping with whomever the top competitor was, their breakups often coinciding with her transfer. We called her the debate-utante.

Until this moment, she'd never noticed me before, an arrangement I'd been okay with. Of course, in addition to my tournament victory, it was nearly time for her to transfer schools again and Portland State was one of the few she hadn't worn out her welcome at.

My team stood back and laughed as she twisted one finger through her thick blond curls, prattling on about democracy in Asia, the conflict in the Middle East and the shoes she got at the mall. I did all I could to appear actively disinterested, but it only seemed to make her more determined. She offered bad arguments gleaned from judging high school rounds: *War makes people depressed which decreases their sex drive which slows the spread of AIDS; therefore war is good because it stops AIDS. Congress is ultimately powerless to reform health care because it is too busy dealing with constant filibustering from the NRA. Ketchup is a vegetable.* She even became the fifth person to claim to me that they'd witnessed the infamous round in which a Japanese team mistranslated the phrase *intelligent design should not be taught in high schools* to mean that *designing artificial intelligence should not be taught in high schools*, and ran a case about robots designed by high school students rising up and overthrowing their masters.

I was beginning to envy Bill.

All I wanted was to get away. I even tried to flag Sofie down as she passed. I could stretch out a strained thanks and congratulations if I needed to. But she looked at me with the standard contempt, took Dave's hand, and made for the door.

Eventually I went to the bathroom and never came back.

Tick.

Our finals schedule interfered with the tail end of the tournament schedule, so I didn't see Sofie again until after the summer. Her hair had grown out.

She nodded hello in the briefing room, but that was all she communicated to me that weekend. We didn't even face one another in round.

The weird part was I felt slightly disappointed. I'd grown so accustomed to facing and annoying Sofie that things just didn't seem complete without it.

Tick.

After three beers at a tournament social at University of Chicago, I told her exactly that. She smirked and walked away.

The next morning we awoke next to one another with matching hangovers and missing pants.

"I have to go," she said, a panicked look in her eye.

"Wait just a second," I said. "What just happened here?"

She already had one hand on the knob. But then she turned and dashed back to the bed, avoiding eye contact. She quickly thrust a kiss at me. "I have to go," she said, whirling and clamping one hand over her mouth as she ran out the door.

Bill later told me I'd accepted a drinking challenge from an Irish team last night. That was the last he'd seen of me. I expected that to be the last I saw of Sofie.

But there came a knock at my door the next evening. And then the next weekend in Ohio. And then again at UC San Bernadino. And then the next week, there was only a knowing glance at the tournament dinner as a cue. There was no discussion or questions. In fact, until she said she loved me, we barely spoke at all.

Tick.

The more I think about it, the more I lean towards believing that this could in fact be a rescue relationship and that debate is our mutual damage. It so alters the thinking of its devotees that they are often rendered incapable of social navigation outside its borders. There is too much explaining required, too many apologies for accidentally bruised feelings and misunderstandings about moral stances. And being involved in a civilian discussion of anything interesting is like listening to a tape player running out of batteries. They lack the information, the proper tools of analysis, and most importantly the cutthroat showmanship.

I once went on a date with a girl who worked at the school library. She had short, reddish brown hair with glasses and she hummed to herself as she checked in books. I'd felt that someone as enraptured with knowledge as she would be able to hold her own in a conversation. But over the course of several drinks it became clear she was more of a warehouse than a factory, as nearly the only thing she said the whole evening was to ask me if there was anything I didn't already have an opinion on.

This is a common story told between rounds. If competitors date, they rarely do it outside of the sport. Mostly they get by with one-night stands after tournament socials. Highly attended championship tournaments with open bars and large blocks of hotel rooms, like Euros or Worlds, are to debaters what spring break in Cancún is to fraternities.

In that respect, the fact that Sofie and I have been sneaking away for most of this term practically makes us married. That we don't ever discuss it only showcases our emotional dysfunctions.

Would that mean that I love her as well?

Tick.

I might, if I can look at it properly. She is educated, attractive, and there are moments when her personality is somewhat less than aggravating. But what does that all mean? Is it love?

Is it the initial steps on the way to love?

I truthfully don't know the answers. And for the first time, I'm finding myself incapable of articulating bullshit to respond anyhow. All I do know is that I feel comfortable here and don't want it to go away.

Tick.

"Well, aren't you going to say something?" she whispers.

"I…" But I stall. It's been too long and I still have nothing. Before me is a gaping, black abyss beckoning me to jump on faith that heaven lays at its floor. All I can do is breathe, counting the agonizing passage of the milliseconds.

There is a point reached in which we have so trained ourselves to see the opposing sides of everything that there is no inherent value to anything because it has an opposite of equal value. That means that at its core, the only thing driving action of any form is human ego, something that is far more than casually suspect in its own right. Reaching that point is paralyzing because the only way forward is to acknowledge the arrogant irrelevance of your actions and existence—and yet boldly proceed forward anyhow. Whether I love her or not, whether I exist or not, the universe will go on ambivalent. The earth will go on ambivalent. Even my more immediate surroundings and personal acquaintances are unlikely to notice. So why should it matter? What possible justification could there be? Why do I care?

The only answer is that it matters to me because I do love her, or at least something in the vicinity of love or affection. And that, regardless of the intellectual implications of being only a single, inconsequential entity in the vastness of creation, effectively I am the center of my own universe as I must experience the world from my own viewpoint. And that if I don't take action, then I risk losing her. A simple cost/benefit analysis points to only one conclusion.

Tell her you love her. And do it now.

But before I can open my mouth, she is laughing. "Oh my god, I had you," she cackles. "You totally thought I was serious didn't you?"

"I, uh…No."

"Don't try to deny it," she giggles. "I had you."

"You didn't."

"Come on, Evan, you should know better by now. We're above love. Unlike most people, we're smart enough that we can see right through it."

"I know that. Don't you think I know that?"

"I totally had you. Hook, line and sinker."

"You didn't."

"I did so," she whispers drowsily, snuggling her head down into my armpit where her face is hidden from mine. "Whatever. Sleep now." She doesn't say another word.

Several moments later I feel a single tear drip down onto my ribs and then I fall asleep.

SPECIAL THANKS TO JANE
ENDACOTT, THE TAILOR BILLINGS
SOCIETY, JENNIE JORGENSEN,
JENNIFER ORR AND VOLNUTEAR
COPY-EDITTTERS BROOKE
COWARD, TIFFANY ALLEN AND
RENE ALLEN.

JENNIE JORGENSEN

Although this is her first large-scale illustrated book, creating books has been a passion of Jennie's since she was a kid. Along with drawing, she also dabbles in printmaking, painting, graphics, photography and glassblowing. Jennie currently lives, works and is generally as busy as a bee in beautiful Boise, Idaho.

ABOUT THE AUTHOR

JOSH GROSS

Ace reporter, produced playwright and internationally recognized rock-n-roll superstar Josh Gross is a frenetic enthusiast of all things communicable that infuses chutzpah into all he endeavors despite ardent detractors. He lives, works and is generally up to no good in Oregon.